The Summer Of Wild

By Jessi Hansen

Copyright © Jessi Hansen 2024
ISBN: 9798869175830
Image: Ammentorp @ 123RF.com

The Lonely Summer Bucket List

- [ ] GET A TATTOO
- [ ] Sneak into the movie theatre
- [ ] SKINNY DIP AT THE LAKE
- [ ] Play a round at the golf course
- [ ] DINNER AT THE COUNTRY CLUB. DRESS FANCY.
- [ ] Smashing Trout Concert
- [ ] JUMP OUT OF THE TREE AT THE CREEK
- [ ] Send a *scandalous* photo

Chapter 1
The Third Wheel

Wilder Cox has been the third wheel in my relationship with Cash Allred since we started dating freshman year of high school. In fact, I can't think of a single relationship milestone Wilder wasn't present for.

He pretend-gagged when Cash asked me to be his girlfriend at lunch the first week of high school.

He shot death glares at me the first movie night I was invited to at Cash's house.

He grumbled from the backseat when Cash got his driver's license, and I was assigned the front seat of Cash's brand-new truck.

He gasped when he walked into Cash's room after we had sex for the first time, and we were still naked.

He groaned and moaned all through senior prom because his date, Kerrigan Lewis, drank too much in the limo and spent the whole night puking in the bathroom. Instead of slow dancing with just Cash, I had to slow dance with Wilder, too. People started asking us if we were a throuple after that. We are *definitely* not.

And right now, he's goading my boyfriend into jumping out of a large oak tree into the shallow creek below.

Some things never change.

Wilder Cox has been—*and always will be*—the third wheel in my relationship with Cash Allred.

"Come on!" Wilder yells from a sturdy branch above the crystal-clear creek. "You're only young once, Cash. Do you want to spend it lying on a rock with your girlfriend? Or do you want to jump out of the fucking tree with me?"

Cash sighs beside me. "I'd rather not break a leg, Wild. Or my face."

"Your dad's a plastic surgeon," Wilder waves off. "He can fix your face."

Cash chuckles and sits up. I glance at his toned stomach as the sun bathes my boyfriend's body in a golden glow.

Cash Allred is beautiful. The kind of beauty that makes my heart ache every time he drops me off at home and his taillights disappear down the road. Sandy blond hair, eyes bluer than the sky, and a smile that's always stopped me dead in my tracks. Four years later, I still pinch myself every time I remember the moment I was eating a peanut butter and jelly sandwich and he blurted out, "Will you be my girlfriend?"

Yes, Cash. Yes then. Yes now. Yes always.

Cash leans forward and places a chaste kiss on my lips. "I'm gonna go for a dip. I'll be back in a minute."

I prop myself up on my elbows and watch as Cash jogs over to the creek, the muscles in his back constricting with the swing of his arms. He's sexy. The kind of sexy that makes things achy and needy *down there*.

I hate that this is our last summer together before he starts school at Johns Hopkins in the fall. His dad pulled some strings, so Cash will be leaving me—and I guess, Wilder—behind for Baltimore in three short months to pursue medicine. Cash's dad wants him to go into plastics, but he's more interested in pediatrics. Cash has never met a kid he hasn't absolutely fallen in love with. Sick kids are no exception.

"Geronimo!" Wilder yells before jumping off a flimsy branch above the creek bed, and my eyes slide from my handsome boyfriend to his harebrained best friend.

Cash's back tenses. The water is too shallow. We both know it.

I close my eyes as Wilder disappears under the water. A loud *splash* echoes off the shade trees as I inhale sharply.

I slowly open one eye and sit up straighter, waiting for Wilder's dark, idiotic head to appear. When it doesn't, I stand and rush over to the creek.

Cash is already wading in, swimming toward Wilder's lifeless form beneath the clear water as I cover half my face with my hands.

The moment Cash grabs his arm, Wilder shoots out of the water, sputtering with laughter. "Your," more laughter, "faces *right now*. I wish I had a camera."

I breathe a sigh of relief as Cash punches Wilder in the arm. "No one is going to believe you're really hurt if you keep pulling asinine stunts like this one."

Wilder's eyes widen in disbelief. "Did you just say *ass*?"

"No," Cash quickly replies. "I said asinine."

"You better hope Daddy doesn't hear you cussing," Wilder teases him. "He might make you put some of your trust fund dollars in the offering plate Sunday morning. You know, as an atonement for your filthy mouth."

I roll my eyes and walk back to my towel. I'm not sure why Cash is friends with Wilder. I mean, they've been inseparable since kindergarten. Todd Chester dumped his chocolate milk on Cash, and Wilder gave Todd a bloody nose in retaliation. That single experience bonded them for life.

Cash is the nice guy, and Wilder is... well, *wild*.

At some point, don't we outgrow our friends? Or, at the very least, friends that don't have the same morals and values we do? Cash spends every Sunday morning sitting in a front-row church pew with his parents. Wilder spends Sunday mornings trying to find his jeans off the floor of some random girl's bedroom. They have nothing in common. They don't even like the same music or partake in the same hobbies. So, why is Wilder always around? And why is Cash fine with it?

"Don't think too hard, Blondie," Wilder clears his throat as he reaches for his towel next to me. "Wouldn't want you to use the last of your brain cells wondering why Cash would rather spend all his free time with me and not you."

Blondie. I hate that nickname. Wilder told Cash I was nothing more than a *blond bimbo* hoping to *cash* in on the Allred fortune when we started dating. He shortened it to Blondie when Cash defended me. Four years later, I'm still here. And so, unfortunately, is Wilder.

"At least I have brain cells," I quip. "You drink all yours away every weekend. Is that because your dad left you for his second family? Must suck to know you weren't worth sticking around for."

"I may have daddy issues, but at least I get laid," he retorts as he flashes his dark eyebrows at me. "When's the last time Cash fucked you? What month are we on now? Two? Or is it three? *I've lost count.*"

"You're a disgusting pig," I sneer. "Who keeps track of their friend's sex life?"

"Me," Wilder gives me a shit-eating grin. "Do you think he's punishing you for not going to

Baltimore with him? Instead, you decided to stay here for college. Does he know it's because your dad lost his job and your parents are about to lose the house, too?"

Red. All I see is red.

"I hate you," I seethe. "*I hate you, I hate you, I hate you.*"

Wilder smirks. "Don't worry, Blondie, the feeling is mutual."

"You better not go around spreading rumors," I warn.

Wilder wipes his tanned chest off with his towel. "Oh, those aren't rumors. Your sister told me all about your family woes last night."

I swallow hard. "Isla wouldn't."

"Tell me, Blondie, do you also have a birthmark on your ass?" Wilder licks his lips.

My heart begins pounding in my chest. Isla has a birthmark on her right butt cheek. "You slept with my sister?"

"Oh, no," Wilder crouches down, glancing at Cash still swimming in the creek. "I *fucked* your sister in the backseat of my mom's car. Did you know doggy style is her favorite position?"

"Stop," I say. "Isla wouldn't sleep with you. She's dating Frank."

"Is she?" Wilder tilts his head to the side, his hazel eyes full of mischief. "She never mentioned him. The only thing she kept saying was, '*Harder, Wilder. Harder.*'"

"You're lying," I say as I shake my head. I know my sister. She wouldn't cheat on Frank. But then, how does Wilder know about Dad's job? And the house?

"Don't worry, I'll keep your secrets," Wilder winks as he stands. "*For now*."

He tosses his towel at me as Cash walks over to us. I instantly throw it back at him.

"You sure you don't want to jump out of the tree?" Wilder slaps Cash's back.

"I'm good," Cash answers him.

Cash dries off as I tug at the corner of my towel, tension building in my chest. If Wilder tells Cash about my parents, it'll be one more thing Cash's parents hate about me. Sure, they're nice to my face, but Cash tells me what they say behind closed doors. *We're too young to be this serious. I'm from a middle-class family so I can't possibly understand their world. If I really loved Cash, I'd pack my bags and move with him. I should get better grades. I shouldn't try so hard to impress them. I should drive a nicer car.*

I don't realize I'm gnawing on my lower lip until Cash's fingers find my chin. "You okay?"

"She's good," Wilder answers for me.

"Why are you even here?" I snap at him.

Wilder holds his hands up in defense. "Woah. Must be that time of the month."

"I think I'm going to walk home." My hands shake as I begin stuffing the sunscreen and my water bottle into my bag.

"No," Cash lays a comforting hand on top of mine. "I've gotta meet my dad anyway. I'll drive you home."

"And me?" Wilder butts in.

"And you," Cash furrows his brow. I ignore his curious stares as I roll up my towel and slip it into my bag.

The drive home is short and quiet. Wilder doesn't say anything from the backseat—*for once*—and Cash keeps his hand on mine until he stops in front of my house.

"My parents won't be home until later," I tell him. "You want to come inside?"

Cash runs a hand through his damp, blond hair. "Sorry, babe, I have to meet my dad at the Country Club."

Rejection. That's what this is. It's been two months and 13 days since I last saw Cash naked.

"Huh," Wilder's annoying voice echoes through the cab of the truck.

"What?" Cash twists in the driver's seat to look at him.

"Nothing," Wilder answers before shooting me an *I-told-you-so* look. "Tell your dad I say hi."

Wilder hops out of the truck as I grab my bag.

"Have fun with your dad," I say to Cash. He leans over the middle seat to kiss me, but I turn my head to the side. The moment his lips connect with my cheek, my heart dips in my chest. Does he not want me anymore? Did I do something wrong? Is he really punishing me for staying here when he wants me to go to Baltimore with him?

"Love you," he says into my hair.

I get out of his truck and shut the door harder than I mean to. Cash takes off down the road. He didn't even notice.

"So," Wilder pushes his blacked-out sunglasses up the bridge of his nose with his middle finger. "I guess three months it is."

"Why are you always so mean?"

Wilder tosses his towel over his shoulder and shrugs. "For the record, any guy who turns sex down is either gay or not interested anymore."

I hug my bag to my stomach. "Yeah, well you fuck anything in a skirt so excuse me if I don't take your word for it."

"Wow," Wilder raises his eyebrows. "I didn't realize little miss goody two-shoes said the word *fuck*. I guess you're not as innocent as you pretend to be."

"I'm not pretending to be anything," I say with defeat. "I don't know what game you're playing, but if you're going to tell Cash about my parents, can you wait until after his birthday?"

"Why?" Wilder frowns.

"I'd like one last birthday with him before my entire world blows up in my face." I step around Wilder and start heading toward my house.

"Hold on," Wilder grabs my shoulder. "Why would your world blow up if he knew your parents are struggling?"

I take a deep breath. "Because Wilder, I'm not you. I don't get to be the screw-up best friend. Cash has an image to uphold, so I have to be the perfect girlfriend."

"You think he only likes you because you look like you have your shit together?"

"I don't know," I say as I cross my arms over my chest. "Kind of feels that way sometimes."

"Cash would never look down on you," Wilder defends his best friend. "If anything, he would help you guys out. And he wouldn't make you feel bad about it either."

"We don't need help," I raise my chin. "We'll be fine." *We're Winthrops.*

"Alright," he shrugs. "See you tomorrow, Blondie."

"*Ugh*," I groan as Wilder begins the slow trek to his house three doors down. "I'm so tired of you being the third wheel!"

Wilder scoffs as he walks away. "You're the third wheel, Blondie. Not me."

Chapter 2
The Backpacking Trip

Dinner at 6?

That was the text message Cash sent me three hours ago. After responding, I frantically raided my closet, searching for the *perfect* outfit. One that will surely make Cash want to have sex tonight. Or at least have a hard time saying *no* when I invite him inside.

Now, I'm standing on the sidewalk, waiting outside my house as the warm breeze curls itself around my bare legs.

It's been months since Cash last took me on a date. I've tried not to bug him. I know he's nervous about going to Baltimore. His dad expects perfection, which means Cash isn't allowed to be mediocre. His father would never allow it.

I've chalked up his busyness to prepping for life at Johns Hopkins, but a part of me wonders if he's avoiding me.

I check my phone before peering up and down the street. When my eyes land on the one person most likely to ruin my mood—*and day*—my heart plummets to the concrete below.

No, Cash didn't.

"What's wrong, Blondie?" Wilder flashes his eyebrows at me. "You look *disappointed* to see me."

"*Please*, please tell me you're just passing by," I place a hand on my hip.

"Nope," he holds up his phone. "Cash told me to meet you guys here."

"Why?" I stomp a foot. "Why can't *I* do anything *alone* with *my* boyfriend?"

"Don't ask me," Wilder shrugs off. "Ask your boyfriend."

I tug on the pink miniskirt I'm wearing. The one I should have left hidden beneath my jeans in the back of my closet. I didn't realize this wasn't a date. It's just another *share-my-boyfriend-with-his-best-friend* rendezvous.

"Ah," Wilder grins. "You're trying to seduce Cash."

"What?" I wrap my arms around myself. "Why would you say that?"

Wilder points to my legs. "Miniskirt."

"It's June," I scrunch my face as my stomach twists in knots. If Wilder can see right through me, why can't Cash? "It's hot outside."

"And the cleavage?" he smirks as his hazel eyes rake over my exposed chest.

"Stop looking at my boobs!" I seethe.

"Relax, Blondie," Wilder rolls his eyes. "You're definitely not my type."

"Oh," I slap my knee with my hand, "that's right. You like girls with low self-esteem who can't help but sleep with emotionally stunted assholes afraid of commitment."

"Don't talk about your sister that way," he licks his lips.

My blood boils. "You're ridiculous."

"You're the one begging your boyfriend for attention."

"Am not."

"Are too."

I take a step closer as he slips his sunglasses out of his back pocket. "Why are you like this?"

"Like what?"

"Confrontational. Egotistical. *Unhinged*."

"I'm trying to help you," he adjusts the glasses on his face. "I'm being helpful."

"You are not," I reply. "If you were, you'd go *home*."

"He's going to break your heart," he warns with a chuckle. "Because guys like Cash don't go off to college *without* their high school girlfriends and—"

"You know why I can't go," I interrupt.

"Honestly, Blondie, don't you think you deserve someone who desires you the same way you desire them?"

"Excuse me?" Wilder is giving me serious whiplash right now. And who says *desires*? What is this? A historical romance novel?

"You have what I'd like to call a *high* sex drive. And Cash? He has a *low* one. You're incompatible. If you don't have sex in common, how the hell are you going to survive twenty years down the road?"

"Huh," I frown. "I never realized how shallow you are."

"I'm not shallow. I'm trying to help you."

No, he's not. He's trying to get rid of me for the summer, so he has Cash all to himself.

"If I didn't know any better," I raise my chin, "I'd think you have a thing for Cash. And you're jealous he'd rather have sex with me instead of you."

"I'm man enough to admit that if I had an inclination for men, Cash would be at the top of my list. Turns out, I'm a fan of pussy."

"You disgust me."

"You annoy me."

"Ugh!" I throw my hands up in the air. "I want one night with my boyfriend. Why can't you disappear?"

"Because Cash told me he has something important to tell us."

"What?"

Wilder smiles victoriously. "He didn't tell you that part, did he?"

No, he didn't. He just asked me to grab dinner. Why wouldn't Cash tell me he had something to share? Why do I always have to find out from Wilder?

"*Because you're incompatible*," Wilder whispers.

"I hate you," I sneer.

"I'm aware."

"Why can't you—"

"Why can't you admit that what you and Cash once had is a thing of the past?"

I shake my head. "Don't you have a hobby? Something to live for other than ruining my life?"

"I didn't realize I had that much power over your life," he purses his lips. "Although, living in your head rent-free does make me feel giddy. And that's not an emotion I feel very often."

"You know what?" I hold my hands out at my sides. "Enjoy dinner with Cash. *Alone*."

"See ya, Blondie," he says as he raises his hand to his face and gives me a childish wave. "Wouldn't want to be ya."

I march up the stone pathway to my house, done with Wilder *and Cash*. They can have each other. But then I hear a *honk*, and the part of me that's madly in love with Cash and *not* annoyed with Wilder looks over my shoulder. Cash is jogging toward me with a big smile on his face. I stop in my tracks, my heart clanging against my ribs.

"Hey," he says when he reaches me. "Where are you going?"

"Uh," I clear my throat. "I was going to check the time."

Cash laughs. "Babe, you could have just looked at your phone."

I nod, my heart warring against itself. I love Cash. I always have. I always will. But if he doesn't love me anymore—if he's going to forget about me when he goes to Baltimore—then I need to prepare myself. I know I won't survive the devastating heartbreak, but at least I won't be blindsided by it.

"Right," I play off.

"You ready?" He holds out his hand.

"Ready," I swallow hard as I weave my fingers through his.

"You look really nice," he tells me.

My heart melts like an ice cube under hot water. "So do you."

When Cash opens the passenger door to his truck, I'm surprised to see Wilder sitting in the back seat, his sunglasses on top of his head. Guess he really can see right through me, can't he?

"So," Wilder slaps the back of Cash's seat as he fumbles with his seatbelt. "Are you taking us to the Country Club?"

Cash laughs nervously. "Uh, no. I thought we could grab burgers at the diner."

I stay silent as Wilder smirks. "You embarrassed to be seen with us, Cash?"

"No," Cash sincerely replies as he turns the steering wheel, checking over his shoulder. "Just not my scene."

"Right," Wilder clicks his tongue. "Could have fooled me with the polo shirt and khakis."

"Don't knock the khakis," Cash chastises him. "I played golf earlier today with one of my dad's surgeon friends. Just trying to make connections."

"Yeah," Wilder huffs. "Cause that's more important than spending your last summer before college with your friends."

No one talks after that, and the awkward silence makes my palms sweat.

I wish I knew what Cash wanted to talk to us about. What if he's going to Baltimore sooner than he originally planned? He's supposed to leave in mid-August, but maybe he moved the date up by a week or two. I don't think I'm going to be alright if that's what he's decided. *Cash is leaving.* He's going to be miles from where I am. We only have the summer before he's gone, and long distance will either make or break us.

"You guys want to listen to something?" Cash asks as he turns the volume up on his radio, unfazed by the silence.

Wilder groans. "Anything but Smashing Trout. I can't believe you actually listen to that shit."

Cash chuckles. "It's upbeat and catchy. And they're a local band. Don't hate on them."

"I can play the guitar, too," Wilder scoffs, "but that doesn't mean I'm going to record myself and make everyone within a twenty-mile radius listen to it."

"What would you recommend then?" I turn in my seat. "Ooh, let me guess. Your personal favorite, the vocal stylings of the one and only, Wilder Cox, sans guitar."

Wilder hides a smile. "You make me sound pretentious as fuck."

"Pretty sure you remember every word to 'Wild Cox Summer'. Or," I glance at Cash, "shall we bring out the video evidence?"

"I don't know what you two are talking about." Wilder crosses his arms and peers out the window. I notice the white material stretches along his toned chest. His *very* toned chest. *Stop looking, Ingrid!* But before my brain registers what's going on, Wilder notices where my gaze has landed, and, when our eyes meet, he raises an intrigued eyebrow.

"I think you do, Wild," Cash interrupts our weird moment. "You know we secretly recorded it."

Wilder doesn't answer right away because he's still looking at me, and I'm still looking at him. And this bizarre energy bounces between us for a split second before I look away, mortified.

I can't believe I was checking out Wilder—*gross*—and he caught me. *Even worse.*

I can explain this. I know I can. My body is simply *revolting* against itself because my boyfriend has suddenly taken a vow of celibacy after years of regular sexual activity. I just... *I'm horny*. And Wilder is not the worst thing to look at... *sometimes*. Until he opens his mouth, reminding me how disgusting he is, and how wrong it feels to even consider what his unclothed chest looks like.

"I think we should all move on from freshman year," Wilder exhales heavily. "And focus on what you want to tell us."

Freshman year. We barely survived. I started dating Cash, and Wilder pissed Cash off because he didn't like me. They didn't speak for months, and the year eventually ended with Wilder's terrible rendition of the alt-rock classic 'Wild Cox Summer', which we all briefly bonded over before he started calling me Blondie, officially. Thinking back now, more went on than I probably knew. Cash has always fiercely defended his friendship with Wilder. I learned early on not to say anything where Wilder is concerned. Even when they're feuding.

"I, uh, think it'd be best to wait until we all have some food in us," Cash cryptically answers.

Weird. It's weird he won't just tell us. This whole car ride is really strange.

Cash parks in front of the diner, and I breathe a sigh of relief at the same time Wilder does. I whip my head around to look at him, narrowing my eyes as he unbuckles his seatbelt. He gives me a challenging wink before I scoff and open the car door. I try to get out, but I forget to undo the seatbelt, so I let out an awkward, "*Argh!*" as my upper body is slingshot back into the seat.

Wilder's voice carries through the cab as I struggle to get out of the seatbelt. "You're such a loser."

"Takes one to know one," I grumble as Cash reaches over the middle seat to release the clip. I lick my lips and smooth my hair down before stepping out of the car and onto the solid ground below.

Cash holds my hand as we wait in line to order. I'm hyperaware of how close Wilder's front is to my back. I keep shifting forward, trying to put an inch of space between us, but he just follows to annoy me. He's *relentless.*

"Two cheeseburgers, two orders of fries, two sides of ranch, two Cherry Cokes, a grilled chicken salad for me, and a cup of water," Cash orders as he pulls out his dad's credit card to pay.

But Wilder reaches over me and hands the cashier his debit card. "On me today."

I roll my eyes. The last time Wilder paid for my dinner, I had to listen to him bitch about it for *months*. Eventually, Cash paid him ten dollars so he'd shut up about paying for a meal I didn't ask him to. We will not be repeating that grueling incident today.

"Actually," I clear my throat as I reach inside my purse. "I'll pay for mine."

I shoot Wilder a *fuck you* grin as I hand over the cash.

"Don't say I never do anything nice for you, Blondie," Wilder holds his hands up in defense. "I tried."

"What is with you two today?" Cash furrows his brow, his dreamy blue eyes perplexed.

"Nothing," Wilder and I both say at the same time.

After we pay, we grab a booth in the back, and Cash tells Wilder to sit next to me.

"Uh," Wilder's mouth drops open. "I'm not sitting by Blondie."

"I'm not sitting by *you*," I snap back at him.

"Come on, you guys," Cash groans. "I have something really important to tell you. Can you get along for five minutes? Please."

"Fine," I grumble as I slide into the booth first. Wilder follows behind, making sure to rub his black jean-clad thigh against my bare one. My skin crawls with revulsion.

"I'm going to grab napkins," Cash informs us. "Try not to kill each other while I'm gone."

I watch Cash go as Wilder twists to face me. He slides his greasy arm behind my head and gives me a sinister smile. "You were checking me out in the truck."

"Was not," I deny. *Deny, deny, deny.*

"While I'm flattered your sexually deprived mind would even consider me, I don't fuck my best friend's girlfriend. Or exes, for that matter," Wilder taunts me. "But if you'd like to request nudes, I'd be more than happy to send you dick pics to help," his face moves closer as his lips barely graze my ear, "get you off."

I take a deep breath as I squeeze my purse strap, picturing Wilder's neck in my hands as I cut off all the circulation to his tiny brain. "Fuck off, Wilder."

"You've turned into such a potty mouth lately," he sits up straighter. "I hope that's my influence rubbing off on you. Ha! *Rubbing off.* Are you going to be thinking of me later while you rub one off?"

"*You wis*h," I cross one leg over the other, ignoring the blazing ache situated there. *For Cash.* Not for Wilder. Wilder's like a creepy stalker who stands outside your bedroom window at night and watches you through the slit in the blinds.

He throws his head back and laughs, obviously amused with himself.

"So," Cash interrupts our tense exchange as he tosses napkins at us. "We need to talk about this summer."

Wilder removes his arm from behind me but keeps his disgusting leg resting against mine. I kick his ankle with the heel of my sandal, inflicting pain. His jaw tenses as he moves his grotesque limb off mine. Glad he got the message.

"What about it?" I say to Cash.

"My dad offered to pay for a backpacking trip," he begins. "*Through Europe.*"

Wilder and I both lean forward.

"Really?" I smile wide. "He's going to pay for all of us to backpack through Europe?"

"Um," Cash swallows hard. "No. Just me."

My mouth drops open as I stare at my boyfriend, stunned. It's our last summer together and he's ditching me for Europe. He's not going to be here. He's going to leave me behind while he gallivants across the globe.

"When do you leave?" Wilder asks him, his tone both solemn and hurt.

"Next weekend."

Wilder and I sit perfectly still as the waiter sets our food in front of us.

Chapter 3
The Goodbye Party

My older sister, Isla, and I have never been close. She graduated two years before me, and we ran in different social circles in high school. Isla was a mathlete who spent all her free time doing extra credit work and volunteering around the community. She didn't really want to feed the homeless on Thanksgiving every year, but she knew it would look good on her college apps. So, she donned a red apron and put a smile on her face as she spooned mashed potatoes onto plates. Isla, while smart and resourceful, has always been rather selfish.

Even now, as she drives me to Cash's parent's house for his *I'm-going-to-Europe-for-two-months-without-my-girlfriend* party.

"I don't understand why you're so butt hurt," Isla pushes her scarlet hair off her shoulder. "This is a great opportunity for Cash."

Yeah, *for Cash*. Not for our relationship. Not for me.

Also, a fun fact: Isla and I share a car when she's home from college. Which is why she's currently driving me to the party.

"Would you let Frank go on a European vacation without you for eight weeks?" I ask her.

Frank Bertinelli. He was Isla's TA for one of her classes at Brown last semester. They had a secret relationship for months before classes let out for the summer. Frank then followed Isla home. He is currently bagging groceries at the local grocery store to make ends meet and to stay *close by*. And by *close by*, I mean getting sex regularly. Unlike me.

"Frank and I aren't like you and Cash," Isla boasts.

"What does that mean?" I cross my arms over my chest. Typical Isla. She's always thought Cash was out of my league. And, because she's Isla, she hasn't kept those thoughts to herself. I'm paraphrasing here, but she once told me the only thing I had going for me was being pretty. I didn't get straight A's like she did, but I did graduate with a 3.6 GPA. Not bad for someone who only has her looks going for her.

"Frank is my best friend," Isla begins as I roll my eyes in disgust. "You and Cash aren't really friends. You're more like Mom and Dad. You love each other, but you don't want to spend all your free time together. Frank and I, well, we're inseparable."

Is this her way of telling me her relationship is better than mine?

And I'm not sure what she's talking about. Mom and Dad spend the majority of their free time watching reality TV *together*.

"But what if it was a *great opportunity* for Frank? Would you let him go?" I push.

"I'd go with him," Isla proclaims.

"What if you couldn't?"

"Frank would never leave me."

Give it four years, Isla, and a dwindling sex life. Her answer might change then.

Honestly, how does she expect a relationship built on secret library sex to last once the newness has worn off?

Spoiler alert: it won't.

"Well, I'm so glad Frank and you are on the same page," I fake a smile.

"Thanks, Ing," she pouts playfully. "I appreciate that."

Ing. I hate that nickname almost as much as *Blondie*.

Isla stops in front of Cash's parents' house. "Call me if you need a ride. Frank's working late tonight, so I'll be home catching up on—"

But I don't hear the rest because I grab my bag, hop out quickly, and shut the door behind me.

As Isla drives off, I stare up at the imposing Allred mansion— a white, colonial-style home with navy shutters and massive columns. Every spring, Mrs. Allred has the red front door touched up for scuffs and dings. After she had it repainted last year, Wilder ran his car keys down it when Cash ditched us for dinner at the Country Club. I was Wilder's getaway driver. We laughed the whole way home.

Come to think of it, that's probably the only time Wilder and I have ever worked *together* instead of *against* each other. Kind of feels like Cash is ditching us again. I wonder what Wilder will do in retaliation this time.

I knock on the red, touched-up door with a heavy heart. This might be my final time at the Allred residence. Once Cash leaves for Johns Hopkins, he doesn't plan on returning. He's made it clear he'll be taking summer classes between semesters and building a life in Baltimore. Sometimes, I wonder if what he wants is to get away from his parents. They put too much pressure on him. Pressure that's made it hard for him to be a normal teenager. Then again, maybe he's trying to get away from me.

"Ah," Mr. Allred says as he opens the door and peers down at me over his glasses. "Cash is in his room."

"Thanks," I say quietly as I scurry past him and up the grand staircase. It's stunning, really. Mahogany steps and an ornate banister to match.

When I reach Cash's room, the door is propped open. I peer inside before making myself known. He's sitting at his desk, staring at his laptop screen. The Leaning Tower of Pisa stares back at him.

"Hey," I clear my throat as I step inside.

Cash closes his laptop. "Hey, babe."

I stand, awkwardly, by the door as he runs a hand through his blond hair. "You, okay?"

He shrugs. "Not sure."

I close the door behind me, toss my bag onto his bed, and slowly make my way over to him. I'm not going to lie, approaching Cash scares me. He's rejected me so much over the past two months that now I'm second-guessing something as natural as comforting him.

But when I reach him, he opens his arms and I fall into his lap like I used to. The moment he buries his face into my neck, all the worry melts away.

"Everything is going to be fine," I promise him.

He doesn't respond. Instead, he tightens his arms around me and kisses my shoulder softly. I close my eyes, savoring the moment. It's been a long time since he's touched me this way. Since he's let me in. Since he's held me. My heart wants to soar in my chest, but I think I've read enough books and watched enough TV shows to know that whatever we're doing is coming to an end. I mean, it has to, doesn't it?

How can we spend the summer apart, and then, four years apart? If we're barely connecting now, how are we going to survive being on different continents? Living in different states?

I should ask him. I should force him to make a plan—to figure things out. But I don't. Because Cash and I don't fight. We avoid confrontation and we sweep things under the rug. We look great on the outside just like the Allred mansion. But inside, we're cold and unemotional. We've talked about marriage and babies and building a house on a piece of land outside of town. The reality is that we've dreamed together but we've never built anything solid together. We can't. Wilder has always served as our third wheel—our buffer. We've never really been alone. Not long enough to truly know one another. We've never even had a hard conversation.

And because I know this is probably ending, I don't say anything when Cash slips his hand under my shirt. Because sex is the only thing Cash and I have ever done alone. The only thing we've ever figured out together. Without Wilder.

I don't stop Cash when he tugs my bra down and cups my breast in his hand. I don't turn my head away when his lips find mine. I don't think about how much this is going to hurt when we both accept the inevitable. This might be the *last* time.

"Can we?" he whispers against my lips.

No. I should say no. He's leaving me. He's spending our final two months together in Europe.

But it's Cash. I love him. I always have. I always will.

So, I stand from his lap and pull my shirt over my head. He does the same as I fumble with the button on my jean shorts.

Once our clothes are shed, Cash walks me back to his bed, his erection straining against my stomach. The space between my thighs floods with heat as he sucks on my bottom lip, carefully laying me down on his cool comforter.

I wrap my legs around his waist while he reaches between us and slides his fingers through my soaked folds.

"Wow," he grins as he begins rubbing circles around the swollen bundle of nerves he's neglected for months.

"It's been a little while," I give him a sheepish smile, "since we, *you know*."

His face flashes with an array of emotions. The most notable one is guilt.

"I know," he sighs. "I've been so stressed with graduation and Johns Hopkins."

All I manage to get out is a weak, "Yeah."

"Shoot," Cash drops his head onto my shoulder. "I don't have a condom."

"I'm on birth control," I remind him.

"I know," he exhales. "But double protection is better than single protection."

"If you're worried, just pull out," I shrug beneath him. It's not like he hasn't done it before.

His blue eyes are torn. I can feel how hard he is against my thigh, but getting his high school girlfriend pregnant would derail all his big plans. And his parents would never forgive him.

I place a hand on his chest and shove gently. "Let's just get dressed."

Before he can protest, I'm sliding on my underwear and shorts.

"Ingrid," he tries as I grab my bra off the floor and put it on. "We can... I can run to the store."

"No," I shake my head, holding in tears. "This is your goodbye party. You can't leave."

He checks the time on the Rolex his father bought him for Christmas. "We have, like, 15 minutes before everyone arrives."

"I'm good," I tell him as I straighten the hem of my shirt. "You should get dressed."

"What's going on?" Cash frowns.

I try not to stare at his still hard *you know what*. "I don't want to be the reason you're not at your party."

"Are you mad?" Cash guesses correctly.

"Does it matter?" I raise an eyebrow. "I mean, you haven't touched me in two months and, when you finally do, you can't figure out if you want to have sex because you don't have a condom. Why have I been on birth control for two years if you don't trust it to work?"

"Ingrid, I just can't deal with my—"

"Parents," I finish for him. "I know. But has it ever occurred to you that what I want matters, too?"

"You know—"

"It's always about you. Where you want to go to school and where you want to live. What your parents want you to do. I mean, this is our last summer together before you leave and you're going to Europe. Didn't you think to talk to me about it first?"

"I didn't think," Cash chews on his lower lip. "I thought you'd be fine with it."

"Our whole relationship has always been about you, Cash. And because I love you so much, I let it be that way. But if you want this to work, you have to start considering what I want, too."

Cash stands and crosses the room. "I will, Ingrid. I promise."

I want to believe him. I do. "You want to do long distance for four years?"

"Do you?" he counters.

"I thought I did."

"You thought?" Cash sounds hurt as the words leave his mouth.

I place a hand on his chest. His rock-solid, sturdy chest. "I love you, but I think you need to figure out if you want to be in a long-distance relationship for the next four years."

"I do," he immediately replies.

"Do you really?

Before he can answer, I hear an unexpected shriek and what follows next can only be described as a shit show.

"What are you doing?" Mrs. Allred covers her eyes in horror.

Cash tries to cover himself as her gaze narrows in on his condom-less length.

"NO CONDOM?!" She roars.

"The door was closed! Why didn't you knock, Mom?" Cash yells back.

And then, as if things couldn't get any worse, Wilder's face appears as he takes a bite out of a sandwich.

Mortification floods Cash's face. "Can you guys GET OUT?"

"I need to go to the pharmacy," Mrs. Allred panics, her blond curls bouncing as she paces. "We need Plan B. I can have Lucille greet the guests while I go. I'll only be gone ten minutes at the most."

"We didn't have sex," I roll my eyes at her. "I'm not taking Plan B."

"GET OUT!" Cash yells again.

Wilder gives me an air fist pump. "Way to go, Blondie. Finally got that D!"

My mouth drops open in shock as Mrs. Allred turns to look at him. "She planned this?"

"Planned what?" Wilder stares at her in confusion.

"Unprotected sex with my son!"

A wicked smile crosses Wilder's face. "Yes, yes she did. She planned this whole thing. I think she's hoping she gets pregnant."

I hate you! I mouth at him. *I hate you, I hate you, I hate you!*

"Can you all please leave?" Cash tries again. Then, he does something completely unexpected. He removes his hands from his nether region and pushes his mom out the door. As it slams behind her, he places his palms on the wood.

Not sure what to do, I reach around him for the door handle.

"Ingrid," Cash says quietly.

I don't look at him. "What?"

"Wait for just a second."

I pause.

"Don't freak out," he whispers. "I will take care of this. She's having a hard time with me leaving."

Tears fill my eyes. Of course, he would defend his mom.

"This was a mistake. I'm sorry."

"Why are you apologizing?" He licks his lips nervously. "You didn't do anything wrong."

"I... I... " I know I didn't, but Mrs. Allred is never going to forgive me for this. When Cash and I started having sex, she sat us both down and made us promise that I'd go on birth control and Cash would always wear a condom. *Double protection* is what she called it. More like an insurance policy if you ask me.

The Allred name cannot be sullied by teenage antics, Mrs. Allred warned us. *Or there will be hell to pay.*

"Go down to your party," I tell Cash. "I need a minute to myself."

He tries to hug me, but I hold a hand up. "No."

"Okay," Cash replies as he runs a tired hand over his face.

Cash gets dressed in a hurry, then fixes his hair in the mirror above his bed. I lean against his bedroom wall, my head in my hands. This is a mess. This whole situation is a big, fat mess. I should have known things would end like this.

I step aside to let him out, avoiding eye contact.

The sound of the door softly closing behind him makes my heart throb.

Cash Allred may be my first love but I'm not sure he'll be my last.

Chapter 4
The Break Up

Cash has been pacing the front porch for the last 15 minutes. I've been waiting for him to knock on the door, but he hasn't worked the courage up yet.

"You should just go out there," Isla dramatically drops her head into her hands. "This is torture."

"I'm sorry my relationship unraveling is torture for *you*," I roll my eyes.

"You're forgiven," Isla purses her lips.

"What should we do?" Mom whispers, oblivious to the mention of my relationship falling apart.

"He can't hear you," I remind her as I cross my arms over my chest, sandwiched between my mother and sister on the couch. "And I don't know. All I know is that he's probably going to break up with me."

"Why do you think that?" Mom furrows her brow. "You know, Fanny did ignore me at the grocery store yesterday. I know we're not friends, but you'd think she'd at least be civil after four years of our kids dating."

"I don't really want to talk about it," I swallow hard.

"Why do you think he's going to break up with you?" Mom asks.

"He's going to Europe," I exhale.

"So?" Mom tries to remain optimistic.

"And then he's going to Baltimore," I raise an eyebrow. "He obviously doesn't want to spend his last summer with me. Why stay together?"

"He might ask you to go to Europe with him," Mom smiles. "It's been four years, Ingrid. He won't throw that all away on a little trip to Italy."

Except, it's not just Italy. It's the whole continent. She's clueless. So clueless.

"Then, why is he still pacing?" Isla points toward the window.

"Cash is... " I trail off as I think about the last four years together.

14-year-old Cash loved to hold my hand.

15-year-old Cash carried my backpack to class for me.

16-year-old Cash took me to the movies and felt me up as soon as the lights dimmed.

17-year-old Cash snuck into my room every chance he got.

Almost 18-year-old Cash doesn't seem to like me anymore.

Cash isn't great with confrontation. Cash isn't great at defying his parents. Except when it comes to condoms, apparently.

I really wish I had a friend right now. Instead of talking to a girlfriend about all of this, I'm stuck sharing the details of this infuriating situation with Mom, whose head is always in the clouds, and Isla, who only thinks about herself.

This is what happens when you spend all four years of high school being Cash Allred's girlfriend. Not to mention the bane of Wilder Cox's existence. I didn't make friends. I didn't have a social life outside of Cash—and Wilder.

Now, Cash is leaving me.

I wish someone would have warned me.

Wait... someone did.

He's going to break your heart. Because guys like Cash don't go off to college without their high school girlfriends...

Wilder. Why did he have to be right about this? The one time I *needed* him to be wrong.

"I can't take this anymore," Isla stands from the couch and rushes to the door. She throws it open and taps her foot restlessly. "Get in here, Allred! We're tired of watching you pace back and forth."

Cash shoves his hands into the pockets of his khaki shorts. He must have been playing golf with one of his father's colleagues before gracing us with his presence.

"Could you have Ingrid come outside?" Mom and I hear from our spot on the couch.

Mom grabs my hand and squeezes it lightly. "Go on now."

My throat dries, and my hands begin sweating as I force myself to stand on shaky knees. I should have found a way to move to Baltimore instead of staying close to home for college. I should have left Cash's room instead of having sex without a condom. I should have made friends and had a social life outside of my boyfriend and his best friend.

I should have done so many things differently.

As I pass Isla, she raises her chin in an unusual display of solidarity. For once, it actually feels like I have an older sister.

"Hey," I say to Cash as Isla shuts the front door behind me.

And that feeling is now gone. She could have left it open in case she needed to intervene.

Cash takes two long strides forward and kisses me before I have a chance to register what's happening.

He's... kissing... me.

He's kissing me.

He's kissing me!

I wrap my arms around his waist as his hands tangle with my hair. Our lips mash together, and I let out a sigh of relief as his tongue slips inside my mouth.

This. This is the Cash Allred I've been missing.

We kiss and kiss and kiss as my hands roam his back and his roam my front. I don't care that Mom and Isla might be watching from the window, or that Wilder could be lurking nearby like the creepy stalker he is.

Cash is kissing me, and it knocks me off my feet.

For the first time in months, the worried knot in the pit of my stomach disappears and I melt into him like wax to a flame. *This*. I've missed this.

But the annoying, pesky voice in the back of my head rears her ugly head. *Why the sudden change, Cash?*

In his bedroom yesterday, Cash and I had our first real talk. The kind where we didn't sweep our feelings under the rug or tiptoe around the issue. It was the first time I've been honest about how I feel and what I want. I didn't expect it to make a difference, but as Cash sucks my bottom lip into his mouth, I realize it must have. He wouldn't be acting this way if it didn't.

When we're both breathing hard and my lips are swollen, Cash finally breaks our long, overdue make out sesh and rests his forehead against mine.

"Hey," Cash finally replies.

I smile as I hug him tight. "I've missed this."

Cash clears his throat as his hands rest on my back. "I leave tomorrow."

My heart dips in my chest. "I know. It's your birthday tomorrow, too."

"We need to talk, Ingrid."

I'm so caught up in how much I've missed kissing Cash that I miss the strange tone in his voice as the words slip out of his mouth.

"What about?" I close my eyes and hold him tighter. He smells like sandalwood and *home*.

"I talked to my parents," he begins.

At the mention of his parents, I notice that he's not really holding me. His fingers are barely resting on my back, and his body is rigid.

I pull away from him and frown. "You talked to them about what?"

Cash's jaw tightens. "I love you, Ingrid."

Nope. That's not a good start.

"What does that have to do with your parents?" I lick my lips nervously.

"They... they think we're too young to be this serious," he answers.

"They've always felt that way," I point out.

"And they think that... that you're a bad influence on me." The second blow.

"Me?" I guffaw. "What about Wilder?"

"They... they think you might talk me out of doing something I've spent my whole life preparing for." He scrunches his eyes closed.

"Like what?" I can feel my face heating with anger.

"Like not going to Baltimore."

"I love you," I defend myself. "And I've always wanted what's best for you. I'd never talk you out of going to school."

He touches my forearm. "I know that."

"Did you defend me? Did you tell them that I wouldn't jeopardize your future? Or mine?"

"I tried," Cash shakes his head, "but you know how my mom is."

Fanny Allred is Satan incarnate.

"I... I'm sorry, Cash. I didn't mean to cause problems for you." Heat builds behind my eyes as I force myself to keep it together.

"My parents think it's best if we spend the summer apart," Cash deals the final blow. "They think it would be good for us to figure out who we are without—"

"You're not going to listen to them, are you?" *Panic*. I'm panicking.

Cash shrugs helplessly. "They're paying for my trip. And for college. What am I supposed to do?"

Choose me, Cash. Tell them to fuck off and spend the summer with me. Who cares about Johns Hopkins? We can find you another school.

"I don't get a say in this, do I?" I guess.

He doesn't respond.

"Do I, Cash?" I try again.

"I... I think it would be good for us to spend the summer apart, too," he sighs.

"You mean so you can go to Europe without any strings attached?" I challenge. "Is that what you want? The freedom to hook up with whoever you want while I stay here and wait for you?"

Cash looks hurt as I jerk my arm out of his grasp.

"No. That's not what I meant."

"What did you mean, then?" I raise my eyebrows.

On the outside, I know I'm projecting. But on the inside, my heart is quivering and breaking apart. Kind of like a glass sliding off the counter in the middle of an earthquake.

"We should take a break, Ingrid. I don't know who I am without—"

"Don't finish that sentence!" I warn.

"—you."

"I think you do," I shake my head.

"I haven't thought much about a future without you in it," he lies. *Liar, liar, liar!*

"You s-should g-go," I choke out as Cash's face falls. "Go on your stupid backpacking trip, and then go live in Baltimore and forget all about me! I know you will. Even Wilder thinks so."

"Wilder thinks that?" Cash chews on the inside of his cheek.

"Yeah," I blow out a tired breath. "It's not just me who sees a change in you. Are you also breaking up with Wilder before you go?"

"I'm not breaking up with you, Ingrid," Cash laments. "I... it's two months apart."

"Are you going to call me?"

"I don't know. I'm not sure I'll have cell service—"

"Email me?" I add. "Send me a postcard?"

"My parents think we shouldn't communicate while I'm gone," Cash reveals.

"Then we're done, Cash. This is over. I'm not spending my life waiting for you."

43

"Don't say things you don't mean." He tries moving closer again, but I back up against the front door.

"I'm not going to spend my summer hoping you realize your parents are wrong. Go to Europe, Cash. Have fun. But I won't be here when you get back."

I try ignoring the tears forming in Cash's blue eyes. I try ignoring my heart banging and clanging against bone and muscle, trying to get to him. I try ignoring the fact that his parents are control freaks who won't let him live his own life. I try ignoring how hurt Cash looks.

But when a tear slips down his cheek, my heart can't take it, and I reach for him. As my arms circle his neck, he cries into my shoulder.

"I'm sorry. I'm sorry. I'm sorry." He keeps saying it, but I'm not sure what he's sorry for. His parents, or his inability to make up his mind.

"You should go," I say, trying to hold in tears.

Cash kisses my cheek before wiping the tears off his face. "I love you, Ingrid."

I want to say it back, but I can't bring myself to. "Have a good trip."

Cash shakes his head. "I'll try."

I watch him go, my heart a battered, beaten, bloody mess.

He gives me a small wave from his truck before driving off.

And because I refuse to cry in front of Mom and Isla, I walk down the stone pathway to the curb. As I sit down, an imposing figure appears like a bad dream that won't stop haunting me.

"I'm not in the mood, Wilder."

He sits on the curb beside me. "At least he said goodbye to you."

I turn to look at him. He's wearing his blacked-out sunglasses, but they don't hide the pain he's in. Pain I'm in, too.

"He came by to break up with me," I flash my eyebrows at him.

Wilder pulls a silver flask out of his back pocket. He takes a long swig before passing it over to me. "At least you know where you stand with him."

I bring the flask up to my lips and take a sip. It's strong. Too strong. I cough as I hand Wilder back the alcohol.

"You were right," I admit. "I'm not going to Baltimore. He's going to find someone who fits into his world better than I do."

"I'm sure he'll find a new best friend, too."

"I don't know."

"Turns out we're in the same boat, Blondie. Both rejected by Cash Allred."

"Want to hear something sad and pathetic?" I smile sadly as Wilder removes his sunglasses.

"Uh, yes," he nods. "Maybe it'll cheer me up."

"You are my only friend now," I admit out loud. "And I hate you."

"So, does that make us frenemies?" Wilder proposes.

"I don't know," I shrug.

"Wait," Wilder grins. "Are you asking me to be your bestie with testes?"

I pretend to gag myself. "Hand me the flask."

Wilder places it in my open palm. "You wanna jump out of the tree at the creek?"

As I swallow another mouthful of whatever Wilder's drowning his sorrows in, I smack the back of his head and say, "Hell no."

Chapter 5
The Bucket List

I stare at myself in the mirror as I brush my hair. The early afternoon sun dances across the vanity and reflects off the mirror. I haven't cried since Cash drove away three days ago. *Not once.* I should be crying, right? Cash is in Europe. The boy I've been madly in love with for four years *dumped me*. Well, maybe I dumped him. Whatever. The dumping was mutual. Why haven't I cried more?

Four years are gone. Down the drain. Over. Dead. Just a memory.

He chose his parents over me. He chose Europe over me. He chooses everything over me. I don't know why I'm surprised. Maybe because I still believe Cash is a good guy. He's still kind and gentle and steady. He always showed up with flowers on my birthday and Valentine's Day and *just because*. He's never forgotten an anniversary. He answered when I called. He drove me everywhere. *Everywhere.* He was the epitome of a dutiful boyfriend.

He loves me. He said he did. And I still love him. But it's over.

So, why haven't I cried more?

I should be crying, right?

"Ingrid!" I hear Mom yell from downstairs. "There's a... *a boy* here to see you!"

I grab my bag and roll my eyes. I dated Cash for four years and Wilder was *always* our third wheel. He's also our neighbor and has been for the past six years. At this point, it's just embarrassing she doesn't know his name. Then again, I've made it a point not to let the words *Wilder Cox* escape my mouth around anyone with the Winthrop last name. But I guess since we're friends now—or *frenemies*—it's time Mom learns his name.

"And that," Wilder's voice carries up the stairs as I race down them, "is why they call me *Wild Cox*."

I slap my hand to my forehead. He did *not* just tell Mom that story. I'm mortified for him. For me. *For Mom.*

"I'll be home by dinner," I yell over my shoulder as I grab Wilder's arm and yank him out the door. I drag him down the porch as fast as I can, hoping Mom doesn't put two-and-two together.

"Where's the fire, Blondie?" Wilder asks as I tug him to my car with force.

"You can't tell my mom that story," I groan.

"But everyone thinks it's hilarious," Wilder whips his head back in confusion. "*Everyone.*"

"No," I shake my head as I unlock my car door. "*Teenage boys* think it's hilarious."

"That's... " Wilder trails off, realization striking him like lightning. "Oh. Yeah. I can see why that might be true. I probably shouldn't mention my legendary nickname to your mom."

"You think?" I raise my eyebrows at him before we both get inside the car.

"Unless she wants to take a ride on *Wild Cox*," he gives me a devilish grin.

"You are ridiculous."

"Tell that to Olivia-Sophia," he claps back.

When Wilder lost his virginity sophomore year to the senior Homecoming Queen, Olivia-Sophia (yes, she has two first names and they're hyphenated), he bragged about it for months. *Months*. Eventually, Olivia-Sophia's friends found out she'd been hooking up with Wilder in secret and asked her why she was sleeping with a sophomore. Olivia-Sophia replied, "They don't call him *Wild Cox* for nothing."

And so, the legend of *Wild Cox* began.

Girls have been flocking to get a peek at Wilder's massive member ever since. I've never seen it myself, so I can't confirm or deny if the legend of *Wild Cox* is true, but Olivia-Sophia was willing to risk her reputation for Wilder's colossal cock. He doesn't have much of a personality. One can only assume what he lacks in social interactions, he makes up for in bedroom antics.

"You thinking about it?" Wilder whispers as I put the key in the ignition.

"Thinking about what?" I glance over at him as he widens his eyes. "And don't be creepy. I can't be friends with Creepy Wilder."

"Thinking about *Wild Cox*," he says as he flashes his eyebrows at me.

I exhale as I grip the steering wheel in my hands. "If we're going to be friends—"

"Frenemies," Wilder corrects me.

"We need to establish some ground rules," I propose.

"Like?"

"Rule #1: Don't mention your dick."

"Why?" Wilder asks, offended.

"I'm not your bro or one of your ladies of the night," I remind him. "I don't care about your penis."

"If you saw it you would," he sing-songs before gazing out the window.

"Rule #2: Don't show me your dick."

"I don't send nudes unless requested," he assures me.

"Aren't you afraid someone is going to post a picture of it on the internet?"

Wilder purses his lips as he looks at me. "No. Why would I be? Are you afraid Cash is going to post yours on the internet?"

"I, uh, never sent him any."

Wilder laughs. "You guys are so lame."

"Rule #3: Don't talk about Cash."

"That one is easy," Wilder holds his hand out for me to shake.

"I'm not touching that," I recoil in disgust. "I don't know where it's been."

Wilder shrugs. "Twenty minutes ago, it was wrapped around my dick in the shower."

"Rule #4: Don't masturbate and tell me about it."

"You are no fun," he crosses his arms over his chest. "*No fun!*"

"I used to be," I lament.

"Before Cash ruined you," Wilder adds.

My mouth drops open. "What does that mean?"

"Just means you used to be funny and easygoing. You started dating Cash, and suddenly you had a stick up your ass."

"I did not," I argue.

"Did, too."

"Okay," I hold up a hand. "This isn't getting us anywhere. Rule #5: Don't argue over stupid stuff."

"Fine," he grumbles.

"And apologize to me," I demand. "You told Fanny I was purposely trying to get pregnant at Cash's goodbye party, and she forced him to break up with me over that."

Wilder raises an eyebrow. "I'm sorry Cash broke up with you."

"And?"

"But I am *not* sorry that Fanny Allred caught you and Cash together," he chuckles. "If she hadn't,

I never would have believed you convinced Cash to give up his vow of abstinence."

"If we're going to be frenemies," I hold up a hand to stop him, "you have to apologize."

"Alright," he grunts. "I'm sorry I suggested you would try to get pregnant to sink your claws into Cash, and the Allred fortune."

"You didn't say the fortune part," I say, shaking my head.

"No," he rubs a hand over his face. "Not this time. I may have said stuff to Fanny in the past."

"You're unbelievable!"

"I was jealous Cash wanted to play with your boobs instead of hang out with me," he admits. "Big deal. I was just trying to get more time with him."

"I'm sorry my boobs were more important than jumping out of trees and possibly breaking limbs," I lament and roll my eyes dramatically. "It's not like you didn't benefit from Cash's status."

"I didn't."

"Don't lie."

"I would never lie."

"Except to Fanny," I remind him.

"It was an exaggeration of the truth."

"I never cared about Cash's money. I only cared about Cash."

"Yeah," Wilder furrows his brow. "So, did I."

"We shouldn't have fought so much."

"No," Wilder inhales sharply. I think this might be the first time we've agreed on something. "I guess it was all for nothing. In the end, he left us. And instead of saying goodbye, he broke up with you and ignored me."

"I'm sorry he didn't say goodbye to you," I gnaw on the inside of my cheek as I put the car in drive. "You've been his best friend for most of his life. He should have."

Wilder points to the road. "Doesn't matter now. We should get going or we'll be late."

I drive away from the house, frustrated. I know where I stand with Cash. He made it clear he wants to spend the summer apart. Wilder, though, didn't get so much as a *see ya around* text. He's stuck in limbo.

I always thought Cash was a good friend, but I'm starting to wonder if it was Wilder who did all the heavy lifting in their friendship. He never would have left Cash for the summer without saying goodbye. He would have never left Cash *period*.

As I look over at Wilder, I take a deep breath.

"Don't pity me, Blondie," he warns. "I'll be fine."

I know he will be. His dad left when he was 12, which is why he and his mom moved into his grandparents' house six years ago. Wilder isn't like Cash. Wilder will survive whatever happens because he's already been through hell. He's never relayed that to me, but I picked up on enough comments in the past. Wilder's dad leaving hurt him, but he survived. Just like I'll survive the summer without Cash. I've survived living in Isla's shadow and Mom's obliviousness. I've survived Fanny Allred dragging my name through the mud. I've even survived Wilder's smear campaigns.

I'll survive this.

I will.

I think I will.

Oh no.

My eyes fill with tears as I try blinking them away. I *cannot* have a breakdown in front of Wilder. He'll never let me live it down.

But then, he motions to the empty church parking lot on our right and I turn into it.

I put the car in park and take deep breaths. I can cry when I get home. I can cry when I'm all alone. I can't cry now.

"Just let it out," Wilder sighs. "It's better to get it over and done with."

"I'm fine," I lie.

"He broke up with you, Blondie. He's not coming back. You can be sad about it." I know I shouldn't trust Wilder, but I don't have anything to lose at this point. Cash is gone. Fanny Allred made sure of that. There's nothing for Wilder and me to fight over anymore. There's just...

I let a few hot, salty tears slip down my cheeks. One collects along my lips, and I raise a hand to wipe the evidence away.

Evidence that I loved Cash.

Evidence that I thought we had a future together.

Evidence that this feels like a betrayal.

Evidence that this hurts.

It hurts. It hurts like the time Mom forgot me at the grocery store. I sat on a parking lot curb waiting for hours. It wasn't until Dad got home from work and asked about me that she realized she left me at the store.

She didn't even come to pick me up. Dad did.

Being forgotten is like trying to fit a key into a lock that doesn't fit. Or waking up to an empty house on a Saturday morning. Or waiting in the rain for someone to notice you.

I don't want to spend my time worrying about being forgotten anymore. I think I want to have fun again. Like I used to before I started dating Cash.

"We have eight weeks before classes start," I say, startling Wilder.

"And?"

"And I'm tired of not having fun," I force a smile. "We should make a bucket list."

"A bucket list?"

"Yeah," I nod my head. "A Lonely Summer Bucket List. We'll each choose four things we want to do and do one a week until the summer is over."

"I get to pick four things and you have to do them?" Wilder sits up straighter.

"They have to be within reason."

"Get a tattoo."

"Okay," I agree. "Sneak into the movie theatre."

"Skinny dip at the lake."

"Uh," I lick my lips nervously. "Can it be at night?"

"Right," Wilder snaps his fingers. "Rules 1 and 2. Yeah, we can do nighttime if you want."

"Sneak onto the golf course and play a round," I flash my eyebrows at him.

"Dinner at the country club," Wilder grins.

"Ooh," I laugh. "I like that one."

"And we have to dress fancy," he adds.

"Deal," I agree as I clap my hands. "Go to a Smashing Trout concert."

"Fuck no," he quickly shuts me down.

"I agreed to skinny dip at the lake," I remind him. "You're going to a Smashing Trout concert."

"Jump out of the tree at the creek."

"Only if I get to choose the branch," I wager.

"Fine."

"That's seven." I hold up my fingers. "I guess I get to choose lucky number eight."

"What's it gonna be?" Wilder crosses his arms over his chest.

What's something that Cash Allred's girlfriend would never do?

I clear my throat. "Send a nude."

Wilder smiles wide. "Sounds like we have our Lonely Summer Bucket List then. When do we start?"

"Friday?"

"Works for me," Wilder says as he leans back in the passenger seat.

I groan. "I can't believe I agreed to jump out of the tree at the creek."

"I can't believe you suggested sending a nude."

"Life is short," I shrug. "You ready to go pick my stuff up from Fanny?"

Wilder exhales. "Knowing Fanny, it's probably sitting on the curb with the trash."

"I think I'm okay with that."

"Yeah?"

I pull back onto the road. "Yeah. I think everything will be fine."

And maybe it will be.

Chapter 6
The Legend Himself

Frank Bertinelli is a douchebag. A short, round-faced baboon. And he's currently sitting across the dining room table from Dad, lecturing him on the pitfalls of government dependence.

"I'm just saying, Jason," Frank steeples his fingers together, "maybe you should think about settling for a lesser-paying job. Unemployment isn't a good look for this family. Plus, it's embarrassing for Isla every time Jill comes into the grocery store and uses food stamps. I talked to my manager and he's willing to give Jill a job on the night shift stocking shelves."

"But I have a job," Mom interjects with a quizzical look. Mom is a dog walker. Basically, she works out for a living. She just does it with four-legged companions whose owners *give* her money instead of with a trainer who *takes* her money. Mom's not the brightest crayon in the box, but she does make decent money for someone whose business model was written in colored pencil.

"Not a job that can support this family," Frank scoffs. "I mean, you think you can pay the mortgage and keep the electricity on by walking dogs? Come on, Jill. You should know better than that."

Honestly, I'm not surprised selfish Isla would fall for this narcissistic display of pigheadedness. Even Fanny Allred isn't this outlandish and contrived.

"Get out of my house," Dad's face turns red.

"I'm willing to loan you the money to get back on your feet," Frank continues. "But you'll have to—"

"Get him," Dad looks to Isla, "out of my house. *Right now.*"

"He's just trying to help, Daddy," Isla defends her stubby boyfriend.

"Then you should take the job stocking shelves," Dad tilts his head to the side. "And you can start paying me rent."

"And for gas money," I add. Isla spends more on gas in one week than I've spent all year. And Dad's been paying for it.

Dad winks at me. "Ingrid's right. It's time you get your own car and pay for your own gas."

"You've got to be kidding me!" Isla fumes.

"No," Dad shakes his head. "I'm not."

"Now, Jason," Mom clears her throat. "We shouldn't be too harsh on Isla. She did fail two classes this semester at college and—"

"She WHAT?" Dad's mouth drops open in surprise.

"Mommy," Isla's eyes widen, "I thought I told you that I was handling that on my own."

"You're saying that I shelled out thousands of dollars last semester on your education and you failed two classes?" Dad stands from his chair. "And then I have to listen to this asshole"—Dad points to Frank—"tell me I need to get a real job? Are you serious, Isla?"

"It's not my fault," Isla crosses her arms over her chest. "Frank kept me busy in the... the library. I was helping him."

"Helping?" I chuckle. "You mean humping?"

Mom laughs and holds a hand up for me to slap. "Good one, Ingrid."

"Let me make something very clear," Dad glances back and forth between Frank and Isla. "The unemployment I receive is money that I've paid into for twenty-plus years in case of an emergency just like this one. You don't get to come in here and berate me like I'm some opportunistic, greasy-haired TA who was sleeping with one of his students." Isla gasps as Dad continues, "So, the next time the two of you decide to attack your mother and I's choices, I might find myself making a phone call to the dean to let him know that the man he employs to teach and educate students is using the library like a whorehouse."

"Jason," Mom blushes. "I think it's called a bordello."

I drop my head into my hands. I can't believe I have to listen to this ridiculous conversation. I would rather spend my night listening to Wilder pick up girls.

"We're just trying to help, Daddy," Isla sniffles. "We don't want you to lose the house."

"No," I hitch a shoulder, "you just don't want Dad to stop paying your tuition."

"That's not true!" Isla yells at me as she nudges Frank with her elbow. I roll my eyes as she begs for backup.

"You shouldn't even be here for this discussion," Frank glares at me. "It doesn't concern you."

Dad clenches his fist as I push my chair back.

"You're right, Frank the Fornicator," I give him a wink. "I shouldn't be here. I think I'm going to take *my* car and find somewhere else to spend my Thursday evening."

"Can I go with you?" Mom asks.

"No, Jill," Dad shakes his head.

"Maybe next time, Mom," I say to her as I push my chair in. "And dog walking is a noble and honest profession. Don't give it up."

"Thanks, Ingrid," Mom smiles.

I grab my car keys off the kitchen counter and hurry out the front door. As much as I would love to hang around for the Frank and Isla show, I'd much rather be alone. Dad's been burying himself with job interviews and Mom's been fake-smiling through the grocery store, trying to hide from everyone that we're struggling. And I've been forcing myself not to think about Cash. Seems like we're all having a tough time except for Isla. But that's typical in the Winthrop house. Isla always comes out on top. Even when she's in dead last.

There aren't many places to hang out on a Thursday night in our small town. There's the bowling alley or the pool hall. And since Cash and I had our first date at the bowling alley, the pool hall is the only logical choice.

Most of the pool tables are taken as I weave between people and sticks in search of the vending machines. It's been a while since I've been in here. Not since sophomore year. Cash got banned after taking the blame for inciting a brawl. Wilder elbowed Donovan Turner in the face and started a fight. Three pool tables were destroyed in the process. The Allreds made a hefty donation to help *restore* the pool hall to its former glory, but Cash was never allowed back in. I'm pretty sure that's the only time Cash ever stood up for Wilder. The only time I can remember, anyway.

And now, since we're broken up, I guess that means I can start frequenting the pool hall again.

I slip a dollar into the vending machine and watch as a Cherry Coke topples off the shelf, falling to the bin below. As I shove my hand inside to grab it, a shadow falls across the floor beside me.

"On your knees again, Blondie?"

I groan. "Are you stalking me?"

"Always," Wilder grins as I stand.

"Well, stop. It's gross."

"You're gross," he snaps back.

I frown. "That the best you got tonight? Kind of weak for you."

"It's been a long day." He shrugs and motions to the pool tables. "Wanna play a round?"

"I didn't come here to hang out with you," I scoff.

"Do you know anyone else here?" Wilder turns and looks around the room.

"I *know* people," I lie. "I have friends."

"I thought I was your only friend," he flashes his dark eyebrows at me. "Or were you lying about that?"

He moves closer, his disgusting hazel eyes lively and warm. *Ew*. Did I just describe Wilder as warm? What is wrong with me?

"Fine," I give in. "I'll play. But I still hate you."

"The feeling is still mutual," he assures me.

We snag a table in the back next to a group of girls. I ignore their hushed whispers and aggravating giggles as I grab a pool stick.

"You remember how to play?" Wilder asks me, oblivious to the fan club swooning over him at the next table.

I don't really remember how to play, but I'm not telling him that. "You can go first."

Wilder walks behind me, his arm brushing against my side. "Ladies first."

"Ah," I raise an eyebrow and rest my hand on the top of the pool stick as he leans a hip against the table. "Then you should go first."

There's this weird tension bouncing between us as our eyes lock in a battle of wills. It's uncomfortable, and it makes my stomach flutter. Things with Cash were easy. There wasn't hard-to-read energy or heated banter. I didn't want to strangle him one minute, and then laugh at him the next. It was simple. Things with Wilder are complicated. They always have been.

Wilder sinks his teeth into his bottom lip. "You're obnoxious."

"You're the one who wanted to play," I remind him. "I was fine standing in the corner with my drink minding my own business."

He sighs and leans over the table, his focus on the triangular formation of balls in front of us. "I'll go first."

I tap my foot beside him. "Don't embarrass yourself."

Wilder tries to hide a smile. "Do you always have to be this obnoxious?"

I place a hand on my hip as he strikes the cue ball. "Always."

The balls scatter as Wilder stands, triumphant. Several disappear into the corner pocket. "You really should have gone first, Blondie. I'm about to annihilate you."

It doesn't take Wilder long before he's sunk all his balls into the corner pockets without so much as a scratch.

"Well," Wilder steals my Cherry Coke from me. "That was fun. Round two?"

I watch, annoyed, as he guzzles the rest of my bottle.

"You're buying me another," I inform him.

"Only if you win," he smirks.

Before I can respond with a snarky comment, we hear Wilder's name from across the hall.

We both turn at the same time a brunette saunters toward us.

"Well, well, well," she coos. "If it isn't the legend himself."

Standing before us is Olivia-Sophia. The girl who took Wilder's virginity and made *Wild Cox* a legend.

"Aren't you going to give me a hug?" Olivia-Sophia asks Wilder.

He shakes his head. "I... what are you doing here?"

"I'm home for the summer," the raven-haired beauty confesses. "I thought we could catch up."

As my eyes drift between Olivia-Sophia and Wilder, I cross my arms over my chest, confused. Wilder looks... scared. Maybe that's not the right word. Apprehensive? Yeah, apprehensive. Wilder looks like he's about to throw up.

Olivia-Sophia, on the other hand, is eyeing Wilder like a piece of meat. Which makes sense. She's the reason every girl in this place has either seen him naked or wants to see him naked. Except for me, of course. I don't want to see Wilder without clothes on.

In a twist I *definitely* don't see coming, Wilder slips his hand around my waist and tugs me close. As my body knocks into him, I stare up at the cool expression on his face. "Sorry, busy on a date."

Olivia-Sophia narrows her eyes. "Aren't you dating Cash Allred?"

"*Was*," Wilder answers for me. "They broke up. Turns out she's been madly in love with me for years."

"Is that so?" Olivia-Sophia exhales.

"Yep," Wilder quips.

Wait, am I really letting Wilder lie right now? He's tormented me for years. *For years*! This could be a chance to get him back for all the shit he's done to me.

"What a shame," Olivia-Sophia purses her lips.

"I'm sure Wilder is free this weekend," I run my fingers through his stupid hair, tugging *hard* when I reach the nape of his neck.

"What the fu—" Wilder starts, but I cut him off.

"And I'm not opposed to sharing," I wink at her. "There's enough of Wilder to go around. If you know what I mean."

"Oh," Olivia-Sophia's face lights up. "I like you. What's your name again?"

I release of Wilder's hair and offer her my hand. "Ingrid. Ingrid Winthrop."

"What are you guys doing Saturday?" Olivia-Sophia asks as Wilder digs his fingers into my hip.

"Country club!" Wilder interjects loudly. "We have a date at the country club."

"You should come," I say to Olivia-Sophia.

She shakes her head. "No, I don't want to intrude."

"Well," I shrug as I run my hand up Wilder's toned front, his breathing catching as I do, "if you change your mind, we'd love it if you joined us."

"I'll think about it," Olivia-Sophia smiles. "I'll let you get back to your date."

She disappears into the crowd as Wilder inhales sharply. I rest my hand on his chest, his face hard to read. I don't know what he's trying to hide, but he's doing a shitty job of it.

"You ready for round two?" I propose.

"I think you should go home, Blondie," he says as he lets go of my waist and circles the table. "You should go."

"Why?" I swallow hard. "You afraid you'll lose?"

His jaw tenses. "I'll go."

67

He heads for the exit as I follow behind him. He doesn't slow his pace until we're outside.

I grab his shoulder, forcing him to face me. "What's going on, Wilder?"

"You shouldn't have invited her."

"Okay," I lick my lips nervously. "I'll go back in and uninvite her."

As I turn, he grabs my arm. "No. Don't."

"Seriously?" I frown. "What's going on? You're not acting like, well, *you*."

"She's... I don't... I... she..."

"Just spit it out!"

"She's a freak!"

I blink slowly. "What?"

"She's into weird shit," Wilder lets my arm go. "She made me do weird shit, okay? Shit I'm not comfortable discussing so don't ask me about it. Shit I'd never do to anyone."

I think he's traumatized. I think Olivia-Sophia literally traumatized him. And for the first time in my life, I actually feel bad for Wilder.

"Okay," I clear my throat, my mind racing through a thousand different scenarios. "Do you need a ride home?"

"Yeah," he scratches the side of his face. "If you don't mind."

"No," I answer as I hook my arm around his. "I don't mind."

His gaze lands on our linked arms. "What are you doing?"

"Taking you home," I brush off.

"No, why are you touching me?"

I shrug. "Seems like you could use a friend."

Wilder pulls his arm out of mine and grabs my hand. He squeezes lightly, not letting go until we reach my car.

When we're buckled inside, Wilder presses his forehead to the window and takes a deep breath.

I don't know what happened with Olivia-Sophia but I've never seen Wilder like this before.

I didn't think he was scared of anything.

I guess I was wrong.

Chapter 7
The Country Club

I know I really shouldn't, but I click on the Snapchat icon on my phone and prepare myself for *the worst*. Pictures of Cash surrounded by sexy European women with long legs and gorgeous hair lying on sandy beaches in Ibiza or Majorca. And there will probably be videos of him dancing in nightclubs, too, living up his newfound freedom in Amsterdam and London. Why wouldn't he?

He's young, hot, and *free.*
Free from me.
Free to hang out with lots of girls.

All the scenarios racing through my head right now involve other women, of course. My mind can't help but go there. We were together for four years. *Four years*.

Unlike Wilder, Cash has only had sex with one girl. He's never sowed any wild oats (as Mom would say). He's never even kissed anyone else. Maybe he wants to.

Which leads me to the next horrible thought. *He left me*. Like it was easy or something.

How could he walk away after four years? Why didn't he fight for me? Did he just use his parents as an excuse to dump me? I mean, I *know* it's

Europe. If Dad offered to send me on a sightseeing exploration for eight weeks, I'd probably go, too. The furthest I've ever been from home is across the state line to shop for a prom dress. And that's only because Mom got lost. She's not great with directions.

What if he left me because he wanted a free pass in Europe? What does that say about Cash?

Better yet, what does that say about *me*?

The app loads and I notice immediately that Cash has changed his avatar. New Cash apparently wears tank tops and sunglasses. *The audacity.*

Taking a deep breath, I click on his stories and lick my lips nervously. What I'm about to see, I'll never be able to un-see. I should probably do some deep breathing exercises but I'm not really in the mood to connect with my higher self right now. I prefer to view his unattached rendezvous through Europe as snarky, snide Ingrid.

The first story is a picture of Big Ben. Then, the London Eye. And finally, one of Cash standing in front of what looks like a museum. He's alone, but he looks... *happy*. Why does he look so happy?

My heart dips in my chest as I blink away tears. I was prepared to see girls all over him. I was prepared to see him partying. I was *not* prepared to see him doing fine without me. No, better than fine. *Happy*.

"Why are you staring at a picture of Judas?" someone whispers over my shoulder.

Frazzled, I fumble with my phone, nearly dropping it on the concrete below.

"Why do you always sneak up on me?" I hold my phone to my chest, my heart pounding a million miles a second.

"I like to keep you on your toes," Wilder winks.

"Well, *don't*," I snap.

Wilder points to the phone in my hand. "Why are you stalking him? And why are you doing it on Snapchat? He'll know. He checks to see who views his stories."

"He won't know," I say as my breathing evens out.

"Why won't he?"

I hold my phone up. "Secret account."

"You have a secret Snapchat account?"

I nod. "I do. Does that make me pathetic?"

"Depends on what your secret account name is."

"Pam."

"Pam?"

"Yes."

"Then yes, you are pathetic, Pam."

Well, at least he didn't call me Blondie.

I take a moment to look him over. We're crossing off Lonely Summer Bucket List Item #1 tonight. *Dinner at the country club. Dress fancy.* Wilder is dressed in black slacks and a soft green button-up that brings out the minty color of his eyes. Mint, with tiny flecks of gold in them. They're not horrible to look at.

"You like what you see, Blondie?" Wilder rolls his hips suggestively in my direction.

"You have to ruin everything," I groan, "don't you?"

"Why, Wilder," he says with a high-pitched voice, obviously mimicking me, "you look rather dapper this evening."

"Is that supposed to be me?" I raise my eyebrows at him.

"Yes."

"You should really work on that. I would *never* use the word dapper."

"You look nice, too," Wilder tilts his head to the side as his hazel eyes sweep over my body. I shift my weight from one foot to the other as his gaze lingers on my chest. I settled on a white, body-hugging lace dress I wore to Fanny's End of Summer party last year. It was the fanciest thing in my closet. My boobs, however, like to spill out of it.

"My eyes are up here," I remind him with a smirk.

He lets out an annoyed breath. "You ready?"

"No," I honestly admit.

Cash never took me to the Country Club. I wasn't allowed to attend any of the Allred family dinners there. I'm not sure how Wilder managed to finagle his way into a reservation for us, but in the four years Cash called me his girlfriend, he never let me hang around the elite group of people he grew up with. I always assumed it was because he was embarrassed by them. Now, I'm beginning to wonder if he was embarrassed by me.

"Are you okay?" Wilder steps closer, his face full of concern. Or it could be gas. Hard to tell. "You look like you're going to cry."

"Do you ever wonder if Cash was embarrassed by us?" I ask him.

Wilder shoves his hands into his pockets and looks over my head. "All the time, Blondie."

I hug my arms to my chest. "Is that why he broke up with me? Because I was embarrassing."

"I think you give Cash too much power over you," Wilder answers.

I narrow my gaze, agitated. "That's not what I asked."

"I'm not trying to hurt your feelings," he tries softening the blow, "but you broke up. Let him go. What's that stupid saying my mom always says? Something like *let him go. If he comes back, great. If not, move the fuck on.*"

I smile, despite wanting to strangle the only friend I currently have. "Your Mom says *move the fuck on*?"

"No," Wilder grins. "But she really should. She's still pining over that loser Lee. It's been three years. She really should *move the fuck on*."

"Wasn't he married?"

He shrugs. "Yep."

"Alright," I concede. "How do I stop giving Cash power over me?"

"You can start by deleting Pam."

"I don't want to delete Pam," I pout. "She posts pictures of her cat and likes to knit."

"You don't have a cat," Wilder shakes his head.

"I could have one if I wanted to," I defend myself. "And, so what if Pam wants to check up on Cash every other day or so?"

"It's not healthy."

"I can keep tabs on Cash," I brush off. "I can handle it."

"I thought we weren't allowed to talk about Cash?" he frowns. "Wasn't that one of your friendship rules?"

"Yeah," I inhale sharply, shocked he remembered.

"No more talking about him tonight," Wilder asserts.

"You're right," I exhale. "We should get going so we're not late."

Wilder leads the way and opens my car door for me. Touched by his thoughtfulness, I smile. "Thanks."

"I just wanted to look at your boobs again."

"You're disgusting."

"I know," he grins.

Despite myself, I laugh.

Wilder fidgets with the radio as I drive through town, the sun still high in the summer sky.

"How did you get us a reservation?" I glance over at Wilder, curious.

"I know someone."

"You know someone?" I blow out a tired breath. "You must mean a girl because you don't have guy friends."

"My only guy friend is currently in Europe."

"Have you talked to Judas?" I pry.

Wilder rolls his eyes. "We're not supposed to talk about him."

"I know that," I chew on the inside of my cheek as we stop at a red light. "I lost a boyfriend, but you lost your best friend. And I'm sure that must bother—"

"I'm fine," Wilder cuts me off. "And I didn't lose Cash. Cash chose to spend the summer alone. Can't fault the guy for wanting some worldly experience before he's stuck in school for the next eight years straight."

"Okay," I huff. He's impossible. I'm just trying to validate his feelings, but Wilder never has been—and probably never will be—one to express his emotions. He calls it weakness; I call it trauma.

"People leave, Blondie," Wilder continues. "They leave, and sometimes they don't come back. It's a part of life. You just gotta deal with it."

"I wasn't worried about me, Wilder. I was worried about you," I clarify.

"I'm fine," he reiterates.

He says he's fine, but I know better. He wasn't fine when his dad left. He wasn't fine when he found out his dad had another family. He wasn't fine when his mom started falling for the wrong guys. Wilder's default setting is avoidance. And my default setting has always been to avoid Wilder's pain because he takes it out on me.

"Well," I sigh, "if you ever want to talk—"

"I won't."

"I'm here."

"Will your boobs also be there if I need to talk?"

"Why do you always do that?" I grip the steering wheel tighter.

"Do what?"

"Avoid talking about anything serious," I say as I look over at him. "You make a joke instead of just being... *real.*"

"The light is green."

I let out an annoyed grunt before driving through the intersection. Wilder stares straight ahead, not interested in having this conversation. Not that I should be surprised. Wilder and I have never been friends, and I know it's going to take more than friendship rules and a bucket list to change that.

By the end of the summer, I plan on knowing all of Wilder's deepest, darkest secrets.

The winding road leading up to the country club is lined with flowers—tulips, lilies, roses, and daffodils. It's deceptively welcoming. But if you don't pay an exuberant amount of money to belong here, it's decidedly unpleasant.

I run my hands along my white dress as I step out of the car and peer around. My little silver Toyota Corolla stands out in a sea of Range Rovers, BMWs, and Buicks.

"You ready?" Wilder asks as he waits for me at the edge of the car.

Here goes nothing, Ingrid. "Yep."

"Wanna know the secret to fitting in with this crowd?" Wilder whispers in my ear as we head toward the massive wood doors.

"There's a secret?" I swallow hard.

Wilder grabs the door and holds it open for me. "Act like you don't give a shit about anything. They'll never know the difference."

"You want me to pretend?" I tilt my head to the side.

"That's the key, Blondie."

I've never been great at pretending, but I've been doing a lot of masking lately—masking how I feel. With Cash gone, my world is small and sad. So, I fake smiles, and I pretend life is better than it is for Mom and Dad's sake. The last thing they need is an unhinged, brokenhearted daughter. They already have to deal with Isla's self-absorbed, self-serving antics.

I think I can pretend tonight. I can pretend that the one place I was never allowed to be Cash's girlfriend, I can be Wilder's date. I can belong here, even if I don't ever plan on coming back.

"Cox party of two," Wilder winks at the hostess.

The hostess blushes as she grabs two menus. I roll my eyes as Wilder places a hand on my back, pushing me forward.

One foot in front of the other, Ingrid. Hold your chin up. Smile. But not too big. Pretend you're uninterested, but life is easy.

"Why do you look constipated?" Wilder chuckles as he takes a seat across from me.

I smile at the hostess as she hands me a menu. "He likes to joke."

"Oh," she beams, "I know."

My mouth drops slightly open.

"My shift ends in 45 minutes," the hostess tells Wilder. "I'm looking forward to the *thank you* you're going to give me later for getting you a reservation."

With that, the hostess saunters away and Wilder watches her go.

"I'm sorry," my voice squeaks, "but did you trade sex for a dinner reservation tonight?"

"I did," Wilder admits with a shit-eating grin.

"So, you'll be going home with her after this?"

"Her name is Karissa. And yes, I will. You can give her a ride, right?"

I run a hand over my face. "Unbelievable."

"Don't worry, Blondie," Wilder flashes his eyebrows at me. "I'll be thinking about your boobs the whole time I'm *thanking* Karissa."

"You're disgusting."

"Yeah, you say that a lot."

"Because you are."

Wilder hides a smile as I glance around the country club, hoping someone or something can distract me from the utter disgust I feel right now. When my eyes land on Mr. Allred sitting at a table across the way, my heart freezes in my chest.

"I thought you said Cash's parents wouldn't be here tonight," I panic.

"Fanny's in Arizona visiting her sister," he stares at me, confused.

"Then why," I say through gritted teeth, "is Mr. Allred here?"

I motion to my right as Wilder's eyes follow. "Oh my—"

"Who is he here with?" I ask as I crane my neck to get a peek at his dinner companion. But there are too many people in the way. I can't see who it is.

"Uh," Wilder shakes his head. "You're not going to believe it."

"Who?"

"Clementine Church."

I gasp and cover my mouth with my hand. Fanny's arch-nemesis? No, that can't be right.

"What are we going to do, Wilder?"

He smirks as the waitress appears to take our drink order. "We're going to enjoy our first and only dinner at the Country Club, Blondie."

Chapter 8
The Bonding Experience

"What are we going to do, Wilder?" I ask again as my fingers dig into the white, crisp tablecloth.

"You don't think he's... he wouldn't... *no*," Wilder shakes his head.

"Cheat?" I whisper-yell.

"Fanny would," Wilder pauses and lifts a finger, dragging it across his neck, "if he was."

"You mean unalive him?"

"Can't you say *kill*?" Wilder shakes his head.

"I've been watching too many TikTok's," I run a hand down my face. "They'll suspend your account or something."

"For saying *kill*?"

"Or *die*," I shrug. "I think it's triggering for some people. Or it incites violence. Either way, you're not supposed to say it."

"It's going to be a trigger for us if Fanny finds out about *this*," Wilder raises an eyebrow. "Unless she already knows. That doesn't mean we still can't have some fun with it."

"But why would Mr. Allred be here?" I scrunch my face, confused. "In the open. Where everyone can see what he's doing."

Wilder leans forward, a tendril of charcoal falling across his forehead. "What if this is why Cash never brought us here?"

"Because his father is a lying, cheating psychopath?"

"Woah, Blondie," he says as he holds up a hand. "Let's tone it down a notch. Innocent until proven guilty."

"Yeah," I clear my throat. "You're right." That was a little dark and disturbing. Even for me.

I glance over at Mr. Allred and Clementine, shocked to see the former caressing the cheek of Fanny's arch-nemesis. The table next to theirs is empty now, giving me the perfect view of their dangerous liaison.

Why? Why is he doing this to his family?

Cash told me once that his father was a covert narcissist. I didn't pay much attention then. I just assumed he was pissed at his parents and wanted to complain about them. Maybe he was right. Maybe Mr. Allred is an unfeeling, selfish, cheating egomaniac.

Wilder snaps a picture of me.

I look at him. "What are you doing?"

"I want to remember this moment forever," he winks.

"Because?"

"This is the first time you ever admitted that I was right."

"You're dumb," I roll my eyes.

"So are you," he snaps back.

I tilt my head to the side. "What's gotten into you lately? Your comebacks suck, and you haven't made any jokes about sleeping with my sister. Or about me not being good enough for Cash." I can't help but think this has something to do with Olivia-Sophia. Did her return cause Wilder's mojo to... *plummet*?

"Isla was a one-and-done thing," he shrugs. "And Cash dumped you, thereby proving my point correct. You never were good enough for him."

"Ah, there's the Wilder I've grown to love and adore," I tease him.

"Don't use my name in the same sentence as *adore* unless you're talking about adoring my dick."

"You don't need anyone to adore your dick," I scoff. "You adore it every time you take a shower."

"Or think about your boobs," he admits as he hitches a shoulder.

I lean forward and narrow my gaze. "Stop talking about my boobs."

"I can't help it," he grins. "They're hanging out and making me think about all the things I'd like to do to them. Or on them."

"You repulse me."

"You ever wonder why Cash never did anything to them?"

"What? How would you know?"

"He's my best friend. We talk about the weird shit we do in the bedroom. But Cash never talked about your boobs. Is he a butt guy?"

I swallow hard. Cash really wasn't all that adventurous. We never had sex anywhere other than a bed and he hated blow jobs. Wait, I'm not supposed to be thinking or talking about him right now. Not when we have a crisis on our hands.

"Can we focus? *Please,*" I beg Wilder.

His hazel eyes dart to my chest. "It's hard to when you're boobies are calling my name. *Wilder, please touch us. Please do things to us. Please rub your*—"

"Stop!" I yell at him, catching the attention of the couple having dinner at the table next to ours. "*Sorry*," I give them an uncomfortable wave.

Thankfully, the waitress appears with our drinks and asks for our order. I take a moment to hide behind the menu and gulp in a few sobering breaths.

Once the waitress is gone, Wilder exhales. "We have two options, Blondie. Confront Archibald Allred about his alleged affair or take some pictures and use it to blackmail him."

I briefly close my eyes. "Confront or blackmail? Those are the only two options here?"

"Unless you have a better one."

I chew on my bottom lip, conflicted. I always knew Fanny hated me, but I used to think Mr. Allred liked me. He invited me to movie nights, let me tag along when the Allreds took their boat out on the lake, and paid for a limo to drive us to every high school dance we attended. I didn't know he thought I wasn't right for his son until the summer before senior year. I overheard him and Cash talking when they thought I was in the bathroom. He told Cash I was a pretty girl but that I wasn't ambitious enough to be a surgeon's wife. I've always known I'm not as ambitious as Cash. I mean, not many people are. Cash wants to save lives. Me? I want to own my own business someday. My dreams don't include holding a scalpel or curing cancer, but they're just as important.

"Earth to Blondie," Wilder kicks me under the table.

"What?" I grumble.

"You come up with a better plan?"

"I... " but I trail off. I don't have a better plan. What other choices do we have? Walk up to the table and ask Mr. Allred why he's on a date with someone other than his wife. Or secure photographic evidence that he's a cheater.

"Confront or blackmail?" Wilder taps his fingertips on the white tablecloth.

I lift my chin. "Blackmail."

Wilder raises both eyebrows. "Blackmail it is, then."

I watch as Wilder slips his phone out and discreetly snaps a few photos of Mr. Allred and Clementine Church. Then, he texts them to me.

"Now what?" I frown as I scroll through them.

"Now, we wait for the right opportunity to present itself," he crosses his arms over his chest.

"And when will that be?"

"You ask too many questions, Blondie," he smirks. "Can't you just go with the flow for once?"

"I'm the one who always goes with the flow," I remind him. "How many idiotic things did I tag along for?"

"You complained every time," Wilder tries to hide a smile.

"I just wanted to be alone with Cash."

Wilder sits up straighter. "We've broken every friendship rule you made for us, and we haven't even gotten our food yet."

"No," I shake my head, "not every rule."

"I can show it to you," he waggles his eyebrows suggestively.

"I'm good," I say as I grab my drink and pull it towards me. "I don't want to break any more rules tonight."

"I'm pretty sure rules are meant to be broken, Blondie," he argues.

"Did you really sleep with Isla?"

Wilder's eyes bore into mine. "No."

"Then how do you know about the birthmark?" I wonder aloud.

"Frank," he divulges.

I grit my teeth. "What did Frank the Fornicator do now?"

He chuckles. "Frank the Fornicator?"

"It's a long story," I shudder.

"Frank the Fornicator drank too much at the bowling alley and started telling everyone about Isla's birthmark. According to Frank, she likes doggy style, and he likes to stare at her birthmark while he fucks her. He also mentioned that your dad lost his job and you guys might lose the house."

"We're not going to lose the house," I tell Wilder. "Not yet anyway. I think my dad will do anything to hold onto it just to spite Frank."

"Your parents will figure it out," Wilder assures me. "They seem like nice people. They helped my mom out a few times with groceries."

I smile. "They did?"

"Yeah," he lowers his voice. "My mom was waiting for her food stamps card to come in the mail when we first moved in with my grandparents. She didn't want to ask my grandparents for money since they live on a fixed income, and they were giving us a free place to stay. Your mom was walking by with one of her dogs, and she saw my mom crying on the front porch. Jill didn't even know her, and she gave my mom a hundred bucks for food."

"You and my mom are on a first-name basis now?"

"Jill and I had a bonding experience the other day," he jokes. "Over *Wild Cox*."

"I can't believe you told my mom that story," I groan.

"Did she figure it out?"

"I hope not," I say as I twirl the straw in my glass.

"If you guys need cash for groceries or anything," Wilder plays with the fork on the table beside his plate, his eyes refusing to meet mine, "let me know. I owe you one."

"We're doing okay," I tell him. "But I'll keep it in mind in case something comes up."

Our food arrives and we spend the rest of our dinner at the country club in charged silence. To drown out the awkwardness, I scarf down my chicken fried steak and mashed potatoes while Wilder kills off his burger in a few bites.

"You ready to go?" Wilder yawns.

"It's only eight," I chastise him. "And you're already falling asleep?"

"I was up early."

"Doing?"

The corner of Wilder's mouth tips up. "Adoring my dick in the shower."

I resist the urge to gag myself. "No more *Wild Cox* talk."

"You want dessert?"

"No, I'm stuffed."

"Good," Wilder looks around. "Because Karissa is heading our way. Must be time to go."

Oh, right. Wilder traded sex for our dinner reservation. I'm not sure why, but there's this scratchy, annoying feeling in my chest as Karissa runs her hand over his shoulder.

"I'm off. You ready to go?"

"Yep," Wilder jumps up. Guess he's not tired anymore.

I sneak a peek at Mr. Allred's table. He and Clementine are sharing a slice of chocolate cake. I grab my phone and take a picture of him spoon-feeding the woman he's so obviously cheating on his wife with.

"Blondie," Wilder whistles. "Let's go."

But Mr. Allred hears the whistle and glances around. When he spots me, our eyes connect and he looks *uncomfortable*. I know I should look away, but I can't. I can't look away as we stare at each other, neither one refusing to back down.

When Cash finds out about this, it's going to destroy him. I shouldn't care, but I do. I don't want Cash to get hurt. Even if he's hurting me right now.

I break eye contact with Mr. Allred and grab my purse off the table. Wilder and Karissa are waiting by the door as I hurry over to them.

"Everything alright?" Wilder says quietly.

"Everything is fine," I force a smile.

"So," Karissa links her arm with mine and drags me away from Wilder. "How is chemo going?"

"What?"

"Wilder told me," Karissa lays her head on my shoulder. "He said your dying wish was to have dinner with him at the country club. And since you've been in love with him since kindergarten, how could I say no when he asked me to get you a reservation?"

My jaw clenches as Wilder hides a laugh behind his hand. I can't believe he would stoop *so low*. But if Wilder can have fun with this, then so can I.

"I was devastated," I inhale sharply, "when I found out that I was sick. I mean, I had just told Wilder how I really felt about him. It took me so long to work up the nerve to tell him that I wanted him for more than," I lower my voice to a whisper, "*Wild Cox.*"

Under the parking lot lights, I see Wilder's mouth drop open.

"When they told me it was terminal," I wipe away a fake tear, "he made love to me, and it was the most beautiful experience of my life. He was so gentle and kind. After we were done, he cried."

Wilder gasps. "I did not."

"Shh," I hold a finger up to my lips as Karissa rubs a comforting hand on my back. "It's okay. This is a safe space."

"I didn't fucking cry," Wilder defends himself.

I nod to Karissa and mouth, *he did*.

"I shouldn't say anymore. I don't want to embarrass him."

"Of course, not," Karissa sighs.

"Now that I only have weeks to live, I just wanted to enjoy a quiet dinner with my first and only love before I'm bedridden," I swallow hard, wiping away another fake tear.

"True love," Karissa corrects. "He's your true love."

"Yes, my true love." There's a beat before I continue. "You'll take good care of him, right?" I ask Karissa as I grip her hand in mine. "When I die, you'll make sure he's taken care of, right?"

"I'll... I'll try." *Huh*. She sounds uncertain.

"It would mean—"

"Blondie," Wilder snaps and opens the driver's side door, motioning for me to wrap it up. He always ruins everything.

When I reach him, he puts his arm out, blocking me from getting in. "What was that?"

"You're a despicable human being," I whisper as I give him a horrified glare. "I can't believe you would lie to her about something like that. There are actual people in the world who are going through a terminal illness diagnosis."

"You're just as despicable. You lied, too."

"Maybe," I lick my lips as my eyes settle on his mouth. "I don't want to pay for your shitty decisions, Wilder. I paid for Cash's for years. When

Karissa finds out the truth—and she will—I don't want to be around for it."

"I'm not Cash," he steps closer. "I'm not the good guy, Blondie. I'm not the guy who does the right thing all the time. I'm a lot of fun, though."

What is he saying? That he thinks I'm trying to replace Cash with him? That I hold him to the same standard as the asshole who ditched me for Europe.

"Don't worry, Wilder," I purse my lips. "I know exactly who you are."

"Good."

"You're the guy who cons girls into sleeping with you by telling sad, pathetic stories," I breathe through my nose. "I feel sad for you. You have sex with girls one time, then move on. You've never even been in a relationship. Does it have something to do with Olivia-Sophia?"

"Mind your fucking business," Wilder warns.

"Don't sleep with her," I plead. "Don't sleep with Karissa."

"Why?" His hazel eyes scan my face.

"Because," I place a hand on his arm. "You might be the fun guy, but we both know you're worth more than a dinner reservation."

Wilder stands perfectly still as I run my hand down his arm and grab his fingers. I move them off my car and slip into the driver's seat.

Wordlessly, he closes my door behind me, walks around the car, opens the passenger door, and gets in.

We both look over at each other as I turn on the ignition, a strange surge of electricity crackling between us.

I'm not the good guy, Blondie. I'm not the guy who does the right thing all the time. I'm a lot of fun, though.

But what if he is? What if he's the good guy? What if he's just confused and lost and traumatized?

"Let's go, Blondie."

I glance in the rearview mirror and pull out of the parking spot, my heart a conflicted mess.

Chapter 9
The Fanny Show

My boobs hurt, there's gigantic zit on my forehead that's pulsating, and I'm bloaty. By my calculations, in 1-3 days Aunt Flow will arrive. Hooray. I love getting my period while already being an emotional wreck.

I roll over and stare at my alarm clock. I got a part-time job at the waxing salon for the summer. I'll be answering phones for Loretta Van Buskirk while she takes her extended lunch from 11-2, Monday through Friday. Pierre, her nephew, will be filling in while Loretta socializes with the girls over cocktails and couscous at Bordin's, the fanciest restaurant in town. Come to think of it, I should probably schedule a Brazilian. With Loretta—not Pierre. Pierre gives me the creeps. But I'm not having sex because Cash dumped me and he's in Europe. So, what's the point?

Skinny dip at the lake.

Oh, right. Bucket list item #4. I guess I should probably get that part of me waxed before Wilder *gulp* sees me *gulp, gulp* naked.

Unless we skinny dip at night. Then, I wouldn't have to worry about buzzing the bush. Honestly, sometimes being a girl is exhausting. I think I'll put Brazilian wax on the back burner for now. We'll see how things go.

My phone starts vibrating on my bedside table. I grab it and see *Mom calling*. "Hello?"

"Ingrid?" Mom whispers on the other end. I have no idea why she's being weird, but this is just a typical Thursday for the Winthrops.

I hobble out of bed and open my bedroom door, peering up and down the hallway. "What?"

"We need to talk to you," she says quietly into the phone. "Come downstairs."

Oh, joy. Another family meeting. And because I know Isla snuck Frank the Fornicator into her bedroom last night, I'm sure he'll grace us with his gross presence this morning at breakfast. There goes my appetite. I really need to get my own place.

I don't bother changing out of my Smashing Trout tee and oversized pajama bottoms as I take the stairs two at a time.

I find Mom in the kitchen, rubbing her hands together nervously.

"What's up?" I ask.

Mom glances over my head and places a finger to her lips. "*Shhh!*"

"Okay," I frown.

She motions for me to follow her into the laundry room. When we get there, Dad shuts the door behind us and puts his weight against it.

"Are we being robbed?" I scratch the side of my face. "Are we under attack?"

"Frank's here," Dad grits his teeth. "I have a job interview and I don't want him to know."

"Alright," I tilt my head to the side, confused.

"We need you to create a diversion," Mom crosses her arms over her chest.

"I already snuck my suit out to the car," Dad explains, "but I don't want Frank to see me leave."

"I'm sure Frank is still asleep. They were up all night," I grimace, "moaning."

"I told her she wasn't allowed to let him sleep over," Mom whisper-yells at Dad.

"Isla's paying rent now," he rolls his eyes. "She said since she pays for the room, she should be allowed to have over *visitors*."

"Your house," I yawn, "your rules."

"Grow a backbone," Mom snaps at Dad.

"Jill," he looks at her, hurt.

"Sorry," she shrugs. "Been a stressful week. I lost two clients."

"Why?" I ask her.

"The Porters moved to Tennessee, and the Garber's dog died."

"Oh."

"It's fine," she says as she holds her hands out to the side, pinching her thumbs and forefingers together in a Zen-like motion. "I will get more clients. I will walk more dogs. I will be more successful than ever before."

Mom's a manifester. She's a big believer in speaking things into existence. It's always worked for her. I, on the other hand, see things a little differently. Like Dad, I think we make our own way in the world. I also believe that good things happen to good people. Which is why good things always happen for Mom. She might not be very bright, but she has a heart of gold.

"So, you want me to distract Isla and Frank while Dad sneaks out of the house without being questioned or seen?"

Mom and Dad look at each other and nod before saying, "Yes," in unison.

"You do realize this is your house, right?" I question.

"We're just trying to get through the summer," Dad exhales. "Then we're sending Isla back to college. Where she belongs."

"The college that you pay for," I raise an eyebrow. "And she's currently failing."

"Can you please just distract them?" Mom pleads. "I don't want your father to be late. This is a very important interview."

"I will distract them," I hold up a hand, "but you two should seriously consider how this looks. Living under the tyrannical reign of your eldest daughter and her lecherous boyfriend. It's very Henry the 8th."

"I thought he started his own church to divorce his first wife and then killed Anne Boleyn. That's what happened in that Showtime series. I don't see how that's the same as what's going on here," Mom furrows her brow.

"I didn't mean it literally," I try explaining. "I meant in the sense that we're living with a tyrant who beheads anyone who disagrees with them. But instead of beheading, Isla cuts us down with her words."

"We'll discuss this later," Dad interrupts. "I have to go."

"Fine," I cross my arms over my chest. "I will distract Queen Isla and Frank the Jester."

"But wouldn't he be King Frank?" Mom scrunches her face.

"Over my dead body," Dad mutters under his breath.

I leave Mom and Dad hiding in the laundry room and stomp up the stairs. I want Isla and Frank the Fornicator to hear me coming because I don't want to interrupt more moaning. It was bad enough listening to it all night long.

When I reach Isla's room, I knock hard. Then again. And again. I keep knocking until she throws the door open and glares at me.

"What do you want?" She snarls.

"I think I might be pregnant," I lie. "And I need your advice."

Isla places a hand on my shoulder. "You came to the right people."

I enter the Lair of Debauchery and shudder as Frank sits up. Without a shirt on. His chest is so hairy, it looks worse than Loretta's wastebasket full of waxed bushes.

"What's wrong?" Frank rubs his eyes.

"Ingrid might be pregnant," Isla informs him.

As she closes her bedroom door, shutting me inside, I curse Mom and Dad for not putting Isla up for adoption when we were younger and making me an only child.

"Loretta's Laser Hair and Wax Removal," I say into the phone. "How can we whack that bush for you today?"

Laughter. Peals of laughter fill my ears.

"Why are you calling me at work?" I groan.

"Whack that bush?" Wilder chortles. "What are they paying you to say that?"

"Minimum wage," I grumble.

"I'm calling because you haven't answered my texts," he clears his throat. "I wanted to make sure we're still on for the movie theatre tomorrow night."

"Wow," I smirk, "you're actually calling in advance to solidify plans. I thought your random hookups were a spur-the-moment type of thing.

Wait! Does this mean that you're madly in love with me? You did cry after our hypothetical first time."

"I shed tears of horror because you repulse me so much," he replies.

"If you expect me to believe that," I scoff, "you should really stop telling me you think about my boobs while you have sex with other girls."

"Are we still on?" He ignores my jab. "I need to know if I'm borrowing my mom's car."

"We are still on," I tell him. "Why don't you have your own car?"

"Because, Blondie, I've been saving for the past three years to pay for college," he answers.

"You make enough at the lumber yard to pay for all four years of college?"

"Yep," he boasts.

"But you only worked in the evenings."

"It's called investing," Wilder chirps. "You should try it."

"Is that all?" I shake my head. "I have to get back to work."

"Enjoy whacking all those bushes, Blondie."

"I just answer phones!" I rush to get out, but he's already hung up.

As I replace the handset on the receiver, the front door chimes. In walks Pierre's 1 o'clock. Fanny Allred.

I resist the urge to roll my eyes and grab a clipboard. When she reaches me, she gives me a victorious grin.

"Ingrid, I see you're spending your summer working," she winks as I hand her the clipboard. Loretta is making us update everyone's information. "How wonderful."

I don't respond. I don't even open my mouth. Because I'm terrified the words *your husband is sleeping with Clementine Church* might escape.

And then, as if on cue, the door chimes again and a familiar form saunters in. Clementine Church in the flesh. As if this day could get any better.

She gives Fanny a sinister smile.

Oh, this is going to be good.

"Fanny," Clementine greets Cash's mom as straight, black hair cascades over her shoulder. "How good to see you."

Fanny's jaw tenses as Clementine gives her air kisses on each cheek.

"You, too, Clementine," Fanny fakes a smile before hurrying over to a chair and hiding behind the clipboard.

"How can I help you?" I say to Clementine.

"I need an emergency wax," she states quietly. "I have a big date tonight. Is Loretta in?"

"No," I shake my head. "But Pierre is here. I think we can squeeze you in at 1:30."

Clementine tucks a strand of hair behind her ear, distracting me with her beauty. The woman is ethereal. Black hair like silk. Blue eyes like sapphires. Smooth, luxurious skin. I get why Mr. Allred is attracted to her, and why Fanny loathes her.

"I'd much rather see Loretta."

"I can get you in at four," I flip through the schedule. "You just need your usual?"

She leans in. "Hollywood wax. The whole shebang."

Wow. Didn't see that one coming. No wonder she wants Loretta. I wouldn't want Pierre waxing my anus either.

"Got you penciled in," I smile as I hand her an appointment card. "See you soon."

As Clementine heads to the door, she stops suddenly and makes a beeline for Fanny.

"I heard Cash is in Europe for the summer," Clementine's voice drips with honey. Ooh, she likes to play with fire. And I'm here for it.

"Yes," Fanny forces out as she finishes filling out the intake form. "Backpacking before college."

"I'm so jealous," Clementine dramatically touches her cheek. "Before Coy died, he always said he'd take me to Paris."

"Did the coroner ever figure out what killed a perfectly healthy 34-year-old man?" Fanny narrows her eyes.

"Came back inconclusive," Clementine responds.

"Interesting," Fanny nods slowly, her blond, curly hair hovering over one side of her face. "I'm sorry it happened so soon after you married."

"It's been hard."

"Has it?" Fanny frowns. "You didn't waste any time buying a new car, and furnishing your house before the ink was dry on the death certificate. The grass hadn't even started growing back on the lawn where he used to park his car before you were out dating again. With that fortune you inherited, I can't imagine why it's been so hard. Someone might even think his death was... intentional."

Woah. Did Fanny just accuse Clementine of murdering her husband?

"We both know money doesn't buy happiness," Clementine holds her head up.

"No," Fanny shakes her head, exposing her icy blue eyes. "But money can buy loyalty. And this town is loyal to me."

"Is it now?" Clementine taunts Fanny. "I don't think everyone is." *Uh oh.* This could turn violent.

Fanny grips the clipboard so tight that her knuckles turn white. "If you have something to say, say it."

"See you and Archibald tomorrow night," Clementine grins, her pearly whites sparkling beneath the harsh fluorescent lighting. "Don't forget it's bikini night at the club."

With that, Clementine glides out of the salon and disappears down the street.

"I want the Hollywood," Fanny slams the clipboard down in front of me. "I want it all gone. Every last inch of it."

"I'll let Pierre know," I say as I let out the breath I was holding.

"You do that," Fanny snaps.

This is just the Fanny show, and we're all living in it.

Chapter 10
The Movie Theatre

I take a picture of the dashboard, zooming in on the odometer reading and gas gauge. Queen Isla is taking my car tonight for Girl's Night Out while Frank the Fornicator works the late shift at the grocery store. I didn't think Isla had any friends, but I guess she's made some lifeguarding at the pool this summer. I give it a month or two before they see the real Isla—selfish, self-absorbed, and insensitive. Then, they'll drop her faster than Wilder drops his pants for a back alley blow job.

"Have fun," I force a smile as I hand Isla the keys. "And don't forget to put gas in it when you're—" but she slams the car door shut, cutting me off, "done using it."

"That was brutal," Wilder predictably pops up over my shoulder.

"Why are you standing on two feet?" I narrow my gaze as I turn to face him, my eyes shifting from his stupid tanned face to the worn sneakers he wears everywhere.

"Because I'm not a dog?" He tilts his head to the side, confused.

The sound of car tires burning out on asphalt causes me to roll my eyes. Queen Isla and her theatrics. When will her tyrannical reign end?

"No," I shake my head, focusing back on Wilder, "why aren't you in a car? Your mom's car, more specifically."

His eyes widen. "Shit."

"You had *one* job," I groan. "And you couldn't even do it?"

"She had to rush into work," he explains. "The hospital is short-staffed. I was helping my grandpa mow the lawn when she left. I forgot. I'm sorry."

"It's fine," I blow out a tired breath before glancing at Dad's car in the driveway. "Let's go ask Jason if we can borrow his."

"You're sure?"

I lick my lips. "You owe me, Cox. You owe me big time."

"I'll make it up to you," he nods. "I promise."

I hold up a hand. "Don't promise me anything. No one keeps their word anymore."

"Cash sure did a number on you," he shakes his head as he slips his phone out of his pocket, probably checking to see if his heartless bestie sent him a message.

"Touché," I raise an eyebrow at him.

Mom and Dad are binge-watching The Bachelor when we find them cuddled on the couch with a six-pack of beer and an empty pizza box. Honestly, if I don't find a man who watches trashy reality TV with me while stuffing my face with junk food, then what's the point of living?

Side note: Cash Allred doesn't eat greasy, processed, or junk food, and he always refused to watch reality TV with me. The warning signs were *so* obvious. How did I miss them?

"Jason!" Mom slaps his knee. "This is the girl! I read on that blogger site that he chooses this one."

"Why do you always ruin it, Jill?" Dad drops his head.

"Um," I cough, announcing my presence. And Wilder's.

"Oh!" Mom sits up, eyeing the boy standing next to me who is *not* Cash. "Are you going to introduce us to your latest suitor?"

I place a hand on my hip. "No, Mom. This is Wilder. You've already met him. He's been our neighbor for, like, six years."

Mom shrugs as she takes a swig from her bottle. "I like his hair, but he has deep-set eyes. You know what they say about deep set eyes, Ingrid."

"No, I do—"

"According to face reading experts on the TikTok—"

"Here we go," I mutter under my breath as Dad and I share a look.

"—deep set eyes belong to calculating people who thirst for power."

"Jill," Dad groans, embarrassed.

"They're also slow to act," Mom continues. "If you're hoping he's going to make a move, you might be sorely disappointed. But that doesn't mean you can't be the one to make it."

"Thanks for... *that*," I blink slowly. "Anyway, Dad can we borrow your car to go see a movie?"

Dad points to the kitchen. "Keys are on the counter."

"You should read Reality Murphy's blog," Wilder says to Mom. "Sources are saying it's Kristin who wins the final rose. Not Joanna."

Mom gasps. "Really?"

"Really," Wilder shrugs.

"Thanks," I say loudly, interrupting Wilder and Mom's weird, reality TV gossip. I grab the keys, then Wilder's arm, and drag my *latest suitor* through the foyer.

"I love your family," Wilder chuckles as I shut the front door behind us. "They're a nice blend of crazy."

"They're a mess," I shake my head. "It's even worse when Queen Isla and Frank the Fornicator are around. My parents are *terrified* of them."

"Well," Wilder hitches a shoulder, "every story must have quirky side characters."

I scoff. "Isla is not quirky. She's deranged."

"She's like the evil stepsisters of The Winthrop-verse."

"Okay," I laugh as I walk beside him to the car. "What does that even mean?"

"Isla gives off big main character energy, but she's too selfish to ever be the hero. She's just an intriguing side character who pushes the heroine into the garden to meet her saving grace," Wilder winks at me. "A pumpkin that turns into a carriage."

"I'm sorry," I clear my throat, "but beneath this flagrant fuckboy facade, are you actually human?"

"No," he stands perfectly still before stiffly raising his arms. "I am robot," he rattles off in a monotone voice. "Sent here to destroy you."

"Why are you so weird?"

"Because I have deep-set eyes," he raises his eyebrows at me. "Didn't you hear Jill?"

"No, deep-set eyes denote a thirst for power crippled only by your inability to act quickly. Doesn't explain why you're weird."

"You really believe that face-reading stuff?" Wilder throws a thumb over his shoulder. "Do I have deep-set eyes?"

"Hmm," I study him curiously. There's a tiny mole beneath his left eye. Soft greens and bright golds in his hazel irises. Long, dark eyelashes that flutter against his tanned skin every time he blinks. Under the gentle glow of the fading sun, he's kind of beautiful.

What?

No.

I *did not* just think the word *beautiful* about the world's ugliest man-child. *Gross.* Wilder Cox is a sadistic, slithering serpent. Yeah. He's disgusting. Slimy and sleazy. But also sort of attractive when his mouth is shut.

Ew. Not again!

I don't know what's going on here. My brain must be malfunctioning because I think Wilder might be hot.

This is... this is not how I saw this summer going. This is not how I saw our weird friendship going.

I can't be attracted to Cash's best friend, can I? The guy who *tortured* me for years. No, *no*. That's almost as insane as using the words *Isla* and *selfless* in the same sentence.

"I don't think you have deep-set eyes," I finally say. "Jill's a little off her rocker. She spends all day with her furry friends, and they sniff each other's butts to greet one another. What she lacks in social graces though, she makes up for in heart."

"Am I calculating?" he asks, changing the subject.

I shrug. "Maybe. But you're an only child who grew up in a fatherless home while his mother worked long hours. You had to fend for yourself. What might appear to some people as calculating, might have been your only means of survival."

"Wow," Wilder exhales as he scratches the back of his neck. "That's dark and depressing. Even for you."

"Fine, you are calculating," I give him a hard time. "Better?"

"Get in the car," he rolls his eyes. "Or we're going to miss the movie."

I park around the back and lock the doors as soon as I get out. Wilder shoots me a strange look as I walk around the front of the car, surveying the area.

"Why are you looking at me like a psycho?" I whisper to him as the orange light overhead flickers.

"Because we live in the safest town in America. We haven't had a murder in... at least ten years."

"Better safe than sorry," I mumble as I drop the keys into my purse. I peer around, taking in the piles of stacked cardboard boxes and rows of dumpsters. *Creepy.* This alley is creepy.

"Josie said she'd leave the back door propped open for us," Wilder says quietly.

"Did you also promise her sex in exchange for a favor?" I challenge.

He stares down at me, something strange building in his stupidly gorgeous hazel eyes. "You jealous?"

"*Psh*," I wave off. "Me? Jealous of all the girls you string along? The ones who have no idea you jump from bed to bed without a care in the world. No, never. Why? Why would I be?"

"A simple *no* would have sufficed," Wilder smirks.

He starts walking, leaving me a few steps behind. I jog to catch up.

"Have you ever done this before?" I ask him, looking around for any sign of life. "Snuck into the movie theatre?"

Wilder slows as we near the door left ajar for our devious entry. "No."

"Why not?"

"Are you going to talk the whole time we're trying to sneak in, Blondie?" he grumbles.

I shake my head. "No."

"Oh, so you do know how to use that word."

"I am *not* jealous of Karissa and Josie and whoever else you're bumping nasties with this week."

"Could have fooled me," Wilder replies as he grabs the door handle and pulls it open slowly. I sneak a peek over my shoulder. Still no one around.

"Coast is clear," he says quietly as he motions for me to head inside.

"I'm not going first," I inform him. "You go first."

"I got us the open door." He crosses his arms over his chest. "It's your turn to do some heavy lifting."

"Fine," I huff. "If I had a harem of desperate lovers, I, too, could have gotten us an open door. But I'm too scared of STDs, so I guess I'll go in first."

Wilder follows behind me as we tiptoe our way into an empty movie theatre. The lights are dimmed low, so I feel along the wall, careful to take the small staircase one at a time.

"Just admit it, Blondie," Wilder continues his tireless tirade. "You're jealous."

"Let it go, Wilder." I crane my neck to look at him. "I'm not jealous. I just hate the idea that you're using your genitals to make our Lonely Summer Bucket List easier."

"I'm touched you're concerned for my dick, but it's fine."

"You're so annoying."

"At least you never walked in on me like the dozen or so times I've walked in on you and Cash," he barely mutters loud enough for me to hear.

I slow my pace. "You've only walked in on us twice."

"Twice that you saw," he shoots back.

"I swear Wilder Andrea Cox," I grit my teeth.

"Who told you my middle name?" His voice sounds a little panicky. Almost as if he's afraid I'll tell everyone his best-kept secret. "It's *Andrew*.

The nurse entered it wrong on my birth certificate and my parents were too lazy to change it."

"If you recorded Cash and me in a compromising position, I'll never let you—"

"I never recorded you," he interjects. "I would never do that to Cash—*or you*. Why do you always think the worst of me?"

I suck in a harsh breath. "Because you tormented me for years. You made my life a living hell."

We're so close, I can hear his heart beating in his chest. The infuriating need to slide my hand up his toned pecs and place my palm over his Grinch-like organ *nags* me relentlessly. *Do it, do it, do it. Come on, Ingrid, touch him.*

I swallow harshly before giving in and bringing my hand up to his chest. I pause for a moment, searching his eyes in the dark for a trace of disgust. When I don't see it, I cover his heart with my fingers.

"Why is your heart beating so fast?" I ask him.

He shifts his body weight from his left leg to his right one. "Who told you my middle name?"

"I saw it on your school ID," I whisper, letting my hand linger on his chest for a moment before reluctantly slipping it off. "We should go. What theatre number is it?"

Wilder lets out a breath I didn't notice he was holding. "Five."

I lead the way, popping my head out of the empty movie theatre to make sure we don't get caught. As luck would have it, there isn't a single person in the hallway. We hurry across the hall to theatre number five.

A few people are already sitting in the theatre as boring advertisements fill the screen. I cringe when I see Pierre holding a banner that reads, '*Let us whack that bush for you*'. Loretta really needs to get a new slogan.

"Where do you want to sit?" I hear Wilder to my left.

Cash always made me sit in the front, and I'd have a kink in my neck for days after watching movies at an awkward angle.

"In the back?" I suggest.

"Perfect," Wilder nods. "I hate the front. Makes my neck hurt."

I smile to myself as I climb the stairs, then grab a seat in the middle. "You hungry?"

Wilder plops down beside me. "Yep."

"I brought rations."

I hand Wilder a candy bar, sour gummy worms, and a bottle of water.

"No popcorn?" he pouts.

"No popcorn," I confirm. "We were out at home."

We sit silently, our elbows touching.

"You have hazel eyes," I state beside him.

"Okay."

"In face reading," I take a bite of my candy bar, "hazel eyes are some of the rarest in the world."

"You're also a fan of face reading?" he guesses.

"No, but I hear enough of Jill's TikTok to pick up on a few things."

"What do hazel eyes mean?"

"It means you're trustworthy," I reveal. "And a good friend."

"I am an excellent friend," Wilder boasts.

"What happens when Cash comes back?" I chew on the inside of my cheek. "Does our friendship end?"

"I don't know, Blondie."

"What happens if this whole bonding thing really does make us friends?" I push. "What then? Are you going to ditch me for Cash?"

Wilder sighs. "You've been a better friend to me the past few weeks than Cash was in twelve years, but I don't think Cash and I will ever not be friends. We've been through too much together."

Even though he ditched you? Even though he hasn't talked to you? Come on, Wilder. Open your eyes.

"Yeah," is all I manage to get out in response.

The lights dim as the movie trailers begin. I take another bite of chocolate and close my eyes. Cash and Wilder have been friends for most of their lives. Of course, Wilder would choose Cash over me. I can't compete with twelve years of friendship.

Still, it hurts a little. No matter how close Wilder and I get this summer, his loyalty will always be to Cash Allred.

And mine?

Mine is *shifting*.

Chapter 11
The Shopping Spree

Golf Course Attire 101: The more expensive the piece of fabric, the more acceptable at the country club.

That's what Dad said when I asked him, anyway. I figured he was the best person to consult on this topic since he golfed with a client or two back when he had a job. And he wasn't wrong.

"$79 for a skirt?" I whisper-yell to my bored accomplice. "I can't afford this, Wilder."

"We can't play on the golf course without the right clothes," he yawns from his stupid spot on the white, faux leather couch. "The country club has strict guidelines. And since we put it on the bucket list, we have to do it."

"This is dumb," I exhale heavily as I twist in front of the mirror, watching as the pleated white skirt fans out as I do. When my eyes shift back to Wilder, I see his teeth sinking into his lower lip and he's eyeing my backside like it's a piece of meat. "Stop checking my ass out!"

He grins. "Why not?"

I place a hand on my hip and narrow my eyes at him. "Because I'm trying really hard to be your friend and you're being gross right now. I already told you I can't be friends with Creepy Wilder. Get your act together."

"Sorry," Wilder runs a hand over his face. "Been a while since I got laid."

"You mean Josie didn't let you slip it into her hairless beaver after she helped us sneak into the movie theatre?" I feign shock. "That's a surprise."

"No," he crosses his arms over his chest. I try hard not to stare at the black cotton material as it stretches across his toned pecs. "Being friends with you is bad for my sex life. And how do you know it's hairless? Oh, right. You work at the waxing salon where you're up to your ears in whacked bush."

I smile triumphantly, ignoring the bush dig. "Am I really ruining your sex life?"

"Yeah," he groans. "Josie said we *looked cute* while we were watching the movie last week, and she doesn't want to interfere with whatever's going on between us."

Laughter spills out of me. "I'm a cock blocker. I am *your* cock blocker. I love this for you. I love this for *me!*"

"Don't get *cocky*," he winks.

"Was that a pun?" I gasp. "Are you... are you flirting with me?"

"Shut up and go try on the pink skirt," he rolls his eyes.

I raise my eyebrows. "You sure you want a show, Wilder? Cause I can model all day for you if that's what you want. Might make your blue balls even bluer, though."

"What I want is to get out of here," he exhales heavily and points to the khaki pants and polo he's already picked out. "Hurry up."

"Is that because you're afraid you might be seen *looking cute* with me at the mall?" I scrunch my nose.

Wilder stands and walks over to me. When he's an inch from my face, he narrows his eyes. "Let's get one thing straight. I'm not Cash. I'm not going to hold your hand and skip through the mall sipping lemonade and sharing a pretzel from Annie's."

My mouth drops open. "We did not skip. We *meandered*."

"Whatever," Wilder grimaces. "I'm not interested in being your boyfriend, Blondie."

"No," I glare back at him as his minty breath tickles my forehead. Dammit! Why does his breath have to smell good? "You're only interested in one thing. Sex."

"Not with you," he says as he tilts his head to the side. "I don't fuck my best friend's leftovers."

"That's too bad," I trail a finger up his stomach. "Because I give a really," I lower my voice, "good blow job."

Wilder swallows hard. "Oh, if you want to suck my dick, go right ahead. I won't stop you."

"Let's go then," I call his bluff. "Right now. Dressing room."

His breathing hitches as my fingers slip beneath the collar of his T-shirt. His skin is surprisingly soft and warm.

"I don't have a condom," he clears his throat.

"That's fine," I say as my other hand finds his forearm and I squeeze lightly. "I do my best work *raw*."

His eyes stare back at me as his pupils slowly begin dilating. Holy shit! Does Wilder find me attractive?

"Come on," I tease him. "Let me wrap my mouth around that big, fat—"

"Wilder?" We both hear.

He whips his head around to see who it is, but I keep a firm grasp on him. If it's one of his many conquests—or *potential* conquests—I intend to continue with the cock blocking.

"Elowyn?" he inhales sharply.

The leggy brunette moves through the clothing racks with ease until she reaches us. I drop my hand from Wilder's forearm and lace my fingers with his. For some reason, he doesn't pull away. Instead, he holds on tighter.

"Dad said you didn't want to go on the family vacation to Orange Beach this year," she crosses her arms over her chest. That's when I see it. The resemblance. Dark hair and hazel eyes. The same curve of the nose. His sister. *Half-sister.* The one his father left him for.

"I'm busy," he lies.

Her eyes slide to me, and she holds out a hand. "Hi, I'm Elowyn. Wilder's sister."

I shake her hand as Wilder's grip strengthens on my fingers. "I'm Ingrid. Nice to meet you."

"Ingrid," Elowyn smiles. "I think Wilder's mentioned you before."

"We're neighbors," Wilder explains as Elowyn's gaze drifts to our interlaced fingers.

"And lovers," I joke.

"She's kidding," Wilder quickly interrupts. "She's just a friend."

"I used to date his best friend, Cash," I explain. "Then, Cash ditched us for Europe and since neither of us has any other friends, we're stuck together. All summer long." Wilder shoots me a panicked look. "When Wilder is not busy. Which is usually never."

Elowyn laughs. "I know he's not busy, Ingrid. I also don't blame him for skipping the family vacay. It's too much. Even for me."

"We are busy," I defend Wilder. Why am I defending him? Why do I suddenly feel the need to stick up for my *arch-nemesis-turned-shopping-*

companion? "We're doing a bucket list this summer. And we have a lot of items on it."

"A bucket list?" Elowyn gets excited. "That sounds fun."

"We don't want to keep you," Wilder ruins our tête-à-tête. "Tell Margot I say hi."

"I will," Elowyn smiles. "My mom really misses you. Anyway, It was good seeing you. Both of you."

"Nice meeting you," I say before Elowyn disappears through the racks and Wilder's shoulders slump. "You okay?"

Wilder nods slowly. "Fine."

I glance down at our intertwined fingers. "You want to talk about it?"

"No," he quickly answers.

"You still want that BJ?" I nudge him with my shoulder.

"No."

"I'll let you touch my boobs the whole time your dick is in my mouth," I continue as the corner of his lips tips up.

"You couldn't handle *Wild Cox*," he perks up a little. "It's too big for your tiny mouth."

"I do not have a tiny mouth," I scoff.

"I've seen you try to eat a hot dog," he smirks.

"It's not my fault Costco has massive hot dogs. Everyone has a problem trying to eat a Costco hot dog," I argue.

"*No one* has a problem fitting them into their mouths, Blondie," he shakes his head. "Except you."

"I resent that statement," I inform him as his eyes trail down my torso before settling on our hands.

"I haven't talked to Elowyn in two years," he reveals.

"Why not?" I ask.

He shrugs as I stroke the back of his hand with my thumb. "My dad takes care of her. She has a car that he pays for and a roof over her head. She doesn't have to work the late shift at the lumber yard to pay for college because my dad is going to pay it for her. Elowyn doesn't know what it's like to scrimp and save just to get by in life. She has it made."

I nod in understanding. "I get it."

"It's too hard to hear how easy her life is when all my mom and I have done the past six years is struggle."

"It's not fair," I shake my head.

"It's not," he agrees, "but Elowyn isn't the bad guy. She's just related to the bad guy."

"Agreed," I chew on the inside of my cheek. "She seemed nice."

"She is," he shrugs. "So is her mom, Margot. But it doesn't change anything. Margot knew my dad was married and my mom was pregnant with me when she got pregnant with Elowyn. She knew he had a kid on the way that he needed to take care of. She kept their relationship a secret for 13 years."

"People can be nice and still do bad things," I look up at Wilder. There's a line between his eyebrows that I want to smooth away, but I don't.

"And people can be bad and still do nice things," he adds.

There's a lull in conversation as we stand, hands clasped, staring at each other. I knew Wilder had a rough childhood. I knew his dad left him and his mom struggled to make ends meet. What I didn't know is that Wilder carries around a mountain of pain wherever he goes.

For the first time since we first met, I think I'm beginning to understand him better. I understand why he doesn't let anyone in. I understand why he probably doesn't get involved in relationships. I understand why sex—physical connection—is easier than emotional connection. There's too much at stake.

"I should try on the pink skirt," I tell him as my free hand grabs the end of the pleated golf skirt I'm currently wearing. "But it's more expensive."

Wilder looks toward the cash register and then back at me. "Try it on. Don't look at the price tag. We'll get whichever one you like better."

"But I can't afford either skirt. And I still have to find a shirt."

"I'll take care of it," he assures me.

"How?"

"Don't worry about it, Blondie."

"If you think I'm going to shoplift—"

"We're not going to shoplift," he finally releases my hand. "Just trust me on this." Before I can protest, he adds, "*For once.*"

"I better not live to regret this," I mumble as I head back into the changing room. I switch skirts and find Wilder sitting on the couch again. "What do you think?"

"Pink," Wilder says. "Get the pink."

"Okay," I give in. "Pink it is."

Once I'm changed back into my clothes, Wilder and I find a matching pink polo to wear on the golf course and start heading toward the cash register. He takes the clothes from me before snaking his arm over my shoulders. "Play along, Blondie. *If you can keep up.*"

"What does that mean?" I frown as his hip bumps against mine.

"You'll see."

The cashier, a sulking redhead, smacks on her gum as we near.

"Is that going to be all for you today?" she states plainly.

Wilder drops our clothes onto the counter. "Yep."

"How will you be paying?" she asks him.

"Charge account," he replies. "Archibald Allred."

The cashier removes the hangers from the clothes and shoves the garments into a large plastic bag. "Do you have ID?"

"You must be new here," Wilder chuckles as he flashes his eyebrows at me. "I'm Cash Allred. Archibald is my dad."

NO! I mentally yell at him. He doesn't think this is going to work, does he?

The cashier types away on the screen. "Do you have ID?"

Wilder shoves his free hand into both pockets. "Shit. I think I left it in the car."

"If you want—"

"What seems to be the problem?" An older woman appears behind the desk.

Great. Now, we're surely going to get caught. And then we're going to end up in jail. I just know it.

"He wants to put all of this," the cashier points to our bag, "on his dad's charge account, but he doesn't have his ID."

"What's the name on the account?" the older woman asks.

"Archibald Allred," Wilder answers for the cashier. "I'm in here all the time. Do I need to call my dad and let him know how his son is being treated by his favorite clothing store?"

"Cash, right?" The older woman eyes him suspiciously.

"That's me," Wilder fibs.

"I've seen him in here," the older woman tells the cashier. "He uses his dad's charge account all the time. I'll vouch for him."

"Thank you," Wilder offers the woman a warm smile.

The cashier hands us a receipt and we head out of the store, my heart a pounding, beating mess.

"What was that?" I snap. "We could have gotten caught."

"It was a big *fuck you* to Archibald," Wilder hitches a shoulder as he carries our bag of stolen goods like a trophy. "For cheating on his wife and sending my best friend away for the summer."

"Have you done that before?" I question. "Used Cash's name to get things?"

Wilder stops walking. "No. Never."

"Don't do it again, okay?"

"Why not?" Wilder scratches the back of his neck.

"Because," I tilt my head to the side. "We're better than the Allreds. And we don't need their charity."

"You're not going to let this become a thing, are you?" Wilder challenges.

I don't know what's going on with me. My heart is sloshing around in my chest as I stare into his hazel eyes. I think I might like Wilder. Like, *really* like him. How else do I explain what I'm feeling right now? I don't want him offering sex in exchange for bucket list favors. I don't want him lying and stealing because I can't afford clothes to play a round of golf with him. I don't want him to hurt because his dad chose his second family over him.

The realization hits me like a brick wall. It hurts to breathe, and my heart feels bruised.

"Blondie," Wilder blinks rapidly. "You're not going to let this become a thing, right?"

"No," I answer hoarsely.

"Good," he pinches his lips together. "You want to grab a burger at the diner?"

I nod. "Sure."

We walk toward the exit, my mind racing. I can't like Wilder. Wilder is Cash's best friend. Wilder tortured me all through high school. Wilder is morally gray and mindlessly aggravating. I can't... I can't like him. That's... there are rules. Rules like don't fall for your ex-boyfriend's best friend.

But for some reason, when it comes to Wilder, rules don't seem to apply.

Chapter 12
The Golf Course

"What's the plan, Blondie?" Wilder yawns beside me in his new khakis and polo as we scope out the country club from my car. "Since I'm not allowed to barter my body for favors anymore, you're going to have to start pulling your weight."

"I'm thinking," I snap at him as I adjust the pink pleated skirt on my thighs.

"Don't think too hard," he smirks. "Hate for you to lose *even* more brain cells."

"That joke is getting *really* old," I shake my head. "Get some new material."

Wilder rubs his hand over his face and huffs. *No response.* I'm starting to miss the old Wilder. The one who always had a witty comeback.

"What if we just pay like everyone else?" I suggest.

"We agreed to *sneak* in," he reminds me while rolling his eyes. "Paying for a round of golf is not sneaking in."

"Right," I clear my throat. "That only leaves us a few options then."

"Which are?" he asks.

"First, we become friends with whoever is in charge of renting out golf carts. Then, we save their life from an unknown threat and call in a favor afterward to help us sneak in."

Wilder stares at me, unamused. "In what universe would that even be a possibility?"

"Everything is a possibility," I scoff. "Aliens could literally descend upon us in their massive mothership right now, deploy several circular-shaped saucers to destroy all major cities in an attempt to take over Earth, and our only means of survival is a fighter jet carrying a pilot and a guy who writes computer virus codes."

"Did you just tell me the plot of Independence Day?"

I nod. "I did."

Wilder rubs his temples. "You are... impossible."

"I'm not great at this, okay?" I shrug. "I don't sneak into things. I don't have fun. Or go on adventures. I... I spent the last four years of my life trying to fit into Cash's world and hoping it would be good enough for his parents."

"And where did that get you?" Wilder raises a dark eyebrow.

Where did it get me? It got me here. Sitting in a car beside my arch-nemesis trying to find a way to sneak into the country club to play a round of golf.

"I'm trying Wilder," I tell him. "I really am. I just... I'm not great at this *yet*."

He gives me a small smile. "That's the spirit."

"Another option is to try and blend in with that group over there," I point to what looks like a corporate retreat event, "and hope no one notices we're not with them."

Wilder grins. "That's it! That's our way in. Let's go."

As Wilder walks next to me, I lower the crisp white ball cap on my head and adjust the golf bag strap on my shoulder. Wilder has one hand situated on the strap of his bag and the other swaying beside him.

"Why do you look so confident?" I say to him.

He laughs. "It's called faking it 'til you make it, Blondie."

Fake it 'til I make it? Well, I did do a lot of faking with Cash. I'm sure I can use those skills *outside* of the Allred mansion. In the real world.

I throw my shoulders back and walk with purpose. I mean, I think that's what I'm doing. It seems to work because Wilder and I push our way through the group until we're smack dab in the middle and no one seems to notice we don't belong. Wilder pulls his phone out of his pocket and starts looking through it. I stare at my nails, hoping no one talks to me.

Someone at the front of the crowd tells us to split into fours. I'm not the least bit surprised when a platinum blond cozies up to Wilder and says, "Hey, you must be from another department. We haven't crossed paths before. I'm Hendrix."

I roll my eyes as she offers Wilder a seductive smile and casually tries to hike her belly-bearing top further up her torso.

"Sales," Wilder winks. "And you must be from marketing."

Hendrix smiles wide. "How'd you know?"

"Lucky guess," Wilder replies as his eyes slide down her toned body.

"I'm Ingrid," I wave awkwardly to Hendrix.

Wilder places a hand on my face and pushes me backward. "She's from accounting. Ignore her."

My mouth drops open in shock. Though, should I be surprised? It's Wilder. And we all know he loves dipping his joystick into anything wearing a skirt.

"Hope that rash has cleared up," I narrow my eyes at Wilder before patting his shoulder. "It's going to be a long, hot day on the green. I'd hate for it to *flare* up."

"She's joking," he tries explaining to Hendrix. "She does this all the time. Says outrageous things to make me look bad."

I scrunch my nose as Hendrix takes a step back. "Are you calling me a liar?"

"Yes," Wilder snaps at me.

"You guys need a fourth?" a tall, handsome blond wearing a blue button-down interrupts.

"We do," I tell him as I hold out my hand. "I'm Ingrid."

"Ian," he supplies. "What department are you in?"

"Accounting," I lie.

"Oh, really?" Ian seems a bit uneasy. "My dad's the CFO. I'm sorry if he gives you a hard time. It's... uh... he can be a hard ass."

"It's fine," I wave off. "Being CFO can be stressful."

"Yeah," he agrees before introducing himself to Wilder and Hendrix. Wilder grunts in reply, but Hendrix shakes his hand. I think I see dollar signs lighting up her brown eyes for a split second as she takes him in.

"You ever played before?" Ian asks me.

I shake my head. "No. This is my first time."

"I'd love to give you some pointers," Ian offers.

Wilder grumbles to my right but I don't hear what he says because I'm too busy *ignoring* him.

"That'd be great," I smile up at Ian.

When it's our turn to hop in a golf cart, I laugh as the attendant steps around Wilder and hands the keys to Ian. I skip past Wilder, giving him a triumphant smile, and take the front seat beside my new companion.

Wilder slips into the back behind me and leans over my right side. "Cash 2.0, huh?"

I twist in my seat to look at him. "Are you jealous?"

He swallows hard. "Nope."

"Good," I says as I flash my eyebrows at him.

The cart takes off, and I face forward gripping the seat tight. I'm not sure why, but it feels like that time at the county fair the summer before junior year. Cash and I rode the Ferris wheel while Wilder waited below. I didn't want to get on the ride, but I didn't want Wilder taking my spot next to Cash.

The Ferris wheel circled twice and, right when we were about to go over the third time, we were stopped at the very top. I was holding onto Cash's hand so tight, his fingers were turning white. I didn't want to admit it then, but I was scared. Scared of careening over that ridge and plummeting to the hard dirt below.

Right now, I feel scared again. Not of plummeting to the dirt below, but scared of falling off the Wilder cliff and meeting the rough, choppy waves below.

"You ready to tee off?" Ian nudges me with his elbow as we come to a stop in front of the first hole.

"Yep," I force a smile.

Wilder helps Hendrix off the rear bench, then slips on his sunglasses. I try not to stare, but Hendrix links her arm with his, making my heart sting a little.

"You're up first," Ian hands me a ball and club. "This is called a driver."

"Thanks," I say to him as I place my ball on the little wooden tee and scan the green.

Ian shows me how to place my hands on the grip. I take some practice swings before lining up with the tee and checking the distance to the next hole.

"You've got this, Ingrid," I mutter to myself as I pull the golf club back and rotate my shoulders. "You can do this."

I inhale, then slowly exhale and let my arms propel forward. The club makes contact with the ball and sends it flying across the grass.

"Yes!" I hear Ian behind me. "You did it!"

I chew on my lower lip as the ball stops fairly close to the first hole. Satisfied, I take a step back and let Hendrix go next. She misses the ball a few times but eventually hits it in the right direction. Wilder goes after. He's never been as athletic as Cash, but he manages to get the ball closer to the hole than Hendrix does.

Ian goes last. He winds up the shot and lets it fly. He seems happy when the ball stops a few feet from mine.

"Ready for more?" Ian directs to me as he takes my club.

"Yep."

Wilder makes Hendrix laugh all the way to the golf cart. I strain to hear what they're talking about, but Ian is telling me a story about his first golf lesson and multi-tasking has never been my strong suit. Nothing is harder than trying to be present for two separate conversations.

"And that's when I told my dad I'd never be a professional golfer," Ian finishes as Wilder holds out his hand to Hendrix. She takes a hold of it and smiles at him as she climbs into the golf cart. "Ingrid?"

I glance over at Ian. "Sorry, what?"

"Are you okay?"

I adjust the cap on my head. "I was thinking about how I'm going to get the ball into the hole."

Wilder mumbles something to Hendrix and they both burst into laughter. *Me.* I think they're laughing at me.

Heat builds behind my eyes, but I'm determined not to cry. Wilder's been making fun of me for years. Why does it suddenly bother me so much?

Because you recently got dumped and Wilder is your only friend, my subconscious reminds me.

I shove the negative emotions deep down and walk around the golf cart. As I do, Wilder grabs my arm and stops me. "If you need some help getting that ball into the hole, I've had plenty of practice. *I'd love to give you some pointers.*"

He is making fun of me. I can tell by the way Hendrix hides a stifled laugh behind her hand.

"I don't need pointers," I say to him as I pry his grimy fingers off my arm. "I'm perfectly fine on my own, Wilder. But you? You always have to have someone around. Is that because you're terrified if you're left alone with your thoughts for too long, you might actually see why no one gives a shit about you?"

Wilder's hazel eyes flash with hurt before he hides the pain behind an impenetrable wall.

"I'm sorry," I apologize. "That was mean. I... I didn't mean that."

I don't want to hurt Wilder. Everyone else has done a fantastic job of that. The last thing he needs is more of it from me.

"Yeah, you did," he says quietly. "No one may give a shit about me, but I didn't spend four years of my life begging the Allreds to like me."

"That's fair," I lift my chin.

"Oh, I'm not done," Wilder shakes his head. "There's a bunch of stuff you still don't know. You didn't know about the secret Snapchat account Cash used to talk to other girls. You didn't know about all the times he used me to get out of hanging out with you. He didn't want you, Blondie. He left the country to get away from you. So, yeah, people might not give a shit about me but at least I don't waste my time on people who don't even like me."

My lower lip trembles as I listen to Wilder.

"You're not going to cry, are you?" he pouts, mocking me.

"No," I decide, willing the tears away. "I'm going to play a round of golf and I'm going to kick your ass."

I take a sobering breath and slip into the front seat. I don't know if Wilder's telling the truth about Cash, but I can't think about it right now. I can't let myself fall apart here. Not on Cash's turf. Not in front of Cash's best friend.

"What are we waiting for?" I plaster a smile on my face and say to Ian.

"You sure you're okay?"

"Never better."

Fake it 'til you make it, Ingrid.

This faking thing isn't so bad. Then again, I've had lots of practice.

Chapter 13
The Same Wound

Don't cry, Ingrid. Don't cry, don't cry, don't cry. You picked a fight with him. You knew it was a sore subject. You knew he'd lash out. You said it anyway. Doesn't make what either of us said right. But I started it, and Wilder? He finished it.

Did Cash really have a secret Snapchat account, though? And what did Wilder mean when he said Cash used him to get out of spending time with me? Did Cash not want to be with me before his Europe trip? If so, then why didn't he break up with me? To spite his mom, perhaps. Did he stay with me just to stick it to his parents?

"You're up," Ian reminds me as I squeeze the life out of the putter I'm holding in my hands.

"Right," I clear my throat. Out of the corner of my eye, I see Wilder drape his arm over Hendrix's gloating shoulders.

Ignore, ignore, ignore.

I inhale slowly, trying to keep my breathing even. I'm focusing on this shot. Nothing else. I have three feet. Three feet to sink the ball into the hole. *I've got this.*

I apply enough pressure to push the ball forward. It glides slowly along the turf before effortlessly dropping into the hole.

"Yes!" I hear Ian behind me. He's fist-bumping the air when I look over my shoulder.

Wilder, however, is too busy chatting up Hendrix to notice. I frown as I swing the golf club back and forth. Things are starting to feel like they did before Cash left. Before Wilder and I became cohorts. Back when we traded insults like soldiers on a battlefield. Every sharp jab of the tongue was a swift stab to the extremities.

I don't want to go back to that. I don't want to spend all my free time hating Wilder. I like being his friend. Even if he might not feel the same way.

Hendrix saunters past me to her ball stuck in the sand pit.

"Good luck," I offer.

She scoffs as she tosses her platinum blond hair over her shoulder. "I don't need luck."

So much for us being friends. Then again, making friends has never come easy for me. Most girls at school hated me because I was Cash Allred's girlfriend. And now that Cash is gone, I guess I've become friends with *Wild Cox*. He may not hold the keys to the Allred Empire, but he has a legendary dick everyone is waiting in line to get a turn with.

"Are you sure you've never golfed before?" Ian says in disbelief.

"I have never golfed before," I proudly proclaim.

"You're a natural," Ian laughs. "I'll have to put in a good word with my dad."

"Yeah," I chew on the inside of my cheek.

Hendrix misses the ball and hits the sand at least a dozen times before Wilder jogs over to help her. I roll my eyes in disgust as he stands behind her and places his hands over hers. Then, Wilder sways their bodies back and forth as he shows her how to swing the club.

"You guys close?" Ian guesses as he tips his head in Wilder's direction.

"Not really," I shrug. "We've been neighbors for the past six years."

"So, you're the girl next door?" he laughs nervously.

"I'm the girl a few doors down," I clarify. "I also dated his best friend all through high school."

"There's history then," he scratches the back of his neck.

"You could say that."

"Do you like him?"

I scrunch my nose. "No. Wilder is annoying and disgusting."

Ian smirks. "That sounded like a *yes*."

It might be a yes, but I'm not admitting it to a stranger.

"I don't really care how it sounded," I hitch a shoulder. "Wilder and I are acquaintances who live on the same block."

Finally, Hendrix makes contact with the ball. It flies by us, in the opposite direction of the hole.

"We're going to be here all day at this rate," Ian runs a hand over his face.

By the time we make it to hole 15, there's a line of golf carts behind us. I sigh with relief when I see the beverage cart heading our way.

"I'm gonna go get a drink," I say to the group.

"I'll go with you," Wilder offers.

I swallow hard, not sure what game he's playing at now. "Okay."

We leave Hendrix and Ian behind as we walk over to the cart. We wait behind two middle-aged men, neither of us saying anything. I'm hyperaware of every movement Wilder makes. The twitch of his hand, the way his Adam's apple bobs as he swallows, the tiny droplets of sweat forming on his upper lip. I study him, trying to read him. Trying to figure out why we can't seem to get along for very long.

"Why are you staring at me, Blondie?" He raises his eyebrows at me.

"I'm sorry," I shake my head. "I was thinking about earlier. I shouldn't have said what I did."

"It's fine," he huffs.

I know I shouldn't push him, but I need answers.

"Did Cash really have a secret Snapchat account?" I gnaw on my lower lip.

"No," he clears his throat. "I lied about that."

"Oh," I frown.

"I knew it would upset you, and I wanted to hurt you after what you said to me."

"I do the same thing to you sometimes," I admit. "And the part about him using you to get out of spending time with me, was that a lie, too?"

"I don't know," Wilder wipes the sweat off his face with his forearm. "I started noticing he was spending a lot less time with you over the last year. When he did make plans with you, he always invited me. Almost like he needed a buffer."

"I wonder why," I muse as I cross my arms over my chest.

"Who knows," Wilder shrugs. "Cash and the Allreds are secretive people. They don't like anyone knowing their business."

"It's weird, right?"

"I guess."

"I am sorry, Wilder," I try.

"I know, Blondie."

"I don't want to fight like that anymore," I reveal.

He licks his lips. "Me either."

"Why do we always go for the jugular?" I inhale sharply.

Wilder cocks an intrigued eyebrow. "Sexual tension."

I roll my eyes dramatically. "Not everything is about sex."

"No," he agrees. "Sometimes, it's about connection."

What? Is he implying that we have some sort of connection that isn't sex but sexual?

"I don't get it." I whip my head back.

"We have the same wound."

"And what wound is that?" I tilt my head to the side.

"The rejection wound," he states. "My dad rejected me. Cash rejected you. We've both been rejected by the people we love."

Wilder takes a step forward and orders a beer as I stand perfectly still, the realization that we're not all that different crashing over me. He slips out his fake ID and winks at me as the beverage cart girl hands him over a Coors Light.

"Water," I tell her as Wilder takes a long swig from the silver bottle in his hand.

"You ready to head back and *kick my ass*?" Wilder flashes his eyebrows at me.

"As long as you promise to start hitting the balls for Hendrix," I quip. "I'd like to get home before midnight."

"She sucks, doesn't she?" he laughs.

"Do you find that attractive?" I quiz him. "Women who downplay their intellect and athletic ability."

"Damsels-in-distress?" he rephrases.

"Yeah."

"Honestly, Blondie, I'm barely saving myself from all the shit I'm drowning in. I don't have the strength to save anyone else."

I clink my water bottle against his beer. "Touché."

The next three holes go much faster as the sun begins its descent. Hendrix stole Wilder's beer and downed it before he had a chance to. Since then, she's used it as an excuse to act bolder than she was before. Her drunken advances don't seem to faze Wilder.

Ian ends up winning by one point, and we high-five as Wilder grumbles behind us.

"You did great," Ian compliments me for the millionth time. "Are you staying for dinner?"

"I'm not sure," I glance at Wilder who's grabbing our bags from the golf cart.

"Ah," Ian shoves his hands into his pockets. "You do like him."

"We're friends," I soften the blow. Friends with a non-sex, sexual connection because we have the same wound. *The rejection wound*. Yeah, that's not confusing or anything.

"Well, Ingrid," Ian grins, "hope to see you around."

"Uh, yeah," I force a smile. "Thanks for all the pointers."

I walk over to Wilder and exhale when I see Hendrix curled up on the golf cart seat, passed out.

"Should we wake her?" Wilder asks me.

"Nah," I purse my lips. "Let her sleep it off."

Wilder slings both our bags over his shoulder and points toward the exit. "You ready?"

"Yep," I lead the way. "I think I like golf."

"I had fun. Now I know why Cash liked to ditch us to play."

"He could have invited us."

"I'm kind of glad he didn't," Wilder adjusts the bags on his shoulder. "Can you imagine spending a day with Archibald on the golf course?"

"You're right," I chuckle. "That would have been torture."

"What I said earlier, I don't think Cash was trying to get out of spending time with you," Wilder sighs. "I think his life is complicated. I think his parents put a lot of pressure on him. You and me, we don't have that kind of pressure. We have cool parents. You have your mom and dad, and I have my mom. We have parents who take care of us because they love us, not because they need us to make them look good."

"You always defend him," I cross my arms over my chest. "Even when he leaves you behind for a European getaway and doesn't reply to your messages."

"He's my best friend," Wilder weakly argues. "What kind of person does that make me if I abandon him the same way he's abandoned me?"

We stop in front of my car and I open my trunk. "What kind of person isn't devastated that her boyfriend of four years broke up with her?"

Wilder drops the golf bags into my trunk. "You aren't devastated?"

"Should I be?" I ask him.

He leans against my car. "It was four years. That's a long time."

"If I let myself *feel* the loss," I tug at the end of my hair, "then that means whatever we had is really over. I don't want it to be over. I really love him—*loved* him."

"I thought he loved you, too," Wilder adds.

Tears fill my eyes. *No*, I don't want to cry right now. Not in front of my Wilder. "He left me. He broke up with me and left me like it was easy as breathing."

"I know."

"I just can't understand why." My bottom lip trembles. "Why didn't he want me anymore? What did I do wrong?"

Wilder grabs my hand and tugs me into his arms. I hold on tight as he lays his cheek on top of my head.

"I know what it's like to be pushed aside for something better, Blondie," Wilder confesses. "It's, uh, a different kind of pain. One that's impossible to ignore. You can't just put a band-aid on it and wait for the scrape to heal. It's like a broken bone. It takes a long time to get over, and the bone doesn't always go back into place right away. Sometimes, you have to re-break it. Then, you wrap it in a cast and hope you don't have to wear it forever."

I nod against his chest as several tears escape. "I don't want to re-break it."

"Then don't."

"How?" I pull away and gaze up at him.

Wilder cups my face in his hands and wipes the tears off my cheeks with his thumbs. "When I figure it out, I'll let you know."

"I'm sorry your dad left you. I think he made a big mistake. You are... you're lots of things. But you've been here for me. You know, since Cash left. There's some good in there." I lay a hesitant palm on his chest. "Might have to dig a little to find it but I know it's there."

Wilder's eyes grow impossibly large.

"What?" I whisper.

He caresses my cheek gently before he leans forward and kisses me.

Chapter 14
The Wax Job

His mouth is devastatingly addictive. Every swipe of his tongue against mine—every suck and lick and nip—feels like I'm being devoured whole. *And it's sensational.*

I can't seem to catch my breath as Wilder's fingers cup my chin possessively and the front of his khaki pants rubs against the front of my skirt. I'm wet and sticky and uncomfortable *down there.* I don't think I mind, though. I don't want him to stop. I don't want him to end the kiss. I've never been kissed like this before. Like a thousand fireworks exploding in the sky above us.

My hands slide up his stomach as he sucks my bottom lip into his mouth and I place a hand over his heart, the rhythm a chaotic beat. I know if I checked my pulse, it'd be dancing to the same cadence. *Boom, boom, boom.*

When our lips part, I hear an audible sigh escape my mouth. Wilder tugs the baseball cap off my head and rests his forehead against mine.

I wait for him to say something, but he's breathing heavily, and his eyes are closed. I should say something, right? I should acknowledge what just happened.

"Are you ready to go?" he whispers before replacing the hat on my head and leaving me a writhing, confused mess in the country club parking lot.

What the hell just happened?

I drive home in a fog. Wilder kissed me. He shoved his tongue inside my mouth. But now, he's sitting silently beside me on his phone as if those fireworks exploding—*boom, boom, boom*—never happened. As if it meant nothing.

By the time we're parked outside my house, I've convinced myself that I imagined the whole thing. It didn't happen. We didn't happen. Whatever that was in the parking lot was a made-up scenario. A dream. But then, why is my heart still beating so hard in my chest?

Wilder hops out first and pops open the trunk. He grabs the golf clubs and slings them over his shoulder.

"See you later," he says.

"Are we not going to talk about it?" I ask as I wrap my arms around my midsection.

"It was a weak moment, Blondie. Don't read into it too much," he says as he flashes his eyebrows at me.

"Wilder," I take a hurt step forward. "That wasn't just a weak moment. I... I felt something. I..."

"You're Cash's," he reminds me. "Not mine. You've always been Cash's."

"Well," I shake my head, "Cash isn't here."

"I have to go."

"Wilder!" I call after him, but he's already a house away. Then two. Then, he disappears down his driveway and I still haven't moved from the spot I'm frozen in.

I don't know what's going on. What do I do now?

I lock my car and trudge up the pathway to the front door, thoroughly confused.

I wake to the sound of Isla's latest temper tantrum. I wonder what Her Royal Highness is shrieking about now.

Even though I really want to go back to sleep, I roll out of bed and find my way to the bathroom. Frank the Fornicator is walking out as I try to get in.

"You're going to want to wait to go in there," he informs me. "Just dropped the kids off at the pool."

"Don't you have an apartment?" I cross my arms over my chest. "One with a bathroom that you don't have to share with two women?"

"Isla wants me to stay here," he shrugs.

"In the future, could you please destroy the downstairs bathroom instead of the one with my toothbrush in it?"

Frank the Fornicator mumbles something incoherent as he slithers back to Isla's Den of Debauchery.

I turn and head downstairs to the half bath. The one without Frank's disgusting ass smell permeating the daisy wallpaper.

"You don't get it, Mom!" Queen Isla wails. "I love him! It doesn't matter how we met. What matters is that we love each other!"

"I know that, Isla," Mom replies. "All your dad and I were saying is that Frank doesn't live here, and we'd like you to limit the amount of time he spends at our house."

"Why don't you hang out at his place?" Dad interjects as I tip-toe to the bathroom. This really isn't a conversation I want to be dragged into.

"Because he has three roommates," Isla screeches.

"You also have three roommates," Dad points out.

"Ugh!" Isla dramatically slaps her hand on the counter. "You're not listening to me. You're both missing the point."

"We hear you, Isla," Mom states. "We hear you loud and clear. But we don't want Frank here."

"Then, I'm moving in with Frank," Isla announces.

"YES!" I mistakenly celebrate from the hallway.

Isla whips around to face me. "You talked them into this, didn't you?"

"Me?" I point to myself.

"You're unbelievable," she seethes. "You've always been jealous of me. And now, you've forced Mom and Dad to kick me out because Cash dumped you and you can't stand to see me happy with Frank."

"You volunteered to leave," I roll my eyes as I slowly move one foot in front of the other. The sooner I can get out of here, the happier I'll be.

"They won't let Frank stay the night anymore because of you!" she hollers.

"Sorry," I shrug before taking another step forward. Only a few to go before I'm at the bathroom.

"Sorry?" she gasps. "That's all you have to say for yourself."

"I hope you and Frank have a lovely time with his three roommates," I grin before running into the bathroom and locking the door behind me.

Phew! Made it out alive. For now.

I stare at myself in the mirror for a moment. Isla's words echo in my head. *You've always been jealous of me. And now, you've forced Mom and Dad to kick me out because Cash dumped you and you can't stand to see me happy with Frank.*

As far as sisters go, Isla's the worst. I'd never want her to be unhappy just because I am. If the roles were reversed, she'd make my life miserable. Instead of having the tiniest bit of sympathy for me, she's using my break up to make herself look like the victim. She really is an egotistical tyrant.

I pull my pajama bottoms down my legs and glance at my crotch. I really, *really* need to get a wax. Especially since *skinny dip at the lake* is still a bucket list item that hasn't been crossed off yet.

I think that's what I'll do today. I'll get a wax. Surely Loretta can fit in her favorite employee. Besides, I need a distraction. Something to keep my mind off of the kiss with Wilder yesterday. The one he says not to read too much into. But I'm reading into it anyway. I'm reading into *everything*.

I mean, why did he have to say that thing about us having the same rejection wound? Why did he have to say things that make sense? Why does he see me so clearly when Cash never could?

I know what it's like to be pushed aside for something better, Blondie. It's, uh, a different kind of pain. One that's impossible to ignore. You can't just put a band-aid on it and wait for the scrape to heal. It's like a broken bone. It takes a long time to get over, and the bone doesn't always go back into place right away. Sometimes, you have to re-break it. Then, you wrap it in a cast and hope you don't have to wear it forever.

He said all those deeply profound things and then he kissed me. It was... it was terrible timing after our golf course fight, but still thoughtful and honest. Cash and I rarely talked about our feelings. We talked about everything else. Sports, his parents, music, and Johns Hopkins. We barely scratched the surface.

But Wilder and me? It's like we dove into the deep end of the pool without testing out the shallow end first.

Is it possible to spend four years with someone and never really know them? Then, turn around and spend four minutes with someone else and feel like no one has ever understood you better.

I groan as I drop my head into my hands. Wilder kissed me. And I liked it. Then, he acted like it was no big deal.

You're Cash's. Not mine. You've always been Cash's.

I was Cash's, but Wilder was always there. I was never really *just* Cash's. Wilder and I spent more time arguing than Cash and I did talking.

What if... what if all this time I was dating the wrong friend?

No, Ingrid. Don't do that to yourself.

What Cash and I had was great until it wasn't. It was young, puppy love. Then, it was over.

Now, I'm still fighting with Wilder but there's less arguing and more talking and feelings and words that are deep and meaningful, and then there's the kissing. Explosive, orgasmic kissing.

The best kiss of my life. But I'm not supposed to read into it.

So, I guess I'm going to get a wax. Maybe a painful diversion will clear my head.

I flush the toilet and head up the stairs. The Cave of Corruption is awfully quiet. I throw on a pair of shorts and a tank top before heading out the door hoping to avoid Queen Isla before her tireless tirade continues.

The drive through town on a Sunday morning is serene and slow. Everyone is still slumbering inside their quiet, peaceful houses. Houses not terrorized by Isla and Frank's regrettable relationship.

"What do you mean Loretta isn't in today?" I say when I make it to Loretta's. My eyes widen as Pierre adjusts the skin-tight black sleeves on his shirt.

"She doesn't work Sundays anymore," he rolls his head back and forth on his shoulders. "I have a 30-minute window open now. No charge."

I inhale sharply. I could always wait until Monday to ask Loretta about a wax. But if she doesn't have any openings next week, and Wilder wants to skinny dip at the lake Friday night, then the bush will be on *full display*. And I'm not sure after that racy kiss I want to introduce Wilder to the tangled mess of pubes I've let grow out of control.

"Fine," I swallow hard.

Pierre leads the way into the back. My palms begin sweating instantly. I prefer Loretta and her gentle, grandmotherly touch to Pierre's quick, questionable torment.

"You sweat a lot last time," Pierre fondly remembers. "I'll go get the baby powder."

I want to die. Someone, please hand me the sharp, jagged end of a sword.

"Get on the table!" Pierre hollers from the closet.

I take off my shorts and climb onto the table. Everything is sweaty. My hands, my legs, my armpits.

"You know the drill," Pierre *tsks* me as he swirls the purple wax in the warmer. "Put your feet together."

I close my eyes, mortified, as I press the heels of my feet together and give Pierre access to the part of me I swore he'd never touch again.

It's not that Pierre is gross or unprofessional. He doesn't make uncomfortable comments or let his eyes linger too long in places they shouldn't. It's just that he's a boy. One that graduated three years ahead of me. It feels *weird*.

Pierre spreads the first patch of wax and I grip the sides of the table with force.

"Relax," Pierre instructs. "It'll be over soon."

"Not soon enough," I grunt as he rips off the first strip.

What follows is a painful ten minutes of removing every last stubborn hair *down there.*

"Turn on your side," Pierre exhales when my vagina is hairless.

"Oh," I shake my head, "no. I don't want that area waxed."

Pierre raises an eyebrow. "You need it waxed."

"Is my butthole hairy?" My mouth drops open in surprise.

Pierre grabs the stick from the wax warmer. "You don't really want me to answer that, do you?"

I turn on my side and cover my face with my hands. Being a girl is rough. Especially when you walk into the salon expecting a bikini wax and wind up with the Hollywood.

Chapter 15
The Skinny Dip

It's been four days since our kiss at the country club, and I still haven't heard from Wilder. He's usually the one who initiates bucket list items every weekend. But there's been no contact on his end. So, I decide to take matters into my own hands.

Are you free Friday night? I text him.

No, busy.

That was a fast response.

You have a date or something?

Yep.

With who?

Hendrix.

The girl who sucks at golf?

Yep.

I'm sure she's good at sucking other things, too.

A snarky but necessary reply.

I'm free Saturday, he texts back.

Guess he's ignoring my dig.

I was going to suggest we get a tattoo, but I'm feeling bold.

Skinny dip at the lake?

He doesn't answer right away, which causes a flash of panic to flare in my chest. Maybe that was too bold. But then, I see the little bubble with three dots pop up and I know he's typing.

Pick you up at 6.

Bold is definitely paying off today.

"Your mom let you take her car?" I ask as I plop into the driver's seat with my bag and towel.

"I dropped her off at the hospital," Wilder explains. "She's covering the night shift."

"Thanks for driving three doors down to pick me up," I try. I could have walked to his house, but Wilder was already waiting in the driveway when I stepped outside.

He doesn't respond.

Awkward.

"Smashing Trout is playing at the Civic Center in two weeks," I clear my throat. "I got us tickets."

"Cool," Wilder shrugs.

Cool? That's all I'm going to get out of him? He hates—no, *loathes*—Smashing Trout. And he's suddenly just *cool* with me buying tickets for us? Something is seriously wrong with him.

I inhale sharply and turn to face him. He's gripping the steering wheel with both hands, and his jaw looks tense. Too tense for someone who got laid last night.

Wait, did he not sleep with Hendrix? I don't think he did. He's all wound up, like a swing that's been twisted until its chains can't budge anymore. All he needs is to let go, and he'll be spinning out of control.

Me. I'd like to be the one causing the spinning.

"What's going on?" I ask.

He briefly glances at me before his gaze returns to the road. "What do you mean?"

"Well," I lick my lips, "you kissed me, you didn't want to talk about it, you made it clear I would always be Cash's, and then you've ignored me for the past six days. So, I digress. What is going on, Wilder?"

"I don't want to—"

"Can I just say something?" I interrupt.

"Sure," Wilder exhales.

"I am my own," I swallow hard. "I don't belong to anyone. I'm not Cash's. When we were together, there was a room inside my heart where he stayed for a while, but my heart lives with me. I'm the one who lets people come and go from it. I'm the one who gave Cash permission to occupy a piece of it. It's mine. I don't belong to anyone but myself. I'm not Cash's, and I'm not yours. I am my own."

"I'm aware," Wilder sighs. "That's not what I meant when I said that."

"Then, what did you mean?"

"He saw you first, Blondie," Wilder states. "He saw you a split second before I did."

"I... I don't understand," I say. "He saw me first so that makes me his. What does that even mean?"

"It means the moment he saw you," there's a long pause before he continues, "our friendship would be over if I ever wanted you, too."

Did he just admit—*ambivalently*—that he wants me?

"You're afraid if we talk about the kiss," I clarify, "it'll mean we have to talk about why it happened and that might end your friendship with Cash?"

Wilder drops a hand from the steering wheel to his thigh. "Cash is my best friend. Or was? I'm not sure if we're friends anymore. He doesn't respond to my messages, and he's been running around Europe with some guy named Nick."

"Nick?" I gasp. "Did you Snapchat stalk Cash?"

"I didn't stalk," he rolls his shoulders. "I saw his stories."

"You said we have the same wound," I tread lightly, "but that doesn't mean it'll heal the same way. Cash ditched you, and he didn't even have the decency to say goodbye. You never got closure, and now you're living in limbo. But my mom always says *limbo is closure, too*. Maybe you're hanging onto something that isn't going to go back to the way it was. And it's okay to be heartbroken over it."

"I'm not heartbroken," Wilder scoffs. "I'm annoyed. There's a difference."

"Well, I'm angry," I tell him. "For you. I'm mad about the way he treated you. I'm not that angry for me. Cash... Cash is gone and I'm doing fine without him."

"Yeah," Wilder sits up straighter, his eyes meeting mine for a split second, "you are doing surprisingly well."

"I've only cried once," I shrug.

"You're a ruthless host," he gives me a cheeky grin.

"Hey," I raise my eyebrows, "I don't let people live in my heart rent-free. Once they're all paid up, I like to kick them out."

"As you should."

"If you want me," I lick my lips nervously as I lay a hand over my heart, "there's room. I give you permission to stay a while."

Wilder tries to hide a smile, but the setting sun lights up his face. "Thanks, Blondie."

"How was your date with Hendrix?" I force a change of subject.

"She got drunk and puked all over my shoes before she fell asleep in a booth at the bowling alley," he laughs.

"Typical Hendrix," I tease him. "Drinks too much and then passes out." *See*, I knew he didn't get laid.

His smile fades as we near the lake. "I'm sorry I kissed you."

"Why did you?"

Wilder runs a hand through his dark hair. It's getting longer, and I know he's overdue for a haircut. "Because I wanted to."

I suck my bottom lip into my mouth and bite down. There's a lot I want to say. I want to tell him that kissing me, then going on a date with Hendrix was shitty and stupid. But it's Wilder. He's like a stray dog. He's jumpy and doesn't trust easily. Once he makes himself at home, though, he never leaves. So, I keep my mouth shut and decide not to push. Not tonight, anyway.

He parks near the dock as the sun hangs on the horizon. A family of four is packing up tackle boxes and a cooler as we sit in the car, neither of us moving.

"I know you're not heartbroken," I fill the quiet with noise. "But I wouldn't blame you if you were."

"Are you heartbroken?"

I tuck a strand of blond behind my ear. "I knew it was coming. When Cash stopped having sex with me, I knew."

"I'm sorry I made comments about that," he apologizes. I glance over at him but he's staring straight ahead. "If it made things harder, I'm sorry."

"I think fighting with you was the only way I got through those last two months," I fondly sigh.

His hand slides across the center console and he places it on top of mine. "We do fight a lot."

"It's just sexual tension," I mock him as the family cleaning up their stuff on the dock starts to head toward their car.

Wilder cocks an eyebrow as he gazes over at me. "You couldn't handle *Wild Cox*."

"The legend lives on," I shake my head.

"You ready to do this?" He removes his hand from mine and motions to the lake.

Pierre waxed *everything*. I've never been more ready. "Yes."

"If you need to keep anything on," Wilder clears his throat, "that's fine with me."

"I'm good," I smirk. "But if you're scared to take off *all* your clothes, I'll understand."

"I have nothing to hide," he winks.

The family files into their van as I tuck my bag under the passenger seat and clutch the towel I brought to my chest. I'm hyperaware of every move Wilder makes. He swallows hard, his Adam's apple bobbing as he does. Then, he grabs the door handle and pushes it open. When he does, butterflies flood my stomach and my mouth dries. I take a sobering breath before I get out of the car and take in the fiery sky. Candy apple red, tangerine, and lemony hues dance across the darkening canvas, the setting sun making the calm lake shimmer and glisten. Suddenly, all the butterflies leave and I smile.

"You coming?" Wilder calls a few feet ahead of me, the warm air tickling my skin.

I take several long strides forward in the soft dirt before I reach him. We walk side-by-side to the dock, not a single boat or jet ski in sight.

I slip my sandals off and place my towel on top of them. Wilder tugs the shirt over his head as my eyes land on his toned back. I drink in his golden skin and the way his muscles constrict as he bunches his discarded T-shirt into a ball and drops it beside him. I look away and grab the hem of my white sundress, slowly pulling it up and exposing the white cotton underwear beneath. Wilder's too busy unbuttoning his shorts to pay attention to my undergarments. I probably should have chosen something slightly more risqué to wear but knowing Wilder, he's seen it all. And seducing Wilder isn't on the bucket list. I am my own. I wear what I want.

The moment I reach for the clasp on my bra, I hear a splash in the water. Guess Wilder wasn't waiting around for me to finish undressing. I remove my bra and carefully step out of my underwear, wrapping both of them up in my dress.

I stand perfectly still for a moment in the waning sunlight. A month ago, I never would have taken off all my clothes and jumped into the lake. Cash Allred's girlfriend *would never*. But I'm not Cash's girlfriend anymore.

I am my own.

Grinning, I run towards the end of the dock and jump off the warm wood, pulling my knees up to my chest while screaming, "Cannonball!"

My body makes contact with the cool lake water and I close my eyes tight. When my head finally resurfaces, I search for Wilder. He's floating a few feet from me.

"You're scaring the fish, Blondie."

I tread water, my skin prickling from the adrenaline. "I don't think I care."

"You used to care," he counters, "about everything."

"I spent a lot of time pretending to be someone I wasn't," I admit. "I didn't realize until now that I've spent the past couple of weeks finally being myself again. No wonder Cash dumped me. I was always trying to fit into his world. I stopped being Ingrid Winthrop and started being—"

"*Ingrid With-A-Thorn-Shoved-Up-Her-Ass*?" Wilder finishes.

I slap my arm on top of the water and splash him. "Shut up!"

Wilder disappears beneath the water as air bubbles float to the surface in his wake. I feel around for the bottom of the lake, but we're too far out. I can't reach it.

A hand curls around my ankle, yanking me under. I hold my breath, my arms searching for Wilder. I feel his bicep first, then his shoulder. Then, we're both drifting to the surface.

"I can't reach the bottom," I tell him as he pushes the wet hair off his forehead.

"Come on," he says, grabbing my hand and pulling me along with him. We swim several feet closer to the shore. "Can you stand here?"

My toes graze the sandy bottom. "Yeah."

He lets my hand go as I stand on both feet, the water rocking us back and forth.

We stare at each other as the sun peeks over the horizon, the sky navy and violet and periwinkle now.

His hazel eyes glow gold as the last rays of sunlight flicker against his face. He's handsome. So handsome. But he's not Cash. He's not steady or stable. He's... *wild*. Just like his name. He's frustrating and difficult and hard to handle.

I'm not sure who moves first, but my arms slide around his neck as his fingers caress my back and he draws me closer to him. I can feel him—*all of him*—against my chest and stomach and thighs as I push off the grainy lakebed and kiss him.

Chapter 16
The Trailer Trash

The water kisses my toes as Wilder's palm cups one of my butt cheeks in his hand. I'm not sure when we waded out of the water and collapsed onto the sand, but his lips are moving against mine, and his *you know what* is digging into my stomach and the sky is full of twinkling stars overhead.

We should rinse the tiny grains of sand off our bodies and go home. Pretend this never happened. Rewind. Go back to the second before I pushed off the lakebed and kissed him. But kissing Wilder is like stepping into a warm, steamy shower after a long day in the snow. Muggy, hot, and relaxing. I'm a little intoxicated right now by the taste of his tongue as it tangles with mine and the feel of his hands as they roam my body.

My fingers slip down his stomach and inch closer to the part of him that's rock-hard against my abdomen. Before I reach it, his hand wraps around my wrist and he inhales sharply.

"What?" I ask him as my brow creases and I wiggle on top of him, trying to pull my hand out of his grasp.

"We should, uh, we should go slow, Blondie."

I smile. "We have been building up to this exact moment since freshmen year. I'm done going slow, and you're not allowed to ignore me after this. Not like you did when we kissed."

"I... I'm still not sure if this is something we should be doing," Wilder wars with himself.

That's fine. He can battle with himself. I've already made my mind up.

"Blondie," he exhales as I fight against his strong grip, "we should stop while we're ahead."

"You're rejecting me?" I push off him, my knees sinking into the sand. I raise a devious eyebrow. "You mean, we shouldn't be doing this?" I scoot back, my soaked center rubbing against his massive cock. I'm happy to report the legend is true. *He's huge.*

His eyes widen as I rock backward, rolling my hips as I coat his throbbing dick with my juices. "Are you saying you don't want this, Wilder?"

His hands find my hips, and he digs his fingers in as I slide back and forth, soaking him. "I think we should go slow."

I stop moving on top of him. "Slow or not at all?"

He groans as I slip off him and lay beside him in the sand. "Slow."

"I swear, Wilder Andrea Cox if you—"

"Andrew," he interjects. "It's Andrew."

"—ignore me after this, I'll ruin every single date or hookup you have in the near future. I'll make your life a living hell. Women will run when they see you coming."

He turns on his side and gently rests his hand on my stomach. "And Cash always said you weren't the jealous type."

I reach a hand up to his face and run my fingers along his jawline. "I wasn't. Not until you."

Wilder drops his head to my shoulder and leaves a chaste kiss on my skin. "We can't do this forever, Blondie. Eventually, Cash will come back."

"Why do you keep bringing him up?" I swallow hard. "I'm naked right now and you're thinking about Cash?"

"When my dad left, my mom and I were homeless for a few weeks," he admits. "My grandparents had to get their spare bedrooms ready for us. My grandma gave up her craft room, and my grandpa worked hard to get the guest room cleared out for me. They didn't have space for us right away. We were going to stay in a motel, but Cash told his parents and they insisted we stay with them. So, we did. And I've felt indebted to him ever since."

My breath gets caught in my throat. "That was surprisingly nice of the Allreds."

"Yeah," he agrees. "Fanny spent the whole time lecturing my mom about her choice in a life partner, though."

"Is that why you keyed Fanny's front door after she painted it?" I laugh.

"That," he lowers his voice and presses his lips briefly to mine. "And for you. She said a lot of shit about you that wasn't true. Cash never stood up for you and I didn't feel it was my place. So, I liked to key her stuff or rearrange the kitchen drawers to annoy her."

"You didn't," I touch his chest.

"I moved all the silverware after she uninvited me to a dinner party once. She told Cash I wasn't allowed to come because I was *trailer trash*. But I got the last laugh," he chuckles. "She had a meltdown in front of all her guests."

"That wasn't very nice," I sigh.

His hand roams my bare skin. "I'm not very nice."

"I know."

"We should rinse off," he lets out a breath.

"I'm starving," I tell him.

"The diner?"

I shake my head. "Ice cream."

"First, you get me naked," he teases me with a kiss on the nose. "Then you kiss me." Another one to my throat. "Now, you want ice cream." A trail of kisses along my jaw. "It's almost like you planned this whole thing."

"It's our first date," I quip. "You didn't get the memo, did you?"

He stands and holds a hand out to me. "No, you didn't mention the word *date* when you texted me about skinny dipping at the lake."

"I like to keep you on your toes," I shrug as he squeezes my hand lightly.

We rinse off in the water, removing sand from all the *uncomfortable* places. There's nothing remotely romantic about making out—*naked*—on the sandy shoreline.

"I think there's sand in my ass," I throw my head back and laugh.

Wilder shakes his head, the moonlight bathing him in a radiant shimmer. "Come here."

I step closer, the lake water cooling off my clammy skin. Wilder runs his hands up and down my legs, removing all remaining sand from that area. Then, his fingers find my back, my stomach, my shoulders. His breathing hitches as the palms of his hands glide over my breasts. I close my eyes, the contact sublime. Cash never touched me like this. Never ran his hands all over my body like Wilder's doing now.

"You okay, Blondie?" I hear Wilder's voice.

I lick my lips. "It feels good. So good."

He smirks and drops his hands to his sides. "Let's go before we both do something we'll regret."

"Oh," I cross my arms over my chest, "you're the only one who would regret it."

Wilder mumbles something under his breath. I don't hear most of it, but I catch the words, "trust" and "me."

"We still getting ice cream?" I ask him when we're fully clothed again.

He glances over at me, the moonlight casting a white glow across his handsome face. "If you want ice cream, we'll get ice cream."

I skip beside him. "I do want ice cream."

"You know," he starts as he unlocks my door and opens it for me, "you were all hot and bothered when Cash wouldn't have sex with you. But I didn't have sex with you, and you don't seem the least bit bothered."

"I'm not sure what answer you're looking for here," I say as I give him a playful wink.

He closes my door and walks over to his side. When he plops in beside me, he turns on the ignition. "You were always frustrated with him because... Blondie, please don't make me say it."

"Say it," I goad.

"You never reached uh, the *peak* with Cash."

"Orgasm," I correct. "It's an orgasm."

"You didn't orgasm just now. Why don't you seem frustrated?"

"How do you know I didn't orgasm?" I challenge.

"I've... I know when a girl—woman—orgasms. You didn't." I can't see the red color of his cheeks in the dark as he drives down the bumpy dirt road, but I know he's blushing.

"Maybe you satisfied something inside of me," I shrug. Honestly, making out naked was enough of a high. *For now*. But I'm not telling him that.

"You sure you're not fucking with me?" He sounds uneasy. I wonder if this has to do with Olivia-Sophia and whatever she did to him.

"No," I reply. "I'm not fucking with you. I don't make a habit of undressing in front of boys just for the fun of it."

"Isn't that the point of skinny dipping?"

"Yeah," I wave off, "but you're probably the only person I would ever do that with."

"Really?"

"Really," I hitch a shoulder. "You're the only person I feel comfortable doing a lot of things with."

"Like?"

"Like sneaking into movie theatres or golf courses. Or shopping for overpriced pleated skirts."

"You and Cash never had fun, did you?"

"Cash wasn't allowed to have fun," I frown. He keeps bringing up Cash. It's almost as if he's comparing what Cash and I had to whatever Wilder and I are doing. "The only time we did have fun is when you were around. You always helped Cash step out of his comfort zone."

"I think I help you do the same," he wisely deduces.

"You let me be myself," I swallow hard. "That's a rare gift."

"Is it?" Wilder asks.

"I meant what I said," I inhale sharply. "I don't want you to ignore me after we made out in the sand."

"We made out *naked* in the sand," he corrects.

"It really bothered me that you kissed me, and then took Hendrix on a date," I confess.

"I didn't mean for it to bother you."

"Well, it did," I reinforce. "If we're doing the bucket list and you're seeing me naked, you don't get to see other girls naked."

"Are you asking me to be exclusive?"

I nod slowly. "Yes."

"That would imply that something is going on between us," Wilder shifts uncomfortably.

"I'm not asking you to be my boyfriend," I clarify. "I've never competed well with other girls. If you're not interested in only kissing me, then I don't think we should kiss at all."

"Anyone ever tell you that you're a good communicator?"

I tuck a strand of damp blond hair behind my ear. "Depends on who I'm communicating with."

"Why the clear communication with me?"

"Because I don't want you to think that this doesn't mean anything to me."

"Like a rebound?"

"You're Wilder," I blow out a tired breath. "You're Cash's best friend, but you've also been a permanent fixture in my life since I started dating Cash. I don't want to lose that. Fighting with you has always been the highlight of my day. You're not a rebound. I know we don't always see eye-to-eye, but you're kind of, sort of, my best friend. At the moment, anyway."

"Can I think about it?"

"Can you think about it quickly?" I laugh nervously. "I'd really like to do more than just kiss you in the dark at the lake."

"Even if we were to kiss more often, we couldn't flaunt it around town. There are too many eyes and ears."

I scratch the side of my face. "You wouldn't want Cash to know?"

"Would you?"

I shake my head. "I guess not. This is just really complicated, and you keep bringing up Cash and it annoys me."

"It annoys me, too, Blondie."

"I hate keeping secrets."

"I know you do."

"Maybe we should both think about it."

"Yeah," Wilder says before parking in front of the Big Dipper Creamery.

We get out and keep our distance as we walk over to a window to order.

"Welcome to Big Dipper Creamery," Jensen Olsen smiles at us. He's a year younger than we are, but when you live in a small town, everyone knows pretty much everyone. "What creamy concoction can we fill your cone with?"

Wilder hides a smile. "They pay you to say that Jensen?"

Jensen rolls his eyes. "No, I'm supposed to say, 'What creamy mess can we drizzle on your milkers', but that's just embarrassing."

"Milkers?" I laugh. "Who came up with that?"

Jensen throws a thumb over his shoulder. "The owner. She was looking for a *hip* word to call milkshakes. She decided on milkers."

"What is wrong with this town?" Wilder runs a hand over his face. "If it's not bushes, it's milkers."

I let out a small giggle as Wilder's eyes lock with mine. "You think that's funny, Blondie?"

"I would like a vanilla milker," I wink at Wilder. "And can you drizzle some marshmallow cream all over it?"

Jensen's face burns red. "One vanilla milker drizzled in marshmallow cream coming up."

"That wasn't very nice," Wilder *tsks* me.

"I'm not very nice," I return as I nudge him with my hip.

The expression on Wilder's face is hard to read. "I'm starting to think hidden beneath your good girl facade is a rebel."

I purse my lips. "I guess that depends."

"On?"

I turn to face him. "On how much clothing I'm wearing."

Wilder's teeth sink into his bottom lip. "You're a tease."

Jensen hands me my milker before taking Wilder's order. When he's gone, I lick the marshmallow cream off the rim of the Styrofoam cup. "I'd let you drizzle your marshmallow cream all over my milkers, but you have some thinking to do."

His fingers find the hem of my white sundress. "So do you."

"I guess we better get thinking then," I flash my eyebrows at him.

Jensen returns, and hands over a chocolate-dipped cone before Wilder pays. I don't bother offering to foot the bill. If Wilder wants to hold it over my head, I'm sure I can think of a *creative* way to pay him back. In fact, I'd love to owe him. I can think of a few ways to settle the score right now as our eyes stay glued on each other.

I didn't think I'd survive this summer. Now, I'm not sure how I'm going to survive once the summer is over.

Chapter 17
The Insecure Hookup

I eat my cereal in silence. *Silence*. It's blissful. Queen Isla and Frank the Fornicator haven't been back since Isla decided to move out a week ago.

We have a bet going.

Mom thinks she won't be back at all. Dad says he's giving it a month because she wants to prove a point. I think they're both wrong. Any day now, Isla is going to waltz back in with her stupid red suitcase. My sister cannot—and will not—share a bathroom with four boys. How she's managed this long is beyond me.

"Hey!" Mom chirps as she walks into the kitchen, scaring the living daylights out of me.

I gasp in response and hit the bowl in front of me. It tips over and a trail of milk trickles into my lap as Mom tries to hide her laughter.

"Didn't mean to scare you, Ingrid," she chuckles and covers her hand with her mouth.

"Could you grab me some paper towels *please*?" I groan as milk soaks into my cotton shorts.

Mom reaches for the roll and tosses the whole thing at me. "Your father and I are headed to brunch with the Crockett's, then we're playing Bridge."

Geez, Mom and Dad are getting old.

"Brunch and Bridge?" I raise an eyebrow. "You're turning into Grandma and Grandpa."

"Watch it," Mom points a finger at me. "We'll grill burgers for dinner tonight, so you're on your own for lunch."

"As long as Isla doesn't crash my solo party this afternoon, I'll be good."

"Be nice," Mom raises an eyebrow at me. "She's still your sister."

"I love her but I don't like her," I declare as I stand and walk over to the sink. I deposit the remnants of my breakfast into it.

"You two have never gotten along," Mom exhales. "Even as girls."

"She's selfish," I shrug, my wet shorts sticking to my legs.

"She's just different from you."

"I love that you see the world through rose-colored glasses, but I'm going to take a shower before I say something I might regret. Have fun with Betty and Boris."

"I'll tell them you say hi," Mom calls after me as I jog up the stairs.

I shut my door, and strip off my soggy shorts. I toss them into the laundry basket the moment my cell phone vibrates on the vanity. I cross the room and see it's a Snapchat notification. I decide to ignore it and pull my shirt over my head. As I do, I hear a knock on my bedroom door.

"Yeah, Mom?" I say.

The door creaks open and Wilder's face comes into view. Not the person I was expecting.

Quickly, I hide what I can of my naked body with the T-shirt in my hand.

"Uh," Wilder covers his face with a hand. "Your mom said to just come up."

Oh, Jill. You knew I had to shower. What were you thinking?

"I-It's fine," I choke out. "It's not like you didn't see me naked less than 13 hours ago."

Wilder stands awkwardly in the doorway, unsure of what to do.

"Um," I clear my throat, "can you come in and shut the door? I don't know if my parents are still here."

"They were heading out when I was walking up," he explains.

"Oh," I frown as I clutch the T-shirt tighter to my chest.

Wilder closes the door and shoves his hands into his pockets. "I've been thinking."

"You're going to do this now?" I laugh nervously.

He runs a hand through his hair. "I... well, I was sort of hoping to get this off my chest."

"While I'm not clothed?" I remind him.

His eyes roam my bare legs. "I think I want to do it while you're naked."

"Really?"

Wilder crosses the room in a few strides. When he reaches me, he cups my face in his hands. "I want you, Blondie."

My throat dries. "Really?"

Black pupils eat up his hazel irises. "I think I've always wanted you."

"Really?" I say for the third time.

"I don't want to think about Cash or what happens to our friendship. I just want you."

Before I blurt out that I want him, too, he leans down and kisses me roughly. I drop the T-shirt in my hand and wrap my arms around his waist. He holds my face as his lips move against mine. Everything is a blur as he walks me back to my bed, his hands leaving my face and finding the backs of my thighs. He lifts me and I instinctively wrap my legs around him.

He kisses me like he's been starving for years. Starving for something real and *right*. Starving for something I know only I can give him.

He climbs onto my bed and carefully lays me down as he breaks our kiss. Wilder's breathing hard, his lips swollen and red.

"I want to make you feel good," he whispers.

There's a jolt in my chest, a feeling I've never experienced before. I raise a hand to his cheek and rub my thumb along his warm skin.

"I want to make you feel good, too," I swallow hard.

The corner of his mouth tips up. "Yeah?"

"Yeah," I smile up at him, surprised by the tenderness in his expression.

He kisses me once more before he slides down my body and I thank the waxing gods I got that Hollywood.

I feel his fingers first. They slide through my aching folds until he finds my clit and gently strokes. My body relaxes on my unmade bed as he explores, making everything sticky and wet. Breathy moans leave my mouth as the minutes tick by. As Wilder rubs and massages and plays. It's exhilarating and euphoric. Every nerve ending in my body explodes from his tantalizing touch.

But then, he does something Cash never did. He tugs me to the edge of the bed and throws my thighs over his shoulders. I prop myself up on my elbows as his tongue darts out and he tastes me.

I watch the erotic scene unfold as he sucks my clit into his mouth and buries his face between my legs. My arms shake from the pleasure rolling through my body. When I can't hold myself up anymore, I collapse on the mattress and squeeze my eyes shut tight.

"You okay, Blondie?" I hear Wilder's voice over the buzzing sound in my ears.

"Y-yes," I rasp as he slides his fingers inside me.

"You ready to come?"

I nod my head, unable to form words.

He kisses the inside of my thigh before his mouth closes around the swollen bundle of nerves begging for release.

It doesn't take long between his warm mouth and his teasing fingers before my stomach muscles tighten and my back arches off the bed and I squeeze Wilder's head between my legs.

I'm a writhing, panting mess when he lays beside me on the bed and kisses my forehead. "You good?"

I force my eyes open. "I think you broke my vagina."

Wilder laughs before running his hand down my stomach. "It was that good?"

"I'm pretty much ruined for all future men and I haven't even felt your dick inside of me," I groan.

"Then my work here is done," he teases me.

I curl into him, shivering. He grabs the comforter at the edge of my bed and tosses it over me. He snuggles against me and draws little circles on my back with his fingertips. I want to ask him if this is normal. If he does this with all the girls who welcome them into their beds. But I know the answer won't change anything.

He wants me.

He wants me here and now. So, I push all those dangerous thoughts aside and sigh.

"What are you thinking about?" he asks me.

I bite my lower lip. "I was thinking about how weird this is."

"Is it weird?"

I shift and lay my head on my arm to look up at him. "It doesn't feel weird. I just... I never thought we'd be here. It never crossed my mind. Did it ever cross yours?"

Wilder's eyebrows knit together. "I thought about it a few times but I never imagined it would actually happen."

"You thought about it?" My eyes widen in surprise.

"You're not the worst thing to look at," he admits. "Especially in a bikini."

"Thank you," I smile as I stretch beside him.

"For?"

"The mind-blowing orgasm," I guffaw as I sit up and stare down at him.

He sheepishly grins. "You should feel honored. I don't normally do that."

I can't hide the smile that spreads across my face. "Are you saying I'm *special*?"

His fingers find my back and he runs them along my cool skin. "You know you are."

I'm not sure what's going on with my heart, but it's going haywire beneath my ribcage. "Take your pants off."

"What?" He scrunches his face.

"I said," I laugh as I reach for the button of his jeans, "*take off your pants*. Unless you don't want a blow job. I am a little out of practice."

Wilder shakes his head as he unzips his jeans and shimmies them down his legs. I climb off the bed and yank them down to his ankles as he works on getting the black boxer briefs over his rock-hard dick.

I inhale sharply as his massive cock lays against his stomach. It was gorgeous in the setting sun last night. But this morning, in the daylight, it's even more glorious. Thick, long, the tip red and wet. I need it. I need it in my mouth.

"Stop drooling," he quips.

"It's," I sigh as I move closer and run my fingers over it, "beautiful."

"Don't call it beautiful," he chides me.

"Then what," I flash my eyebrows at him as I begin stroking it in my hand, "should I call it?"

"Um," he grins as he tucks his arms behind his head, "magnificent."

"Stunning."

"Exquisite."

"Delightful."

Wilder chuckles as he grows even larger in my hand. "I'm out of words."

"I could go on for hours about its beauty," I wink at him.

"I've never had this much fun before," he reveals.

"You mean in life or the bedroom?"

"Both."

I chew on my lower lip and watch his dick harden with each stroke. "Me either."

"Blondie," he says quietly.

"Yeah?" I say as my eyes return to his face.

"Why do you look sad?"

"I'm not sad," I shrug. "I just... I never realized how little fun I had before you. Before we became friends."

"We're not just friends," he corrects. "We're... we're more than that."

"I know," I nod. "I'm going to need you to shut up because I'm going to put you in my mouth now."

"Okay," he exhales with a smile.

I take him slowly, savoring the salty taste of his head, the veiny ridges of his shaft, and the feel of his heavy sack in my hand.

It's been a while since Cash last let me suck him off, but giving head comes back almost like riding a bike. I relax my jaw, bob my head up and down, and run my tongue along Wilder's pulsating shaft. I take my time, the same way he did with me. I explore with my mouth and fingers, inching him closer and closer to the back of my throat as saliva drips down my hand and all over Wilder's balls.

When he gets close, he rests his hand on my head. "Blondie, I'm going to... I'm going... if you don't... want to swallow..."

But I keep sucking, wanting to taste him the same way he tasted me.

A low growl leaves his throat as he spills into my mouth, the warm, salty liquid coating my tongue.

Wilder's stomach muscles constrict as I swallow and let his throbbing cock fall from my lips.

"Come here." His voice is gravelly and hoarse.

I lay my head on his T-shirt-clad chest and close my eyes. "Did you like that?"

"I loved it," he answers as he secures an arm around me.

"I was a little out of practice." *Oh no*. I don't want to be *that* girl. The insecure hookup who wonders if he's comparing conquests.

"It was mind-blowing," he reassures me as his phone starts ringing from the pocket of his jeans on the floor.

"Shit," he grunts. "I forgot about my mom."

"Your mom?"

I sit up and pull Wilder with me.

"My grandpa wasn't feeling well so I volunteered to pick my mom up from the hospital."

"Go!" I shove him.

"I..." he trails off as he hops off my bed and scrambles to find his pants. "I don't want you to read into this, okay?"

"I'm not," I assure him.

"I didn't expect this to happen," he confesses as he zips up his pants. "I was only planning on telling you I want this. Then, I was going to go pick my mom up."

"Wilder," I shake my head at him, "I know."

He kisses me goodbye, his hands tangling in my hair. He doesn't let me go as he tilts my head to the side and deepens the kiss.

"I'll call you later," he promises before running out of my room.

I watch him go, feeling sated.

My phone vibrates again. I push off my bed and walk over to it.

The same stupid notification.

When I open Snapchat—Ingrid's, not Pam's fake account—I have a snap from Cash. My heart races as I click on it. It's a selfie of him standing in front of the Eifel Tower. But that's not what causes my heart to dip in my chest. It's the message attached.

I miss you, Ingrid, and I wish you were here with me.

Chapter 18
The Tattoo Shop

I still haven't told Wilder that Cash sent me a selfie. Or that he said he misses me. It's been four days. I don't know why I haven't just blurted it out yet. I guess I don't want to pop our bubble. Our blissful, happy, orgasmic bubble.

It's like I'm holding bottled-up lightning. Rare, electric, and extraordinary. I don't want to let it go. I want to hold onto it for as long as I can. I want to hold onto Wilder as long as I can. Before his wildness gets the best of him, and he realizes I'm just another trap. Another cage. Another round pen, holding him in.

I'm not willing to let Cash release my bottled-up lightning. Not while he's thousands of miles away.

The phone rings, making me jump, and I reach for it. "Loretta's Laser Hair and Wax Removal. This is Ingrid. How can we whack that bush for you today?"

"Ingrid," I hear Mom on the other end of the line, "how's your day going?"

"Uh," I clear my throat. "Good. What's up?"

"Your father and I are thinking about getting away for the weekend."

"Okay," I lean back in my chair. "Are you asking for my permission?"

"No, honey," Mom chuckles, "I wasn't sure you'd feel comfortable staying home alone. I thought I'd call Grandma and have her stay with you."

Home alone? For a whole weekend. Without anyone bothering me.

"I think I'll manage fine without Grandma," I assure her. "But thanks for thinking of me."

"You're sure?"

"I'm sure," I grin.

Me, an empty house, and the whole weekend to myself? I know what I'll be doing. *Wilder.*

"Okay," Mom exhales. "I'm making a grocery store run. Anything you want while we're away?"

"I'll use up whatever's in the fridge," I tell her.

"Sounds good, Ingrid. Love you."

I hang up the phone as a plan formulates in my head. If Mom and Dad are going to be gone for the weekend, the *whole* weekend, then that gives Wilder and me plenty of time to *hang* out alone.

I love it when a serendipitous scheme falls into place.

"Ingrid!" Pierre hollers from the back room.

Groaning, I heave myself out of my chair and stomp down the hallway. "Yeah?"

"I need help hauling in supplies from my trunk," he whines.

I glance between the back door and Pierre. "I get paid to answer phones. Not to unload your car."

"I waxed your overgrown garden for free," he reminds me.

"Ugh," I roll my eyes dramatically. "Fine."

I help Pierre with the boxes. He moves twice as many as I do, but what does he expect? I'm free labor and I'm not rushing.

Once his trunk is empty, and I've worked up a sweat, it's time to clock out. I check in Pierre's afternoon wax, then grab my bag. As I do, the door swings open, and bottled-up lightning enters.

"What are you doing here?" I try to hide a smile.

"How do you feel about crossing bucket list item #1 off our list?" Wilder flashes his eyebrows at me.

"Get a tattoo?"

Wilder nods. "I made us an appointment."

"But... but... it's..." I stammer.

"Get it out, Blondie."

"It's Thursday. We don't do bucket list items on weekdays." It is an unspoken rule, but we both work during the week.

He crosses his arms over his chest. "We're making an exception."

"I have plans for us this weekend, anyway," I inform him.

"You do?"

I walk towards the door, stopping when I reach Wilder. I glance around, making sure no one can see me. Then, I place a hand on his chest and stand on my tippy toes, quickly leaving a peck on his lips.

"What was that?" His top teeth sink into his lower lip.

"I believe," I smirk, "they call that a kiss."

His face softens as he stares down at me. It's electric, the way his fingers feel when they brush my arm.

"Who is this?" I hear Pierre's obnoxious voice.

I whip around to face him.

"Ooh," Pierre waggles his dark, bushy eyebrows. "I'd like to wax his body."

"Paws off, Pierre," I try not to snarl. "He's *mine*." Woah, Ingrid. Let's rein it in. He's yours. *For now.*

"I thought you were dating that pale Allred boy," Pierre tilts his head to the side.

"They broke up," Wilder enters the chat.

"Pierre," my annoying coworker says as he holds his hand out.

Wilder shakes it. "I've heard a lot about you, Pierre."

"Oh," Pierre blushes, "I'm sure you have."

I swallow the words threatening to leave my mouth.

"Yeah," Wilder clears his throat awkwardly.

"You should have seen the mess down there before I worked my magic," Pierre continues as his eyes dart from my jean shorts back to Wilder. "I went through a *ton* of strips."

My mouth drops open in horror. I can't look at Wilder. I cannot. I will not. I'm MORTIFIED.

"I think we've overstayed our welcome," Wilder interjects. "Nice meeting you, Pierre."

"*Harassment,*" I mouth at Pierre. "*I'm telling Loretta.*"

Pierre winks at me before his eyes trail up and down Wilder's tall, toned body. "See you tomorrow, Ingrid."

"I didn't do it for you," I rush to get out when we're walking to my car.

"I didn't say you did, Blondie," Wilder nonchalantly replies.

"I did it for me," I make clear.

He stops walking and twists to face me. "I know you had to explain to Cash why you made the choices you did, but I'm not him. You don't owe me an explanation every time you do something. If you want to whack your bush, then whack it. If you want to braid it and put little flowers in it, I really don't care."

I swallow hard. "Did I explain myself to Cash all the time?"

Wilder nods as a strand of blond falls across my face. He gently removes it with his fingertips and places it behind my ear. "All the fucking time."

"I didn't realize," I chew on the inside of my cheek. "I mean, I guess I did. But I didn't..."

"It's okay," he assures me. "I get it. Cash has a way of making everyone feel they owe him an explanation."

"Even you?"

He hitches a shoulder. "Even me sometimes."

"Must be that Allred blood," I tease.

"I am my own," Wilder quips.

"What?" I scrunch my face in confusion.

"You said that," he reminds me. "*I am my own.* The only person you owe an explanation to is *you*."

I lick my lips as his hazel eyes glint in the shifting sunlight. *Bottled-up lightning.* I swear he's bottled-up lightning. Rare, electric, and extraordinary.

"Same goes for you," I smile.

"Eh," Wilder waves me off, "I don't think that's true for me."

"Why not?" I tilt my head to the side.

"I'm not ready to tell you why," he admits.

"Because it has to do with your dad?" I guess. "Or Elowyn?"

"I don't owe my dad anything," Wilder clarifies. "And Elowyn..."

"Your sister isn't so easy to write off, is she?"

"You're not a shrink," he *tsks* me as he shakes his head at me. "Stop analyzing me."

I laugh. "But it's so much fun."

"Come on," Wilder rolls his eyes. "We're going to be late."

The Tattoo Shop on Park Street is a little hole-in-the-wall place, but it's clean and sterile inside. Drawings and images fill the walls as I wander around, trying to figure out which tattoo I want permanently inked into my skin.

"You pick one yet, Blondie?"

"I'm not sure what to get," I exhale. "Or where to get it."

Wilder's hand touches my back before his palm slides down my backside. He squeezes lightly. "Maybe here?"

A heated spear soars from my heart straight to my manicured garden. "You'd like that, wouldn't you?"

His eyes dance with delight. "You know I would."

"I'm thinking I might get something here," I point to my wrist.

"Like?"

My eyes scan the pictures until I see it. A tiny drawing in the upper right-hand corner. I run my fingers over it. "This."

Wilder nods. "Good choice."

I sit in the chair first. My palms start sweating as soon as the tattoo gun's buzzing sound fills my ears. Wilder sits beside me and grabs my right hand, distracting me. He laces his fingers with mine, and I close my eyes, willing myself to relax.

A prickling sensation spreads across my skin as the needle does its work, but I don't pay it any attention. Instead, I hone in on the way Wilder's thumb rubs the back of my hand. The feel of his knee against my hip as he scoots the chair closer. The sound of his breathing barely audible over the ringing in my ears.

"All done," I hear the tattoo artist, Travis, announce.

I open my eyes and stare down at it. A tiny bolt of lightning. "It's perfect."

"You like it?" Wilder whispers.

"I do," I grin. "Are you ready for yours?"

We trade places, and I hold Wilder's hand the same way he held mine. He decided on a forearm tattoo. He wouldn't tell me what it was, but I have a feeling it's not an inconspicuous bolt of lightning.

Red ink splatters against his skin as my eyes slide from his forearm to his face.

"Does it hurt?" I ask him.

Wilder chuckles. "Didn't you just get a tattoo?"

"I did," I laugh nervously, "but it was much smaller than whatever you're getting."

"You're going to like it."

"You should have gotten one of those bicep I-heart-mom tattoos."

"My mom would have loved that," Wilder groans.

"Really?"

"No," he answers. "She's not a big tattoo fan."

"Then why are we getting tattoos?"

"Because," he grins, "I am—"

"My own," I finish for him. "Stop stealing my lines."

"It's a good one," he laughs.

While Travis works away on Wilder's arm, I decide now is a good time to tell him Jason and Jill will be out of town this weekend.

"My parents are going to be away for a few days," I announce.

"Really?" Wilder schools his features into a mask of indifference. I hate when he does that. Things would be so much easier if I could read what he's thinking on his face.

"Really," I reinforce.

"Are you going to throw a party, Blondie?"

I resist the urge to pinch the bridge of my nose with my thumb and forefinger. "No."

"I could hook you up with a keg," he continues. *Clueless.* He's clueless.

"Nope," I subtly shake my head. "I was hoping you might stop by, though."

"For the party you aren't having?" He scoffs. "Why would I do that?"

"Honestly, are you really that dense?" I snap.

"What?"

"She's asking you to come over while her parents are gone for the weekend," Travis womansplains.

"Oh," the lightbulb clicks on for Wilder. "I didn't realize... uh...."

Travis shoots me a wink.

I place a hand on Wilder's forehead. "Are you okay?"

"I think so," he answers. "Why?"

"Because," I remove my hand, "you're unable to form coherent sentences."

"I didn't think you'd want to," his eyes widen as he omits a few words, "so soon."

"I want to," I press my lips together, hoping Travis doesn't realize we're talking about sex. But he probably does.

"Okay," Wilder says.

His tattoo takes a little longer than mine did. I can't make out what the letters are just yet, but I know they're red.

When Travis is finally done, Wilder holds his arm up. "What do you think?"

I cover my mouth with my hand. "You didn't."

"I did."

"But... you're... *why*?"

On Wilder's forearm is the word Blondie in red, block letters. Just like the logo for the newspaper comic strip with the same name.

"I don't know," he smiles wide as he stares down at it. "I wanted something to remember this summer by."

Touched by this thoughtfulness, I almost forget that he has the nickname he gave me tattooed on his arm. *Forever.*

"I thought you weren't supposed to get anyone's name tattooed on your person," I frown.

"It's supposed to doom a relationship or something."

"It's a nickname, Blondie. It's not like I got Ingrid branded across my ass."

"I would pay for you to have my name branded on your backside." I can't hold in the string of giggles that escape.

"I can always get it removed or tattooed over," he says quietly. "This summer is supposed to be fun. This," he holds his arm in front of my face, "is a joke. It's supposed to be funny."

I should probably tell him that I had a lightning bolt tattooed on my wrist in honor of him, but I don't owe anyone an explanation.

Which is also why I decide not to mention Cash's ill-timed snap. I didn't reply, so why bring it up?

We're in our blissful, happy, orgasmic bubble and I'm not ready to let go of the bottled-up lightning I'm squeezing in my hands.

Chapter 19
The Cash Snap

Mom and I are staked out in front of Queen Isla's fraternity house. Technically, it's an overcrowded apartment. But we're using code names. So, we chose 'fraternity house' to discreetly refer to my sister's new home.

"You really think she's in there?" I whisper to Mom.

She zooms in on the window with her phone camera. "Hard to tell. The blinds are open and bodies keep walking by."

"There's no way she's living there with Frank the Fornicator—"

"*Ingrid*," Mom chastises me.

I ignore her and continue, "—and his gross, college-aged roomies who probably don't shower and spend their evenings gaming."

"Speaking of gross, college-aged roomies, are you ever going to tell me what happened between you and Cash?"

I scrunch my nose, trying to figure out how she went from hypothetical un-showered gamers to clean-cut Cash Allred. "We broke up."

"And now you're sleeping with his best friend?" Mom asks pointedly.

I lick my lips. "I'm not sleeping with Wilder."
Not yet, anyway.

"I'm not judging you," Mom holds up a hand. "I'm just trying to understand."

"Cash broke up with me," I repeat, "and he sort of broke up with Wilder, too. Now, Wilder and I are friends. We bonded over our mutual rejection."

"Rejection has a way of bringing people together. Have you heard from Cash?" Mom pries.

I chew on the inside of my cheek. I could tell Mom about the Cash snap. She'd be a good person to run it by because she has nothing to lose. Wilder, on the other hand, well, I'm afraid he'll remember all those times he told me he doesn't fuck his best friend's leftovers. Even after getting a tattoo of the nickname he affectionately calls me, I still don't know how he'll react when he finds out Cash messaged me.

Yeah, I should run it by Mom.

"He sent me a snap."

"What's a snap?" Mom tilts her head to the side.

"On Snapchat, you can send pictures and add messages to them. Once they're viewed, they're gone forever."

Mom scrunches her nose. "Sounds complicated. Why not just send a text? Or, better yet, pick up the phone."

I shrug. "I have no idea."

"Did you respond?"

"No," I shake my head. "I didn't know what to say."

"Did he say anything?"

"Just that he misses me."

"Maybe he regrets breaking up with you," Mom offers.

I roll my eyes. "He should have thought about that before he ended things."

"I know we don't run in the same circles as the Allreds," Mom shrugs, "but Cash didn't seem to care. He always came over for dinner when I invited him. He never acted like he was above us, or we were beneath him. He was polite and nice."

"Are you defending him right now?" I cross my arms over my chest, appalled.

"No," she holds up a defensive hand. "I was just saying that sometimes parents can influence their children's decisions. They can push them into doing something they really don't want to do."

"Cash can make his own choices," I argue. "He made them for years." *Years.* He knew Fanny didn't want us dating. He kept our relationship going anyway. What would have changed now?

"Ingrid," Mom sighs, "I'm not saying he was the right choice for you. What I'm trying to get across is that you don't have to hate him. You don't have to carry around years of hatred for him. It doesn't change anything, and it only weighs you down. And you don't know his side of the story. You don't know what he's dealing with behind closed doors. You don't have to hate him."

"I don't hate him," I admit. "I think I'm... *relieved*."

"Relieved?"

"I didn't cry—haven't cried, really. Except once. And it wasn't a cry like someone who'd just gotten out of a four-year relationship would have."

"Why do you think that is?"

I think about the fancy dinner Wilder and I had at the Country Club. Sneaking into the movie theatre. Playing a round of golf. Skinny dipping at the lake. The tattoo I have covered with a long sleeve so Mom can't see it.

When I was with Cash, I never had any fun. I didn't laugh with him. I didn't flirt with him. I didn't spend every waking moment wondering when he was going to touch me next because it felt like a spark—a raging fire—every time his fingers made contact with my bare skin. I didn't feel like that with Cash.

Cash made me anxious. That led me to constantly second-guess myself and wonder if I was good enough.

I've never felt that way with Wilder. When I'm with him, I feel... free.

"I'm relieved because I didn't like who I was when I was with Cash," I tell my mother.

Mom reaches over the center console and wraps her arms awkwardly around me. "Do you like who you are now?"

I lay my head on Mom's shoulder as I take a sobering breath. "Yeah, I think I do."

We stay like that, holding each other in front of Queen Isla's fraternity house until Mom's cell rings and Dad wants to know if we want to celebrate his new job over burgers at the diner.

I knock on Wilder's front door and take a step back. In all the years he's lived a few doors down, I've never been inside his house. I've never even walked up the driveway.

Wilder's front door is a simple tan color, unlike the Allred's flashy, bold red door. The door creaks on its hinges and a woman with messy blond hair answers.

"Yes?"

"Hi," I shift from one foot to the other, aware that I'm speaking to Wilder's mother for the first time in my life. "I was wondering if Wilder was home?"

Her hazel eyes—more golden brown than minty green—assess me shrewdly. "Yeah. He's in his room."

She steps aside to let me in, and I realize she has no idea who I am.

"I'm Ingrid," I tell her as she closes the door behind me. "I live a few doors up. My mom is Jill Winthrop."

"Ah," Wilder's mom smiles. "I thought you looked familiar."

"It's nice to finally meet you," I tell her.

"Taya," she places a hand on her navy scrubs. "I'm Taya."

We shake hands as my eyes land on the ID clipped to the pocket of her shirt. Taya Thatcher. Not Cox. So, she changed her last name after her divorce. Interesting.

"It was nice to meet you," I say to her before I head down the hall in search of her son.

The Thatcher house is very different than ours. It's homier. Dozens of family photos line the hallway, and it smells like fresh bread.

I stop when I see a DO NOT ENTER sign nailed to a door. I shake my head as my fingers rap on the faded white paint.

"What?" I hear Wilder's voice.

I push the door open and flash my eyebrows at him. "I'm not interrupting one of your masturbating sessions, am I?"

He closes the book he's reading—wait, he reads?—and sits up straighter on his bed. "What are you doing here?"

"I was in the neighborhood," I try to hide a smile.

"Har har," he rolls his eyes.

"You see what I did there?" I bite my lip to keep from laughing. "Because I live three doors up?"

"I figured it out," he shakes his head, mockingly, at me.

"My dad got a job," I cross my arms over my chest. "And I wanted to tell you."

Wilder stands from his bed and walks over to me. "That's amazing. Your parents must be excited."

I nod as Wilder's fingers slide under my chin. The world stops spinning and time slows as his eyes roam my face. His long, dark lashes kiss his skin as he blinks in slow motion, and goosebumps raise on the backs of my arms as he leans forward and sucks my lip into his mouth. My eyes slam shut and my breathing hitches as he steals the air from my lungs. He kisses me gently, savoring the moment, and I slip my hands under his T-shirt, tracing the ridges of his stomach muscles with my fingertips.

"I'm heading—" Taya gasps.

Wilder quickly breaks our kiss as I slip my hands out from his shirt.

"I'm sorry," Taya apologizes. "I was just... how long has this been going on?"

I glance over at Wilder, who's trying not to laugh.

"Uh... I guess a few weeks," he admits.

"She was dating Cash, right?" I can't tell if Taya is disappointed or not.

"Well," Wilder hitches a shoulder, "Cash dumped her, didn't say goodbye to me, and ran off to Europe for the summer."

Taya holds a hand up. "I don't want to know anymore. Just... use a condom, please. And don't have sex while your grandparents are home."

I run an embarrassed hand over my face as Wilder gives me a shit-eating grin. Whatever he's thinking, it cannot be good.

"Oh, we like to have sex at the Winthrop's," Wilder lies. "Jason and Jill even bring us snacks afterward."

"They do not!" I tell Taya. "And we don't... we haven't had... we're..."

"Spit it out, Blondie," Wilder raises an amused eyebrow at me.

"Blondie?" Taya's eyebrows knit together as her eyes dart from me to the new tattoo on her son's arm.

Wilder smirks. "Relax, Mom. It's not a big deal."

"You got a girl's name tattooed on your arm and I'm not supposed to freak out or anything?" she questions him.

"Technically," Wilder winks at me, "it's her nickname."

"Oh," Taya purses her lips, "and that's supposed to make it better?"

"Mom," Wilder places a hand on her shoulder, "it's fine. Go to work."

"We're not done talking about this," she points a finger at him. "It was nice meeting you, Ingrid, and finding out that my son got your nickname tattooed on his arm."

Wilder shuts the door as soon as Taya's out of sight and then leans back against it. "I thought she'd never leave."

"You keep saying the tattoo isn't a big deal," I bite my lower lip, "but I'm starting to think you like me. You *really* like me."

"Eh," he plays off, "you're okay."

"I'm just okay?" I laugh. "I'm better than okay. I'm literally a symbol etched in permanent ink on your arm. You *like* me."

"I'd *like*," he leaves the door behind and stalks toward me, "for you to shut up."

"But I can't!" I squeal as his arms wrap around my waist and he lifts me off the ground. In one fluid motion, he has me pinned beneath him on his bed. "You like me."

"Fine," he gives in as he pecks my lips. "I like you. But if you tell anyone, I'll deny it."

My fingers graze the area above his tattoo. "I think I can prove it, even if you do deny it."

"What about you?" he challenges as his knee slips between my legs and his hand slides under my shirt, tugging my bra down.

As his fingers massage my hard nipple, I lick my lips. "What about me?"

"Are you going to tell me what the lightning bolt represents?"

"Bottled-up lightning," I answer.

"Bottled-up lightning?"

"Rare, electric, and extraordinary."

"Am I supposed to know what that means?"

He rolls my nipple between his fingers, making me groan.

"No."

I slip a hand behind his neck and bring his face closer. Then, I kiss him. I kiss him knowing that no matter how hard I try holding onto something wild and majestic, it can't be tamed—can't be caged in.

My phone vibrates in my back pocket as Wilder slides my long-sleeved shirt over my head. I ignore it and reach for the clasp on my bra. As soon as it's undone, Wilder yanks it off me and reaches for the button on my denim skirt.

I fumble with his shirt, forcing it over his head. We laugh as we lightly bump foreheads.

Again, my phone vibrates. I grab it from my pocket and toss it to the side.

Wilder drags the denim skirt and underwear down my legs. I watch, propped up on my elbows, as he discards his jeans and crawls onto the bed above me.

"Didn't your mom say not to do this while your grandparents are home?" I inhale sharply as he grips *Wild Cox* in his hand and runs the tip of it through my soaked core.

"Rules," Wilder smirks, "are meant to be broken, Blondie. And, if I remember correctly," he teases me as places the tip of his long, hard cock at my entrance, "you love breaking the rules."

My heart is beating out of control in my chest as he slowly pushes into me.

But then, my phone vibrates again.

And as Wilder's eyes slide from my face to the phone, I watch bottled-up lightning explode in front of me.

"Why is Cash messaging you?"

Chapter 20
The Raw Explosion

Wilder

What the fuck?!

My eyes *have to* be deceiving me. Cash is sending Blondie snaps? You've got to be fucking kidding me.

"Why is Cash messaging you?" I ask her.

I realize this is the worst possible time to ask Blondie why her *former-flame-slash-my-best-friend* is sending her love notes from across the pond.

But *what the fuck*!

Her brown eyes widen in surprise, and she shifts beneath me, reaching for her phone. As soon as it's in her hands, and I'm still balls deep in her, she fumbles to unlock it.

"I-I don't know," she stammers. "I... I haven't talked to him. I don't know why he keeps sending me snaps."

"*Keeps*?" I groan, trying to decide whether to stay inside her or pull out.

Keeps as in he has continuously tried reaching out. Or *keeps* as in they've been continuously exchanging messages?

"I'm deleting the app," she licks her lips nervously.

"What about Pam?" I raise an eyebrow. *Pam*. The fake account she made to stalk her *former-flame-slash-my-best-friend*.

"Pam is dead," she says without looking at me.

"There," she shows me the screen. "Account deleted."

I swallow hard. "Account? I thought you just said you were going to delete the app."

She pushes the phone to the edge of my bed and wraps her legs around my waist. Her skin is warm like the sun on a summer day at the lake. The fact that I just used a simile to describe her skin does not go unnoticed. She's fucked me over. In the worst way possible.

"I don't care about Cash," she looks me straight in the face, her hands cupping both cheeks. "I don't care what he has to say or why he's trying to get ahold of me. All I care about is right now. Here. With you."

I know better. I know better than to fuck Blondie. Cash made it perfectly clear the first time we saw her. We had just moved into this house, and Cash and I were throwing a baseball back and forth in the front yard when he saw her one second before I did. And he claimed her. Because he saw her first. Then, in high school, the first week of freshman year, he stole her right out from beneath me again.

"Wilder?" I hear her voice.

My throat burns and my heart feels heavy. "Yeah?"

"I... I should have told you the first time he sent a message. But I didn't because it meant nothing. I've had more fun with you the past few weeks than I ever had with Cash."

The words feel like a feather. Light and weightless.

I'm still hard inside her. Still warring with myself. Do I fuck her or do I pull out and send her home?

Cash would kill me if he knew. He might have broken up with her, but I know he loves her. He's been talking about marrying her since the first week of freshman year.

This can only end in two ways.

Cash will come back, tell her he made a mistake, and they'll spend a lifetime together bored out of their fucking minds. And I'll just be the summer fling she thinks about when she remembers he'll never satisfy her the way I can.

Or she'll choose me, and I'll disappoint her the way I disappoint everyone in my life. I'll lose Cash, and I'll lose her.

But she's so warm and wet. Everything about her body is inviting. Her plump breasts. Her hard, pebbled nipples. The smell of her skin. Like honey and cinnamon. She's delicious. I want to taste every inch of her.

Cash's piece of shit face flashes in front of me and it hits me that even if she chooses him, I'll never get this chance again. I have one summer with her. I'm not fucking wasting it.

I pump into her, ignoring all the warning bells blaring in my head.

Cash is the only friend you've ever had.
Cash will destroy you.
Cash will never forgive you.
Cash will steal her back the first chance he gets.

She lets out a quivering breath as I move inside her, raw and unsheathed.

Probably should've put on a condom. I would with anyone else. But I didn't think. I never think when I'm with her. I just keep jumping out of the oak tree at the creek, hoping I remember how to swim.

"Wilder," she whispers my name as I thrust in and out of her.

She soaked. My balls are soaked, and I know the inside of her thighs are soaked. I prop myself up on my elbow and use my free hand to run over her body. Over her swollen breasts and her tight stomach. Her toned thighs and the meaty flesh of her ass. She's a wet dream. And I can't believe Cash didn't realize what he had while he had her. I'm sure he realizes now. But I'm not going to let my mind go there.

Maybe I can make this work. Maybe I won't disappoint her. Maybe I can prove to her that the boy who saw her six years ago a split second after his best friend did, can give her things no one else can. I can give her things the Allreds can't.

I've had more fun with you the past few weeks than I ever had with Cash.

I'm fun, but fun doesn't mean financially secure or marriage-worthy. Fun doesn't mean stable or steady.

I'm just a fun, summer fling.

I hear footsteps coming down the hall. I should really stop pummeling Blondie. The sound of her flesh bouncing off mine is surely echoing off the walls. But both Grandma and Grandpa can't hear without hearing aids. And they don't wear them very often. So, I keep up the pace.

"More," Blondie mutters as the floor creaks outside my door.

The footsteps keep going as I slide out of her and flip her over onto her stomach. I wrap my arms around her thighs and spread her wide open.

Wet, pink, and fucking mine.

I push back into her as I press a kiss to her shoulder. I doubt she and Cash did anything other than Missionary. The only thing Cash ever said about their uneventful sex life was that she gave mind-blowing blow jobs. I'm happy to confirm that's true. I usually never get off from a BJ. But with Blondie, I could barely hold it in.

The image of her mouth wrapped around my cock, saliva dripping down her chin, and onto her breasts, does me in and I can't hold back as I explode into her, a guttural groan leaving my mouth.

She wiggles beneath me, glancing over her shoulder as my heart races and blood pumps violently through my limbs.

I slide out of her and crawl onto the blankets beside her. Then, I slip my hand down her stomach and find her swollen, wet bundle of nerves. It's pulsating. Every inhale, and exhale of her breath feels like a dream. I tease her, running my fingers over her slowly. She turns her head into me, burying her face in my chest as her blond hair tickles my chin.

"Faster," she instructs.

I increase speed as her chest heaves up and down. Seconds later, she's coming undone against me. But it's not the quiet moans leaving her throat that make my heart beat erratically in my chest. It's the smile that forms on her lips as she brings a hand up to my face.

"That was amazing," she coos, her eyelids heavy.

She's sated as the last remaining rays of daylight slip beneath the horizon. Shrouded in darkness, I let the mask slip. The one that's always up around her. The one I don't dare let her see in the light of day.

"You hungry?" I ask her.

She nods against my shoulder. "Yeah."

I tug the blankets on my bed towards her and wrap her up in them. "I'll be right back."

I slip my jeans and my shirt back on before leaving her in my bed and heading to the kitchen. Grandma and Grandpa are nowhere in sight as I fill up a glass with water and rummage in the cabinets for something to eat. I grab some pretzels and chocolate chip cookies before hurrying back to her.

She shifts slightly as I set the food down and offer her the glass of water.

Blondie takes a long sip before she grins. "We're going to get in so much trouble from your mom."

"I won't tell her if you don't," I say in the dark as I search for the TV remote and click it on. "You up for a movie?"

"Only if you're taking your clothes off," she quips.

"I can do that," I say, quickly stripping down.

She holds open the covers for me and I roll into them, making her laugh.

"You're so immature," she playfully chastises me.

I kiss her lips mid-laugh, catching her off guard. She immediately responds, placing a hand on my cheek and slipping her tongue into my mouth.

A summer with her.

Just one.

That's all I fucking get.

As my hand snakes up her thigh, a lump forms in my throat.
It's not fucking long enough.

Chapter 21
The Lone Weekend

I've been pacing back and forth on the same piece of worn carpet for the past two hours. The moment Mom and Dad left on their weekend getaway this morning, I sent Wilder a text telling him he could come over. But he's still not here. And I'm starting to worry he's regretting what happened last night.

I didn't mean to have mind-numbing sex with him while his grandparents were down the hall. Or watch a movie and cuddle—*naked*—after I orgasmed so hard, my stomach muscles are still hurting. It sort of just happened.

I also didn't mean to delete my Snapchat accounts for him—my personal and secret one—while he was *inside* me. It sort of just happened, too. I don't regret it, though. He walked me home after the movie ended, and we made out on the front porch until Mom and Dad flicked the light on a million times trying to embarrass us. Jason and Jill thoroughly enjoyed giving me a hard time when I finally came inside.

There's just one problem. When I suggested to Wilder that he should spend the night tonight, he didn't say no. But he also didn't say yes.

He said, "*We'll see.*"

When Cash used to say that, it meant *no*. I'm not trying to project here, but I'm starting to wonder if it also means *no* for Wilder. Wilder is a fuckboy, after all. He's fucked a lot of girls. If I was better versed in fuckboy verbiage, I'd guess *we'll see* means *if I don't have any better offers for tonight, I'll show*. But what do I know?

It's not like we're exclusive. I told him he couldn't kiss me if he was kissing other girls. But it's Wilder. I don't know if he'll listen. Besides, it's just a summer fling. Right? *Right?*

I tug at the end of my ponytail. This is stupid. *Stupid, stupid, stupid.* Sex complicates everything. It's so complicated that I'm pacing my bedroom hoping Wilder Cox, my former arch-nemesis and the bane of my existence, shows up to have mind-numbing sex with me again. I could lie and say I only want him to stop by because I'm dying to see him naked, but that's not the whole truth. I think I might have feelings for him. The scary, real kind that I've never felt before. I like him, but I know it goes much deeper than that.

Wilder Cox will probably break my heart in ways Cash Allred never could. And I know I won't recover.

But we're not going to focus on that right now. We are going to find something to take my mind off this instead of pacing back and forth like a madwoman. I think I'm going to head to work and see if my check is ready. Because falling for the bad boy who's never been in a committed relationship is toxic. Especially considering I just got out of a four-year relationship myself.

Yep, this is doomed to fail. I'm not sure I care at this point. All I can think about is Wilder running his hands through my hair while his dick is in my mouth.

Nope. I'm not doing this today. I'm going to go see Loretta, and I'm going to get my mind off Wild Cox. *Wilder.* Wilder Cox.

Except I should change my underwear first because I'm still not over last night. If you know what I mean.

"Well, well, well," Pierre drawls. "Look what the cat dragged in on her day off. You here for more bush whacking?"

"No," I frown. "I'm here to see if Loretta dropped off my check."

Pierre ruffles around in the desk drawer before handing over an envelope. "Don't spend it all in one place."

I stare at Loretta's flamboyant nephew. I really could use a male perspective. Er—any perspective other than my own.

"Can we talk?" I purse my lips.

"You and me?"

I nod. "Yeah. I have a problem."

"With the gorgeous, tall, well-hung bad boy?"

"He is *so* well hung," I groan as I plop into a chair, "it's all I can think about."

Pierre sits beside me and crosses one leg over the other. "Spill. All the deets."

"We've been fighting for years," I confess. "And all this time I thought I hated him, but I don't."

"Foreplay," Pierre winks. "Sexy."

"Ugh," I run a hand over my face. "We had sex, and it was amazing. But then I asked him to come over tonight because my parents are out of town and he said, and I quote, 'We'll see'."

Pierre sucks in a sharp breath through his teeth. "Those two words are never good."

"Right?" I exhale. "Cash used to say them to me all the time. And I don't want to assume all boys are the same—"

"All boys are the same," Pierre interjects. "But you're young. The world is your oyster."

"I know that," I swallow hard, "but I think I feel things for Wilder that I never felt for Cash. It's not just the sex. It's like I don't have to pretend when I'm with Wilder."

"Didn't the Allred boy dump you?" He taps a finger on his chin.

"Yeah," I shrug.

"Then what's the problem?"

"I just told you the problem."

"No," Pierre shakes his head. "You bitched about having sex with a boy you've been having rigorous foreplay with for years. He didn't ask you to go steady. He didn't ask you to be his girlfriend. Don't make it something it's not."

"You're right," I take a deep breath, my heart aching. "Wilder isn't mine. It was just a second sexual encounter. I can't expect him to—"

"There was another sexual encounter?" he gasps.

I smile. "Yeah."

"People always tell you to be careful with your heart when you're young," Pierre sighs dreamily, "but I say fuck it. You don't get many chances to love recklessly. If you're going to do it, do it now."

"Yeah?" I furrow my brow.

"Yeah," Pierre widens his eyes. "Do it for all of us who couldn't."

"You're still young," I roll my eyes. "You only graduated a few years before I did."

"I may have loved a little too recklessly," Pierre winks. "And now I'm entering my spinster phase."

"I will do my best to love as recklessly as you, then," I laugh.

"If you like him more than you've ever liked anyone," Pierre stands, "tell him."

"What if he doesn't care?" I stare up at him.

"The world is your oyster, Ingrid. Take it by the horns."

"You mean take the bull by the horns?" I rephrase.

"Sure," Pierre hitches a shoulder before sauntering into the backroom.

I glance at the envelope in my hand before hugging it to my chest. Pierre is terrible at giving advice, but maybe he has a point. Maybe we're only young once. Maybe I should put it all on the line while I'm still young enough to recover from the absolute heartbreak awaiting me.

As I walk to my car, I check my phone. No new messages. No missed phone calls.

What if Wilder really does regret having sex with me?

You don't get many chances to love recklessly. If you're going to do it, do it now.

Taking the bull by the horns might not be the worst idea in the world.

I run to my car and hop in. There's one bucket list item I don't need Wilder to do. But I know who I'm going to send it to.

My phone is securely perched in Queen Isla's ring light as I strip off my sundress. After doing some research on taking nude selfies, the internet slews claim the best way to do it is to record a video of yourself posing. Then, I should take screenshots of said video. That's apparently the easiest way to ensure full-body nudes.

I can't believe I'm doing Lonely Summer Bucket List Item #8 in the middle of the afternoon *by myself*. But desperate times call for desperate measures.

Pulling my hair out of a ponytail, I let it fall to my shoulders and drag my fingers through it. I press *record* on my phone and crawl onto my bed. The internet also says to act natural while taking nude selfies, but I'm not sure I can channel *natural*. I'll do my best.

I sit on my knees and adjust my hair, making sure to angle myself a little more to the right. It's my better side. Photogenically speaking.

"What are you doing?" I hear to my left and let out a terrifying scream.

Wilder laughs as I cover my chest with my arms. "What are you doing here?"

He holds up his phone. "You said I could come over."

"Yeah," I say through ringing ears. "I sent that hours ago."

"Sorry." He actually looks apologetic. "My grandpa wasn't feeling well, so I stayed with him until my mom got home from work."

"Is he okay?" I ask.

Wilder tilts his head to the side. "I think so. Are you doing bucket list item #8?"

"I'm trying to," I blush. "I didn't think you were coming so I thought I'd cross off another item."

He grins as he slowly stalks toward me. "I could have taken the photos for you."

"I have to send them to someone," I remind him.

"Who are you going to send them to?" he whispers as he stops at the edge of my bed.

I drop my arms to my side and sit up straighter to reach his lips.

I kiss him softly before revealing, "Pierre."

Wilder chortles. "I don't think Pierre would appreciate them the way I would."

His fingers caress my hip bone as his breath tickles my nose. My heart beats erratically in my chest.

"I'm sure you have a catalog of naked photos from all your conquests," I challenge.

His fingertips slip down my skin, closer to my aching core. "Wouldn't know. I never open their messages. But I'd open yours."

I hate that my heart flutters as his fingers dip between my drenched folds. "I'm sure you say that to all the girls."

"Why are you so jealous, Blondie?" His nose nudges mine.

He strokes my swollen clit as my eyes close tight. "Because I don't want to think about you with other girls."

His fingers slow between my legs. "Then don't."

The moment his hand leaves my body, my eyes fly open. I watch as he yanks his shirt off, and then unzips his jeans. I don't move as he climbs onto the bed behind me and places a possessive hand on my stomach.

"You ever recorded yourself having sex before?" He says into my ear.

I shake my head as he kisses the base of my ear, then my neck. "Have you?"

"No," he says against my shoulder. "This is my first."

A lump forms in my throat as his front brushes against my back. I hate that he knows me so well. Knows that giving me an experience he's never shared with anyone else is all I need to push myself off that reckless love cliff.

Wilder glides the tip of his cock along my ass before finding my soaked entrance. He takes his time, slowly inserting himself into me. When he's in, his lips find my neck and he sucks lightly.

"Wilder," I whisper.

He thrusts in and out, keeping a steady pace as I lay my head back on his shoulder. Everything feels different from this angle. Fuller, harder, bigger.

"Ingrid," he says so quietly, I almost miss it.

My heart spasms and sputters beneath my ribs. He's never said my name before. *Never*. Not once.

I reach a hand up and run my fingers through his hair, not daring to acknowledge what he just said. He kisses my neck again as his fingers find my throbbing clit. He roughly tugs at it, making me whimper.

Between his strong body behind me, my phone in front of us, his fingers playing with my clit, and his massive cock slamming into me, I quickly come undone in his very capable hands.

He follows right after, his mouth pressing to my shoulder as a string of barely audible *Ingrids* leaves his delicious lips.

I don't move, don't speak as he stays inside me and wraps his arms around me.

"Round two?" I tease him as his heart pounds against my back.

"After snacks," he chuckles, pressing his lips to my cheek, my earlobe, my hair.

"Stay with me tonight?" I close my eyes, scared to hear the answer.

"I planned on it," he smiles against my skin, his hands snaking up my stomach in search of my breasts.

"Wilder?" I breathe heavily.

"Yeah?"

"I've never come like this before."

"Like what?" he asks as he kneads my breasts with his hands.

"With... with your dick in me."

He stops moving. "Really?"

"Yeah," I click my tongue. "Uh... is that normal?"

"I don't know," he kisses my shoulder again. "I think it just depends."

"Why is everything better with you?" I let slip out.

His hands leave my breasts and he places one arm around my shoulders, the other around my waist. "I don't know, Blondie."

Ingrid. Say, Ingrid.

"Is it better for you?" I know I shouldn't ask, but I want to know.

"Yeah," he smirks. "Much better. You're also the only girl I'd ever have sex with without using a condom."

"What?" I twist to face him. He kisses my lips. "You've never had sex without a condom before?"

"No, not before you," he shakes his head, his hazel eyes filled with stunning shades of gold and minty green. "You should feel honored you're the only person I'd be willing to almost make a baby with."

I smile as his eyelashes brush along the mole beneath his left eye. "I'd take good care of our almost baby."

An emotion I can't quite read crosses his face. "I know you would. Now, how about those snacks?"

He pulls out of me, and I feel empty again. I grab my robe as he puts on his jeans.

Empty.

I never realized how empty I felt before Wilder made me feel whole.

Chapter 22
The Blissful Bubble

Everything is hazy and muggy as I slowly open my eyes. It's almost as if someone left the shower on, and steam is spilling out of the open door.

Daylight slips in through the slit in the curtains as I run a hand along Wilder's stomach, his rock-hard morning wood jabbing my elbow. My head is perched on his chest, his heart beating a steady rhythm beneath my ear. I don't know what time it is or how long we've been asleep. I only know that I don't want to leave my bed. I don't want to open the curtains or check the time on my phone. I don't want to burst the blissful bubble.

But I know it's coming. There's something looming on the horizon—something dark and murky threatening to bust through the haze and ruin us. *Ruin this*.

I wrap an arm around Wilder, wishing holding him tight would erase all my fears. Fears that something external—not internal—is going to blast us apart.

Instead of worrying about it, I turn my head and kiss his warm skin, savoring the moment. His arm moves and his hand cradles the back of my head. I tilt my neck to look up at him. He's smiling—actually smiling—back at me. I try ignoring the nagging feeling in the pit of my stomach telling me things won't always look this clear in the morning light, but it's relentless.

As if on cue, my stomach lets out a ravenous roar and Wilder laughs. "You hungry, Blondie?"

Ingrid. Call me Ingrid.

I stretch beside him and nod my head. "Yeah. I worked up an appetite last night."

After we recorded ourselves having sex, Wilder and I made popcorn and watched it back as we lay in bed, laughing at all the weird sounds leaving our mouths. In the moment, everything was hot and sultry. The playback, however, was more like a badly scripted adult film.

Except it wasn't scripted. And in the moments when I stopped focusing on how awkward my hips rolled and how funny I sounded, I saw what was really there. Two people who spent years fighting each other before finally giving in to whatever forces kept shoving us together.

"You still thinking about that recording?" Wilder nudges me lightly.

I place a hand on his beating heart. "I'm going to keep it forever."

"I want a copy then," he smirks.

"Why?" I lift my head.

"So, I can keep a copy forever, too."

My heart aches. The kind of ache knowing some moments are perfect, but perfect moments don't last forever.

I've never been this afraid of losing someone before. Not even Cash. I've never been afraid that all the things Wilder and I do in secret—like sneaking into country clubs and kissing beneath the flickering porch light—will end. That *we'll* have to end. That if or when Cash comes back—when the dark and murky thing hovering above us explodes back into our lives—Wilder will choose him and I'll be left heartbroken.

"Why the long face?" Wilder asks me.

I lick my lips nervously as I think back to my conversation with Pierre yesterday.

If you like him more than you've ever liked anyone, tell him.

What if he doesn't care?

The world is your oyster, Ingrid. Take it by the horns.

If only it were that simple. If Wilder wasn't Cash's best friend. If I wasn't Cash's ex-girlfriend. If we didn't live in a small town that runs rampant with rumors, gossip, and expectations.

"Blondie?" Wilder's voice slashes through all the noise.

"I like you," I tell him.

The corner of his mouth tips up. "I know."

"No," I shake my head as his fingers caress my cheek. "I really like you. I've never felt this way about anyone and I'm so afraid that... that..."

"That what?" he says hoarsely.

"I'm afraid that you're going to break my heart," I tell him. He lays perfectly still as I inhale sharply. "Say something, *please*."

Wilder shifts so more of his body is touching mine. "I don't want to break your heart."

"But if Cash comes back," I argue, "we can't... we can't keep doing this."

"We can't?" he whispers.

I search his hazel eyes, more green this morning than gold. "You're his best friend and I... I don't know how we can do this if you're... if he's..."

Wilder kisses my forehead. "Let's not worry about that right now, Blondie. Let's just take it day by day."

I squeeze my eyes shut tight. "Okay."

"You still hungry?" There's that wall. The one he always builds around his heart when I get a little too close.

"Yeah," I answer as I slip out of his arms and search for my robe.

"Blondie," he calls after me, but I ignore him and tie the silky material around my waist.

When I turn around, I have a smile plastered to my face. "I'm not a good cook but I can make toast."

"I like toast," Wilder raises his eyebrows before he tosses the blankets off him, and I physically ache from how beautiful his naked body is.

He slides his jeans up his long legs as I hone in on the dimples in his back, right above his perfect ass.

I lead the way down the stairs and to the kitchen. Wilder stops in the hallway and stares at the only Winthrop family photo taken professionally when I was eight.

"You were cute," he says before he runs a hand down the length of my arm and tangles his fingers with mine.

"It's too bad we went to different elementary schools," I wink at him. "We could've started fighting sooner."

"Is that what you think we did?" Wilder grins.

"Pierre said it was rigorous foreplay," I hitch a shoulder.

"I think Pierre might be on to something," he chuckles. "You talk to Pierre about me?"

"One time," I state pointedly, "because you said *we'll see* about spending the night with me."

"What's wrong with *we'll see*?"

I laugh and cup his cheek in my hand. "Those aren't exactly the words a girl wants to hear when she offers her house *and* her body to a boy."

"Blondie," he sighs, "I live with old people. I had to make sure they would be okay without me for a night."

"What about all the nights you spend with all the other girls?" I cross my arms over my chest.

"You act like I've fucked a thousand women," he shakes his head at me, dark locks of hair curling around his ears.

"No," I purse my lips. "More like a few hundred."

"You really think that low of me?"

I shrug. "I don't know. I don't want to know. I think it's better I don't find out how many other girls touched your body before I did."

He squeezes my fingers. "At least you didn't witness Cash popping your cherry. Or the last time he fucked you."

"I'm sorry," I apologize, annoyed with myself. Why can't I stop thinking about Cash coming home or all the girls that Wilder's stuck his legendary *Wild Cox* in?

Because you're jealous.

"Toast?" I force a smile.

"Blondie, what's going on?"

"Nothing," I lie. "I'm fine." No, I'm not. But I'm not sure how to tell him that I want to yank out the hair of every woman who saw him naked long before I did.

I think I need help. This cannot be healthy.

I pull out the toaster as Wilder hops up onto the kitchen island. I plop in two pieces of toast and grab an array of jams—grape, strawberry, and blueberry—and butter.

"Come here," Wilder holds a hand out.

I exhale before letting my feet carry me over to him. "I'm not crazy."

"I never said you were," he rolls his eyes before running a hand through my hair.

"Why did you stop to look at the picture in the hallway?" I decide to change the subject as I situate myself between his legs.

He glances down at my cleavage before meeting my eyes. "I guess because I don't remember what it used to be like. I can't remember a life before living with my grandparents. It sucks knowing my dad lives a town over with the family he picked over me but doesn't want anything to do with me. You're lucky that you have parents who love each other."

I chew on the inside of my cheek. "I'm sorry you had to go through that."

"My grandpa was a better father to me than my dad ever was," Wilder confides in me. "But that doesn't change how I felt growing up knowing my dad wanted something else. That we weren't good enough. That we didn't—or couldn't—offer what Margot and Elowyn did. I mean, I'm happy Elowyn grew up in a loving home, and that she doesn't have a clue how hard it is to deal with all these fucking abandonment issues. But he's my dad, too. And it would have been nice if he had stuck by the woman he married and tried to be a good dad to me, too."

"It's his loss," I stand on my tippy toes and kiss his lips. "He missed out. Despite him, you're a loyal friend who takes care of everyone around you."

Wilder plays with my hair. "I'm not loyal, Blondie. I'm fucking my best friend's girl."

"Is that all you're doing?" I challenge. "Fucking? Because what I saw in that video, that wasn't just—"

"You know it can't be anything more," he interrupts. "You've always known that."

"I didn't," I reply as my heart dips in my chest. "I thought we were... we were..."

His fingers find my chin and he lifts my face. "We don't know if he's ever coming back. Cash is going to Johns Hopkins soon and I doubt he'll make a detour here on his way there. But I'm not a loyal friend. I haven't been one for a long time."

"You've been one to me," I run my fingers along his chest.

"But not to Cash."

"Cash left us," I remind him. "And he didn't even have the decency to say goodbye. I'm not going to let you beat yourself up over whatever is happening between us. We deserve better, and I'm not sorry about anything we've done since he hopped on a plane and left us."

The toaster pops and I jump at the sound.

"I'm not Cash's," I reinforce.

"You are your own," Wilder gives me a small smile.

Except I don't want to be my own.
I really, *really* want to be Wilder's.

Chapter 23
The Sister Moment

Queen Isla and her red suitcase are standing on the front porch when I open the door.

"Frank and I broke up," she cries as she steps forward and snakes her bony arms around my confused shoulders.

"Why?" I groan as I pat her shaking back.

"He was hooking up with one of the cashiers at work," she says before sobbing uncontrollably.

I'm not surprised a relationship built on secret library sex between a TA and his student didn't last the summer. The question is: why did Queen Isla think it would?

"I'm sorry," I offer half-heartedly.

"He said I was difficult," my older sister sniffles. "Can you believe that?"

Me? Uh, yeah, I can believe that. But she's my sister, and only I'm allowed to call her difficult.

"What a dick," I shake my head as Isla lets me go.

"He's a total dick," Isla hiccups, her green eyes filled with unshed tears.

"Come on," I motion toward the kitchen with a nod of my head. "Mom just finished making oatmeal cookies."

"The healthy kind?" my sister pouts.

"The healthy kind," I roll my eyes as I head inside, dragging her along with me.

I'm not sure who's more surprised to see Queen Isla and her red suitcase, Mom or Dad. But by the shift in temperature in the room, I know neither is thrilled she's back home.

"Mommy," Isla sticks her bottom lip out and pouts like she used to when we were kids. "He broke up with me."

Mom and Dad share a look before Mom rounds the kitchen island and wraps her arms around Isla.

"I made cookies," Mom hugs her tight.

My eyes land on Dad, who has an indecipherable look on his face. He winks at me before quietly leaving the room. I want to follow him, but Mom shoots me a *don't-you-dare-leave-me-alone-with-her* look. So, I stay put. Jill Winthrop may have a heart of gold, but she's not cut out for dealing with Isla and her manipulative tactics. My sister may be going through a break up, but she's still heartless.

"Do you want to talk about it?" Mom asks her.

Isla shakes her scarlet head. "No. I want to eat cookies and take a nap."

Mom gives her an apprehensive smile. "That sounds like a good plan." Then, she hands over the cookies and we watch Isla, sans her red suitcase, march out of the kitchen.

We're both shocked when moments later we hear her say, "Ingrid, aren't you coming?"

I point to myself and stare at Mom. "Me?"

"You," Mom blinks slowly.

Swallowing hard, I follow my sister up the stairs and to her room. She throws herself down on her bed and lets out a muffled scream into her pillow.

Not sure what to do with myself, I stand in the doorway.

When Isla rolls over, she pats her bed. "Come sit."

Reluctantly, I meander over to her bed and perch on the edge. "What's up?"

"Well," she huffs, "you've been through a break up so I figured you could make me feel better with your sad, sappy *Cash-dumped-me* story."

And here I thought we were finally having a moment—a real, honest sister moment.

"You're joking, right?" I raise an eyebrow.

"Fine, tell me this will get better, then," she holds a hand out, exasperated. "Remember the advice I gave you when Cash dumped you for his mistress, Europe?"

If I recall correctly, she didn't give me advice. Her exact words were: *Frank and I aren't like you and Cash. Frank is my best friend. You and Cash aren't really friends. You're more like Mom and Dad. You love each other but you don't want to spend all your time together. Frank and I, well, we're inseparable.*

"You didn't give me advice," I remind her. "You told me you and Frank were inseparable. That wasn't helpful, just so you know."

"It's not always about you, Ing," she groans dramatically.

Of course, it's not about me. It's always about Queen Isla.

"Maybe this is a good thing," I offer. "Maybe you needed to get your heart broken."

"That's harsh," she narrows her eyes.

"Cash dumped me," I shrug, "and I've had more fun this summer than I have the past four."

"How is *that* even remotely helpful?"

"Endings suck but they make way for new beginnings." *New beginnings like Wilder.*

"That's the worst advice I've ever been given," Isla crosses her arms over her chest, not a single tear in sight.

"Well," I slap my leg before standing. "I tried."

"Wait!" Isla rushes to get out. "Don't leave me. I don't want to be alone."

I take a step back, suddenly realizing exactly where I want to be right now. And it's definitely not here.

"Being alone isn't the worst thing in the world, Isla. You'll get used to it. And when you're okay with being alone, maybe you'll even meet the right person for you."

I hurry out her door and take the stairs two at a time. Mom and Dad are sitting on the couch, looking terrified, as I jump off the final step.

"How is she?" Dad asks as I grab my car keys.

"She's Isla," I shrug as I grip the door handle. "She'll be fine. She always is."

I slip my phone out of my back pocket and find Wilder's name. I call him, and it rings a few times before he picks up.

"Hey." His voice is deep and husky.

"Where are you?"

"Diner," he answers. "Just ordered some food."

"Mind if I join you?"

I hear him chuckle. "What do you want? I'll order you some food."

"Just fries and a Cherry Coke," I tell him.

"See you in a few," he says as I smile to myself.

When I enter the diner, I see Wilder sitting in a booth first. As he waves me over, I notice two familiar faces across the restaurant. *Fanny and Archibald Allred.* They pretend not to see me and avoid looking at each other. For the first time in four years, I see how miserable they both are. Fanny is pushing food around her plate with a fork, and Archibald is more interested in his cell phone than he is in the woman sitting next to him. Their marriage is a sham. Maybe it always has been. This explains why Archibald spends his free time with Clementine and Fanny spends her days working overtime to assure the town that their marriage is strong and alive.

But it's not.

It's dead.

It's over.

And Fanny gets the short end of the stick. It makes me want to release those pictures of Archibald and Clementine at the country club because even though she's a horrible person, Fanny actually deserves better.

The people who play golf with Archibald at his fancy country club might not care about his affair, but the rest of the town would.

I blow out an annoyed breath and slide into the booth across from Wilder.

"You see who else is here?" I flash my eyebrows at him.

"I saw," he grumbles, his foot sliding along mine beneath the table.

"Does it bother you they're here?" I tilt my head to the side, watching as his shoulders tense.

Wilder shakes his head, refusing to meet my gaze. "Nope."

"You're lying," I tease him. "*Why* are you lying?"

"Maybe I wanted to kiss you," he reveals. "And I can't because they might see."

I lick my lips. "You want to kiss me right now?"

"I'll kiss you later," he glances at me.

I sink my teeth into my lower lip and crawl out of the booth. "Scoot over."

"Blondie," he groans. "You can't—"

"I can sit next to you," I grin. "And I'm going to."

He moves over to let me in beside him. "They'll tell Cash if they see us together."

"I don't care," I gently touch his face. "Cash dumped me. He left you. We can do whatever we want."

Wilder frowns. "You can but I can't."

"If Fanny comes over, I'll deal with her," I promise him. "I haven't seen you in two days. I want to sit next to you. And I want to kiss you, too."

He runs a tired hand over his face. "Work's been busy."

"I know," I drop my hand from his cheek. He catches my forearm in his fingers and runs his thumb along the lightning bolt tattoo on my wrist.

"You ever going to tell me why you got this one?" The corner of his lips tip up.

"I already told you," I smile wide. "It's bottled-up lightning."

"Yeah," he slides an arm behind my neck. "But what's the significance?"

I inhale him. The clean smell of his laundry detergent mixed with the musky scent of working in a lumber yard all day is my new favorite scent.

Wilder makes me want to tell him the truth, even when I know it's risky. Even when I know it gives him a bigger chunk of my heart to inevitably shatter.

"You. The significance is you."

His breathing hitches. "Me?"

"You're bottled-up lightning," I shrug. "Wild, free, hard to contain."

He smiles, the corners of his hazel eyes crinkling. "You got a tattoo for me after giving me shit for getting one for you?"

"Mine is less obvious," I bury my face in his chest.

"You like me," he teases me. "You really, *really* like me."

"I told you I did," I raise my chin and stare up at him. A dark lock of hair falls across his forehead and I brush it off his face with my fingertips.

He reaches for my hand before it leaves his face, and he kisses the inside of my wrist. There's a tenderness to Wilder I never experienced before now. He's wild and free like lightning but he's also gentle and steady like the rising sun. Every part of me wants to dive into the depths of his soul and memorize every scar, every wound, every tear.

"What?" he whispers in the space between us.

I think I might... I think I might be *in love* with him.

"I just missed you," I say.

"I missed you, too," he replies.

"Wilder," Fanny's high-pitched voice interrupts our moment. I swallow the lump forming in my throat and turn to face her. "And Ingrid."

"How are you?" Wilder asks as he carefully removes his arm from behind me.

"I didn't realize you two were friends," Fanny narrows her hawk-like gaze at us.

"We've always been friends," Wilder lies.

"Does Cash know about this?" Fanny challenges as she motions back and forth between us.

"What does it matter?" I answer. "Cash is in Europe."

"I don't think Cash would like knowing his best friend and ex-girlfriend are shacking up in his absence."

"I don't think you have room to talk," I smile as I fish my phone out of my pocket. I open the folder labeled *Blackmail* and show her the images of Archibald and Clementine at the country club. "I'd really hate for these to get out. So, whatever you think you saw here tonight, forget you saw it."

Fanny grips her purse closer to her body. "Those are innocent photos of two people having a business dinner."

I give her a triumphant smile. "That'll be for everyone in town to decide."

"I knew you were trailer trash," Fanny directs to Wilder. "And you," she points a finger at me, "a whore looking to cash in on our family fortune."

"You should go," I smile up at her. "Before your husband forgets he brought you with him tonight."

Fanny glances around the diner, searching for Archibald.

"You should know," I add, "the only trash in this place tonight is you. And I'm glad Cash broke up with me. Because I'd rather be poor, miserable, and alone than spend another second putting on a show like you do. It must be exhausting, Fanny. Always smiling while you're screaming on the inside."

"Watch your mouth, missy," Fanny spits at me.

"I always wondered why you stayed when you were so miserable," I continue. "But then I remembered Cash told me you signed a prenup. You don't get anything if the marriage ends. Don't you think freedom and a chance at happiness are better than a lifetime of misery?"

"Money," Fanny hisses, "doesn't make me miserable. It makes me—"

"Mean," Wilder finishes. "You're mean, and everyone knows it."

"That's rich coming from the boy whose father left him," Fanny smacks her lips.

"My dad left me," Wilder responds, "but that's on him. That was his decision. Despite everything he's done, I still graduated with honors and I'm paying for college outright with the money I earned. You can call me whatever you want, but I've made my own way in this judgy little town.

One day, I'll leave it. You? You'll still be here in twenty years, picking on everyone who doesn't live a life of luxury. You're a bully, Fanny. That's all you'll ever be."

I turn to peer up at Wilder. He's wild and free like lightning, but gentle and steady like the rising sun.

"If you're done," I breathe in, "we'd like to get back to our dinner."

"Have a good night, Fanny," Wilder winks at her.

"You're the reason we sent him away, you know," Fanny grits her teeth as her evil eyes zone in on me. "He never would have gone if we hadn't threatened your dad's livelihood."

My heart stops beating in my chest. "Wh-what?"

"That's right," Fanny places a hand on her hip. "Cash wouldn't leave you until I got Jason fired by framing him for embezzlement."

"My dad would never steal," I defend the patriarch of the Winthrop family.

"That's what Cash said, too," she purses her loose lips. "The only reason Jason's company didn't press charges is because Cash told us he'd go to Europe without you. I saved the day by generously donating all the missing funds as a favor to my son's girlfriend. You know, to keep things *hush-hush*. So, you'll delete those photos," Fanny threatens, "or I'll go back to Jason's company and personally see to it that he does prison time for the money everyone thinks he stole."

My throat dries and my ears begin ringing as I try to breathe through my nose. Fanny stole. She waltzed into Dad's company and stole money. How? Who helped her?

Fanny took the money, and then she blamed it all on Dad. He lost his job because she didn't want Cash and me together. She literally blackmailed Cash into leaving me. She can't be that manipulative and conniving, can she?

"Have a good night," Fanny trills before sauntering away.

"Is she... is she telling the truth?" I ask Wilder. "Did she frame my dad to force Cash to break up with me?"

Wilder's chest heaves up and down. "I don't know, Blondie. I don't know."

Chapter 24
The Back Seat

There's a knot in the pit of my stomach that's making it impossible to breathe. Or think. I'm still in shock. Shock that less than ten minutes ago, Fanny admitted to getting Dad fired and sending Cash away.

The only reason Jason's company didn't press charges is because Cash told us he'd go to Europe without you. I saved the day by generously donating all the missing funds as a favor to my son's girlfriend. You know, to keep things hush-hush. *So, you'll delete those photos or I'll go back to Jason's company and personally see to it that he does prison time for the money everyone thinks he stole.*

I don't know what to think. *Or do*. How could anyone be so heartless? I doubt Isla could even be capable of such evil.

What am I going to do? Should I tell Mom and Dad? Reach out to Cash? Try to get Fanny to confess again, and record her so I can prove what she did?

My head begins pounding as I close my eyes and rest my forehead on the steering wheel in front of me. This is all so confusing.

If Cash dumped me to keep Dad from going to jail for a crime his own mother committed, then that complicates things, doesn't it? How long has Fanny been blackmailing him? What if it's been going on for years?

Maybe I misjudged Cash. Maybe I decided he was selfish and self-righteous without knowing the truth. The *whole* truth. I based everything on a lie. But if I did that, if I chose to see the worst in Cash when all he was doing was protecting me, then I'm a traitor who slept with his best friend. A traitor for having all these feelings for Wilder. For wanting bottled-up lightning when I had stardust. Cash wasn't perfect but can I blame him for his misgivings? He was living with his worst nightmare.

I hear a tap on the car window. I wipe a tear away before rolling it down.

"License and registration," Wilder jokes.

I force a smile through the tears. "Why did you pull me over, Officer?"

Wilder grips the car frame with his hands. "For beating yourself up over shit you have no control over."

My bottom lip trembles. "But he..."

"He had a chance to do the right thing. Like, going to the police with the information he had. Instead, he made you feel worthless. Even if he did it to protect you, Cash went about it the wrong way," Wilder assures me.

I lick my lips. "What if he didn't know how to do the right thing? And then I...I slept with you. I...I feel things for you I never felt for him."

Wilder's hand cups my cheek. "You don't get to feel guilty for making decisions based on other people's dishonest actions. They lied to you. They broke your heart. They made your dad lose his job. Cash has a moral compass. I've seen him use it. He knew what to do but he chose to ignore the problem and go to Europe."

"Maybe he was tired of defending our relationship," I hitch a shoulder. "Four years is a long time. So, maybe it was easier to end things and run."

"Do you regret—"

"No," I cut him off. "I don't regret anything we've done this summer."

Wilder lets out a heavy breath. "This changes things, doesn't it?"

I shrug as headlights from a passing car light up his face. "I don't see how it changes anything. Cash is gone, and Fanny will just continue to blackmail him if he comes home. Cash is... the past. For me, at least. The only thing I feel bad about is that the one friend he did have—*does have*—I couldn't stay away from."

"No," Wilder argues. "I couldn't stay away from you."

"What are we going to do?"

"We need to find a way to prove Fanny took that money," he raises an eyebrow.

"I don't want to think about Fanny anymore tonight," I touch his hand. "Come home with me."

Wilder sucks his bottom lip into his mouth, mulling over my offer.

"Please," I say again. I want to tell him that I can't see a future without him in it. That losing him to Cash will devastate me the same way a forest fire devours a dry mountainside. But those are words that I can't say out loud right now. Because Cash saw Wilder first. And I wish there weren't all these rules about falling in love with someone you're not supposed to. I wish there was a way I could be with Wilder—really be with him—without ruining his friendship with Cash.

But there isn't. This is complicated and confusing. And every time I have sex with Wilder, another part of me falls madly in love with him. Another part of me is gone—*forever*. He's not Cash hanging out in a room in my heart I allowed him to enter. Wilder owns the whole house. He came in and filled every room with his sarcastic humor and his soundless hurt. His wild spirit and his gentle touch. He's made me feel things I've never felt before. I forgot how to laugh—I forgot how to enjoy my life— before him. He used to be the asshole in the back seat of Cash's truck, but now he's the one person in my life who makes everything better.

He makes it better.

"If I go home with you," he inhales sharply, "it's going to make things harder, Blondie."

"I just want to be with you, Wilder," I reply. "After what just happened in there, I just want to be with you. So, please get in the car and come with me."

He nods. "Okay."

I turn on the ignition as he walks around to the passenger side and gets in.

The drive through town is quiet until a Smashing Trout song comes on the radio and Wilder groans.

"Do we have to go to their concert Friday night?"

"Yes," I answer. "It's on the bucket list. We have to do it."

"I still don't get what you and Cash like about them," he crosses his arms over his chest.

I reach over and change the station. "Happy now?"

"Huh," he says.

"Huh, what?"

"They were the first concert you guys went to together," he reminds me.

"I don't think listening to them play at the park on the Fourth of July with the rest of the town counts as my first concert with Cash," I shake my head. "And if it does, you were there, too. It was my first concert with you, too."

"Why do you always do that?" Wilder glances over at me from the passenger seat.

"Do what?"

"Diminish what you and Cash had," he answers.

"I'm not doing that," I furrow my brow. "I remember things differently than you do. You were there for every big moment in our relationship. You watched Cash ask me out. You were there for every movie night at the Allreds. You walked in on me losing my virginity. You are literally in every memory I have of my relationship with Cash. I'm not diminishing anything. I'm just remembering things the way I saw them. When I think about all the things Cash and I did together, you were there for all of them, too."

"I guess I didn't think about it that way," Wilder's hand finds my thigh and squeezes gently.

"Cash never did anything without you," I sigh. "I used to get so angry because I wanted to be alone with him."

"At least you didn't have to sit in the back seat," he states pointedly.

"Well, the front seat is yours now. I don't want it anymore."

Wilder rubs my thigh. "I'm sorry I ruined every moment with Cash for you."

"You didn't," I smile. "You were what made them all memorable."

Wilder sits back in his chair, keeping his hand firmly on my leg.

Silence settles between us, wide and deep like a canyon. I want to know what he's thinking but Wilder likes building walls. The kind of walls that are impossible to get over unless he lets you in.

When I park in front of the house, I take a deep breath. "You coming in?"

"If that's what you need," he replies.

"What do you need?"

He twists to face me. "Sometimes, I don't think I need anyone or anything. My dad made sure I grew up relying only on myself. But then, you smile or you say something *real*... it makes... it makes me wonder if what I've always needed is you."

My heart leaps in my chest. "Come inside."

"What about your parents?" he counters.

"Jason and Jill are clueless. We can sneak past them," I smile. "And besides, I had sex with you while your grandparents were walking down the hall. You owe me."

"I owe you?" Wilder chuckles.

"You do," I tease him.

We sneak up the front stone pathway and tiptoe around to the back of the house. We enter through the side door, and I quietly shut it as Wilder checks to see if anyone is in the kitchen. Jason and Jill are camped out in the living room, which means we have to sneak past them and up the stairs. Or rather, *Wilder* has to sneak past them.

"I'll distract them," I whisper. "Watch the third step on the way up. It creaks sometimes."

I dramatically march through the kitchen and into the living room, scaring the living daylights out of my parents.

"Where did you come from?" Mom gasps as I toss my car keys onto the coffee table. "You didn't come through the front door."

Wilder tiptoes behind the couch as I cross my arms over my chest and exhale heavily. "Mom, Dad, we need to have a conversation."

"About?" Dad grumbles as he grabs the TV remote and pauses their show.

"About..." *Think, Ingrid, think!* "About Mom's dog walking business."

"What about it?" Mom frowns.

"We should get you a website. Help attract new clients. Or we could, uh, we could pass out flyers. Make business cards."

Wilder is halfway up the stairs when Mom leans forward. "Ingrid, have you been drinking?"

"No," I laugh off. "Unless you count the Cherry Coke I had at the diner."

"This late at night?" Dad shakes his head. "You'll be up for hours. What do we always tell you?"

"No caffeine after four," I roll my eyes.

"Can we talk about this tomorrow, Ingrid?" Mom runs a hand over her face. "Your father and I are in the middle of our show."

I make sure Wilder is no longer on the stairs before clapping my hands together. "Yes."

I clear my throat before heading towards the staircase.

"And honey," Mom flashes her eyebrows at me. "If you wanted the neighbor boy to come inside, all you had to do was ask."

My eyes widen in surprise. "What?"

"We could see him sneaking up the stairs in the window reflection," Dad points to the living room windows.

"I'll remember that for next time," I say as my mouth dries.

"You're 18," Mom reminds me. "If you get pregnant, you have to figure it out."

"Yeah," Dad winks at Mom. "We already raised our kids. We're not raising yours."

"You guys are hilarious," I fake a laugh.

"He goes home at midnight," Dad sternly states.

"Or?" I raise an eyebrow.

"Or you'll start paying rent like your sister," Mom grins.

Paying rent in exchange for letting Wilder stay the night on occasion? Sounds like a win to me.

"Is that all?" I ask.

"Put a pillow behind the headboard," Mom clicks her tongue. "We don't want to hear—"

"Got it," I say as I hold out a hand, mortified.

"Go on," Dad motions. "We want to watch TV."

Ah, you have to love parents who are more invested in their dating shows than their daughter's sex life.

When I finally make it up the stairs, Wilder is sitting on my bed. I shut the door behind me and slip out of my shoes before walking over to him.

"Thank you," I give him a small smile.

He raises his eyebrows at me. "For?"

I tug my shirt over my head as his hazel eyes drink in my bare skin. "For coming home with me."

His hands find my waist as I reach for the zipper on my shorts. "Are you sure you want to do this? Especially after everything that happened at the diner."

I chew on the inside of my cheek. A lot happened tonight but none of it changes how I feel about Wilder.

"I don't know how I feel about what Fanny did," I honestly tell him, "but I know how I feel about you."

"How do you feel, Blondie?"

I place my hands on his shoulders. "I want you, Wilder."

He gives me a sheepish smile. "You can't steal my lines."

"I can," I reach for the button on my shorts, "and I did."

"You're going to pay for that," he promises as he tugs his shirt over his head.

"Am I?" I playfully bat my eyes at him as he's shoving his pants down his legs.

"You are," he licks his lips.

"We need to, uh..." I trail off reaching behind him to grab a pillow and wedge it behind the headboard. "I don't want anyone to hear."

Wilder grasps my hand in his, pulling me close. "I meant it, Blondie. You're what I need. What I've needed for a long time."

I want to say it. I want to scream it. But I don't. Not yet.

So, I kiss him instead and let the unspoken words linger between us.

I love you, Wilder. I think I've always loved you.

Chapter 25
The Dreaded Concert

I fluff my hair and dab on some red lipstick before grabbing the black sequined purse off my bed. One last glance in the mirror before I head down the stairs prepared to rock Wilder's world. I'm going all out tonight. Black-heeled boots, a short leather skirt, and a gold crop top. I went heavy on the eye makeup and high on the hair. *Volume.* Lots of voluptuous curls. Wilder's not going to know what hit him.

"Have fun tonight!" Mom hollers from the kitchen the moment she hears me. "Call me if you're going to be late."

"Love you!" I yell back before skipping out the front door. I would tell her to wait up, but I don't plan on coming home tonight. I plan on staying at Wilder's. I'll let Mom know *after* the concert, though. I don't want another *we-won't-raise-your-child-if-you-get-pregnant-at-18* speech before I walk out the door.

I make the short trek three houses down to Wilder's as the sun is suspended on the horizon, a ball of fiery reds and golds.

Wilder will be driving tonight, and I'm kind of relieved. He's always the one in the passenger seat, watching my every move while I'm focused on the road. Tonight, I plan on studying him the same way he's been studying me all summer long.

"You look..." Wilder trails off as his eyes rake over my body in the driveway.

I smile as I twist to show him my backside. "I know."

He clears his throat. "You ready?"

"Yep," I nod as Wilder opens the passenger door. I place a hand on his chest and give his lips a chaste kiss before sliding into the seat, my heart beating wildly in my chest.

He walks around the front of the car, and I chuckle to myself as he adjusts his pants. Yeah, he's going to be hard all night long. I almost feel sorry for him. *Almost.*

He keeps one hand on the steering wheel and the other firmly on my thigh as he drives to the outdoor concert venue at the Civic Center across town. I tangle my fingers with his as the sun dips beneath the horizon, coloring the sky magenta and violet.

I take a deep breath as I stare up at the stars. A few are shining brightly as daylight slips quietly away, giving the moon space to glow.

"What are you thinking about?" Wilder asks me.

I glance over at him and see that he's studying me. Even when he's driving, he's still watching me.

"I was looking at the stars," I tell him.

"Do you remember that camping trip we went on with Cash freshman year?" he asks as he squeezes my fingers.

"How could I forget?" I laugh. "We had to share two sleeping bags because Cash didn't tell me to bring one."

"Everyone knows you're supposed to bring a sleeping bag when they're invited on a camping trip," he argues playfully.

"We unzipped both of them," I recount. "And used one as padding on the hard ground and then I squished between the two of you to keep warm. We fought over the single sleeping bag on top of us all night long."

"Yeah," Wilder exhales. "Cash ended up stealing most of it."

"I remember," I roll my eyes.

"And you were shivering," he continues. "So, I wrapped an arm around you."

"You did?"

"I did," he confirms. "You stopped shivering after that."

"I thought you hated me," I swallow hard.

"I never hated you, Blondie."

"Even then?"

"Even then," he repeats.

"But Cash saw me first, right?"

Wilder licks his lips as we come to a halt in front of a stoplight. "Cash was there for me when no one else was."

"I know." My heart feels heavy like a sandbag. "So, we hide this thing between us from him forever?"

"I always wanted you," he ignores my question. "But it was never because Cash had you. I wanted you because I... I..."

He can't say the words out loud. The same words that always get caught in my throat. Words that will make whatever we're doing *real*.

When the summer started, I don't think either of us meant for this to. I didn't mean to fall for Wilder. I didn't mean to drive a wedge between his friendship with Cash. But I did.

"Me too," I clear my throat, hoping he knows I feel the same way. "Cash will come back one day, so I'm only going to say this once because I'm not sure I'll be able to work up the nerve to say it again. When Cash does return, please don't push me away. I know you have a lifetime of friendship with him, but I don't want to lose you. I... I've had years with you, too. I know it's not the same, but you're my only friend. The only person who gets me. I stopped enjoying my life when I started dating Cash. Fanny made me feel like... like I didn't deserve anything good. If Cash did something nice for me, it made her angry. She'd lash out and say things that made me feel bad for being happy. I felt bad that Cash loved me. Then, you came along. I forgot what it felt like to laugh before you, Wilder. If you choose him over me, I get it. If, however, there's a part of you that feels anything remotely like love for me, can you please consider picking me over him?"

"Blondie," Wilder's voice cracks as the light turns green.

"Just think about it," I chew on my bottom lip. "I just need you to think about it."

"I will," he promises as the car starts moving again and my heart feels a little lighter.

Whatever happens, I know that I'll always remember this summer.

The summer with Wilder.

The Summer of Wild.

We push our way through the crowd, trying to get closer to the stage. Wilder's hand stays on my hip as he holds onto me. I try to hide the smile on my face but it's hard to when every part of him is touching me.

When we're close to the front, Wilder drapes his arms over my shoulders and kisses my hair. We don't usually touch like this in public, but if Wilder doesn't care people see us together, then neither do I.

After a few minutes of chanting, Smashing Trout finally makes their way onto the stage.

Whoops and hollers fill the concrete theatre as I wiggle in Wilder's arms, excited I somehow roped him into spending an entire evening listening to the local celebrity band he's abhorred for years.

"I can feel you smirking," he whispers in my ear as the first song begins.

"I can't help it," I grin as I twist to look up at him. "You're at a Smashing Trout concert!"

"Kill me now," he playfully rolls his eyes.

The band plays through several songs as I sway back and forth in Wilder's arms, singing along. I know this isn't his scene, but I'm grateful he still came with me. Technically, it was on the bucket list, but I didn't actually think he'd follow through.

"You should know," I say loudly over the roar of music blasting through the speakers, "this is my first official concert that isn't a town event."

"You mean like the Fourth of July?" he winks.

"Yes!"

"It's mine, too," he says as his lips meet my ear.

The 45-minute set ends too quickly, so we all begin chanting "Encore!"

Smashing Trout gives in and plays one final song. A ballad they wrote a few years ago about the one who got away.

Words pour out of the lead singer's mouth, and I feel my eyes pricking with tears. I haven't lost Wilder yet, but I have this feeling that I'm going to. It's hard to explain. Hard to even fathom as the front of his body molds to my back. But there might come a day when he becomes the *one who got away*.

I stop swaying. Stop singing. I close my eyes and let my other four senses take over. The sweet sound of Wilder's breathing in my ear. The enticing smell of fresh summer air. The salty taste of a teardrop as I lick my lips. The feel of his hand running along my bare stomach.

Every moment with Wilder is charged and momentous. I think that's what happens with summer romances. There's a thin line between savoring every second and feeling like it'll all be ripped apart from you tomorrow. That it'll slip away the same way the sun slips from the evening sky each day.

I wipe a tear from my cheek, and Wilder notices I'm crying.

"Blondie," he chuckles before kissing my shoulder. "It's just a song."

But it's not. It's not just a song. It's the beginning of the end. Or what feels like it, anyway.

Smashing Trout finishes and the lights go down. Cheers erupt as I take a sobering breath.

I've never been afraid of losing something before. Does that mean I've finally found something worth holding onto?

"Wilder!" I hear a scream.

My heart drops. Someone has spotted us. And since Wilder is wildly popular with the girls, I'm sure it's one of his former conquests.

He slides his hand in mine and pulls me toward the exit. But we hear his name again. This time louder and more high-pitched.

Wilder's shoulders tense as the person comes into view. Olivia-Sophia.

She doesn't notice our intertwined fingers at first as she smiles wide.

"I thought you didn't like Smashing Trout," she throws her gorgeous head back and laughs.

I feel small. The kind of smallness that only Fanny Allred could reduce me to. Standing here watching someone else freely flirt with Wilder hurts.

His fingers leave mine and I take a painful step back.

That's when Olivia-Sophia notices me. "I heard a funny rumor about you, Wild. That you've spent the summer running around town with Cash's girlfriend. I don't think he'll be too happy to hear you're been fucking his girl."

Wilder shakes his head. "It's just a rumor. Cash is in Europe and I'm stuck babysitting while he's away."

But Olivia-Sophia isn't stupid, and she can read me better than even Wilder can.

"Does she know that?" Olivia-Sophia frowns.

"What do you want?" Wilder changes the subject.

"I've been invited to Smashing Trout's after-party," she beams. "You should come."

"I'm good."

"I'm going to wear you down," she tells him. "You're going to come crawling back eventually. I let you go once. I'm not going to let it happen again. Besides, you know I like a challenge."

"Let's go," Wilder says over his shoulder to me while motioning to the exit.

I cross my arms over my chest and follow him through the dense crowd.

When we finally get to the car, I reach for the door handle before he has a chance to and quickly climb inside.

"What's going on?" he asks me when he's seated beside me in the driver's seat.

"Headache," I lie. More like heartache.

Every second that passes in the congested parking lot exit feels like a lifetime. I'm holding back tears—barely. I want to curl up in a ball and cry, but I force myself not to.

What feels like an hour later, Wilder stops the car in front of my house. I jump out and shut the door harder than I intend to.

"Hey!" Wilder calls after me. "What's the rush?"

"What am I to you?" I ask once he's out of the car.

"What?" He seems taken aback.

"Am I a friend? More than a friend? Or just Cash's ex-girlfriend you're stuck babysitting."

"She would have told Fanny," Wilder defends himself. "Or maybe Fanny told her about us. Either way, her parents run in the same circles the Allreds do. If she thinks I'm into you, the whole town will find out."

"What am I to you?" I ask again.

"I don't know. I'm trying to figure that out."

Heat builds behind my eyes.

"What am I to you?" I repeat.

Silence. He stands there, perfectly still.

"Come on, Wilder," I fight back tears. "Just say it."

More silence.

"You can't even admit it to yourself, can you?" I yell at him. "You love me. Just say it."

He shoves his hands into his pockets.

"Say something!" I shout. "Anything!"

"I don't—"

"I love you," I force out. "I've always loved you. I know you feel the same way, so why can't you just say it?"

Wilder takes a step forward. "Because I can't."

The first tear falls as I realize summer is coming to an end soon.

And so is my time with Wilder.

Chapter 26
The Free Fall

My eyes are swollen, and my face is puffy thanks to a long night of crying. A night of knowing that no matter what Wilder feels, he won't tell me. Because of his infuriating loyalty to Cash Allred.

Part of me admires his dedication to their lifelong friendship. Wilder isn't the type of person to throw history away on a whim. The problem is that he seems to think Cash owns him and his fealty until the day he dies.

I disagree.

I think Wilder forgets Cash left him without saying goodbye. He forgets Cash hasn't even talked to him. I'm not sure if Wilder's reached out, but I know Cash hasn't. If he did, Wilder would be putting up more walls and trying to shut me out. He hasn't done that yet. So, Cash is still ignoring him. What kind of friendship can survive that type of rejection?

There's a small knock on my door. I groan and shove all the tissues I've used under my pillow.

"Yeah?"

Isla pops her scarlet head in. "There's a creepy boy who's been standing in front of our house for an hour. I think he's here for you."

"Dark hair?" I ask.

"Yep."

"Brooding scowl on his face?"

"Yep."

I guess Wilder is here to talk. I would dress up, but I'm sad and tired. I don't feel like trying to pretty myself up to hear whatever sorry excuse he has for making my heart hurt.

I march down the stairs in star pajama shorts and an old T-shirt of Dad's. I don't even run my fingers through my hair before walking outside.

Sure enough, Wilder is standing on the front lawn, his face hard to read.

"Are you stalking me now?" I cross my arms over my chest, defiantly. "You're scaring my sister."

He doesn't say anything.

"Ugh!" I tug at the ends of my hair. "Stop wasting my time, Wilder! I'm done with the silence. If you have something to say, then say it. If not, get off my lawn."

He steps forward. "You know I want to say it, but I can't. I can't say it until I talk to Cash. Until then, it's not fair to you."

I wrap my arms around my chest. "Has he tried messaging you?"

Wilder shakes his head. "No, but I haven't tried either."

"This is stupid," I shake my head.

He nods, taking slow steps toward me. "It is."

"I'm frustrated," I tell him. "I'm frustrated by this whole thing."

Wilder's hands slide through my hair, tugging my face to look up at him. "I'm sorry."

I shrug, holding my arms tighter to my chest. "You should go."

His lips find mine, and he sighs against my mouth. I war with myself, trying hard not to move my lips against his. But he mumbles, "Ingrid," and I melt instantly.

I slowly slip my arm around his waist and tilt my head to the side, sucking his bottom lip into my mouth. We make out on the front lawn until we're both breathing heavily, and my lips are raw.

"Get dressed," he smiles.

"Why?"

"We're jumping out of the tree at the creek."

My stomach knots. "I... I don't think I want to do that today."

"That's exactly why we're doing it," he grins, his fingers stroking the back of my neck.

"Sounds like torture."

"Are you scared, Blondie?"

I lift my chin. "No."

"You are!" he teases before kissing me again.

"I just don't want to break a bone."

"I'll keep you safe," he promises as his hazel eyes glisten in the afternoon light.

"Fine," I reluctantly give in. "I'll change into my bathing suit."

I pull away to head inside, but Wilder grabs my forearm and runs his fingers over the lightning bolt on my wrist. I wonder what he's thinking as he stares down at it, stony-faced. But I don't ask why he's fixated on it. Instead, I give him a moment to take it in. To feel whatever he needs to. *In silence.*

Wilder clears his throat. "I'll grab towels and the car."

I leave him and hurry inside, my heart clanging against my ribcage. I didn't expect him to show up today. I didn't expect him to try to explain himself. Wilder's never been one to apologize when he's hurt my feelings.

You know I want to say it, but I can't. I can't say it until I talk to Cash. Until then, it's not fair to you.

He's right. It's not fair to me. But it's not fair to Wilder either.

I gather my frizzy hair into a ponytail and slip into a lime-green bikini. I toss on a white tank top and jean shorts over, then grab sunglasses. I'm not thrilled about jumping out of the tree at the creek. I don't want to do it.

I'll keep you safe.

I wish he'd keep my heart safe, too.

The water is surprisingly cool as I dip my toes into the creek. The tall shade trees keep the rays of sunlight from dancing across the turquoise surface and warming it.

"You ready?" Wilder asks me as his hand finds my lower back.

I glance up at the massive oak in front of us. "No."

"It's better to just get it over with," Wilder informs me. "Before you give yourself too much time to think about it."

My stomach twists and turns. "I don't want to do it."

Wilder's fingers find my hand. "If it wasn't safe, I wouldn't let you do it."

"But it's not deep enough," I argue.

"Come on," Wilder tugs me toward the water. "You've never swam far out enough to see how deep it is. Let me show you."

"Cash always said—"

"Cash was screwing with you," Wilder raises an eyebrow. "Probably to keep you on the rocks, far enough away to let him swim without being interrupted."

My heart drops. "Cash really didn't want me around much, did he?"

"I wanted you around," Wilder offers.

The more Wilder tells me about Cash, the more surprised I am that they're friends. Or *were* friends? I can't tell anymore.

Wilder swims beside me, keeping his eye on me as we wade further into the water.

"Try to touch the bottom," he instructs.

I feel around with my foot, but there's nothing solid beneath me. So, I propel myself under, my toes still searching for hard ground.

When I come up for air, Wilder flashes his eyebrows at me. "Now, look up."

The tree branch right above us doesn't look that far up. Maybe six feet. From a distance, jumping out of the tree appears much more dangerous than it is. But up close, it's not that bad.

"You ready now?"

I nod. "Yeah."

We swim back to the rocky shoreline, and Wilder leads the way over to the tree. The low-lying branches make it easy to climb. My feet slip a few times, but Wilder grabs my arm every time, making sure I don't fall.

I carefully walk out onto the branch above the creek and take a deep breath. We're not that high up, but I'm still nervous about jumping.

As if he can read my mind, Wilder squeezes my hand. "I'll be right here."

Don't think about it! Just do it, Ingrid!

I inhale before letting his hand go and jumping off the branch. I let out a scream as I plummet into the water below. The moment my feet hit the glassy surface, I hold my breath and let my body sink into the creek.

A few seconds later, I'm popping up out of the water laughing.

"You did it!" Wilder yells from above me.

I swim out of the way to let him go next. He cannonballs in as I float. The moment his head resurfaces, I swim over to him.

"That was scary," I tell him.

"But you did it," he gives me a breathtaking smile.

I've always been afraid to jump out of the tree, but with Wilder beside me, it was easy. Everything is easier with Wilder.

We swim for a little while until the adrenaline wears off. Then, we slowly meander back to shore.

I lay a towel down on one of the big rocks and sit. Wilder follows suit, making sure his arm touches mine.

The sun manages to slice through the thick branches and light up Wilder's face. He looks relaxed and calm. Something he doesn't appear to be very often.

I know I shouldn't, but I scoot closer to him. And then, I kiss his shoulder. His skin is cool, but I can feel the warmth radiating off him.

"You ready to start college in a few weeks?" He makes small talk.

I hitch a shoulder. "I don't really want the summer to end."

He exhales heavily. "Me either."

And because we're in the middle of nowhere, surrounded by tall shade trees and the warm sun, I untie the bikini top behind my neck. I let the material fall forward as Wilder's eyes drink in my bare breasts.

"What are you doing, Blondie?"

I hide a smile as I stand and slowly pull the lime-green material off my hips.

"Blondie," he laughs. "We could get caught."

"So," I flash my eyebrows at him. "Take your swimsuit off."

He doesn't hesitate and lifts his butt off the damp towel, stripping out of his wet shorts.

I stand over him and carefully kneel, placing both knees on either side of his hips. One hand rests on his shoulder while the other searches for his hard dick. When I wrap my fingers around it, I pump it up and down, making him harder.

"You're beautiful," he whispers as I place the tip of *Wild Cox* at my soaked entrance. I lower myself onto him, and he lets out a loud moan. "Why do you always feel so good?"

I don't answer him because we both know why. Love makes everything better, doesn't it?

My hips rock back and forth on his pulsating cock as he stares up at me, dark black pupils eating up his minty gold irises. He's warm and wet and wild. I lean down and press my lips to his, tasting him.

"I love you," I say in the space between us.

Our stomachs stick together as I roll my hips back and forth.

"It's not like this with anyone else," Wilder says quietly as he cups my cheek in his hand.

"No," I agree.

A warm breeze rustles through the oak trees, I increase speed, rocking my hips faster. I don't count the seconds or minutes as they pass. Don't rush to get him off. I inhale a moment, then exhale. I'm sticky and sweaty, but I don't care. There's a scratchy feeling in my chest telling me to savor every second. This won't last forever, even though I want it to.

As my nipples rub against his hard chest, my stomach tightens. Wilder notices and slips his hand between us, flicking my swollen clit. I come undone on top of him, my walls clenching around his hard cock. He follows right after me, burying his face in my neck, muttering my name. My heart feels as if it might explode from happiness.

Afterward, we lay curled up on the damp towel, my legs twined with his. We don't talk, don't fill the air with useless words. We let our hearts speak as Wilder kisses me deeply, his hands gently caressing every inch of my body.

When I begin shivering from the cool breeze, we get dressed, and then carry the dry towels to his car. I hold onto his hand as he drives, wishing this could last forever. That this feeling of being known and cared for and in love could last forever.

We both get out of the car at the same time once Wilder parks the car in the driveway.

We link arms as Wilder walks me to the front door, the moment sweet and simple.

Just as I'm about to turn to kiss him, I notice a familiar figure sitting on the front porch.

My arm drops from Wilder's as the figure stands and hurries toward me.

"Ingrid," Cash barely gets out before wrapping his foreign arms around me. "I've missed you."

Chapter 27
The Sorry Excuse

Cash is waiting in my room while I stare at myself in the bathroom mirror, my lower lip trembling. I haven't stripped off my clothes or changed out of the bathing suit underneath yet. I've just been staring at myself, wondering what the hell I'm supposed to do.

My body is still crawling with Wilder's touch. My lips are raw from his kisses and *down there* is soaked from the pleasure he teased out of me.

"Can we talk?" That's all Cash said after the excruciating hug he gave me in front of Wilder.

I wanted to tell Cash the truth. That I'm in love with his best friend. But Wilder slowly backed away and headed home. My eyes followed him until he was out of sight. Then, I panicked. I didn't know what to say or do. I still don't know. I haven't said a word to Cash.

I know I can't stay in here forever. I can't ignore Cash or the reason he's home early from his backpacking trip. I have to face it. I just wish I could face it *with* Wilder by my side.

My phone is sitting on the marble sink. I grab it and call Wilder.

He answers on the first ring. "Everything okay?"

I take a deep breath before tears spring to my eyes, wanting to be back at the creek in our blissful bubble.

"No. I don't know what to do."

"Have you talked to him?" Wilder's deep voice echoes through the phone.

"No," I say as I grip the sink with my hand. "I'm in the bathroom hiding."

He exhales heavily and I can feel the weight on his shoulders coming through the line. "You need to talk to him."

Walls. He's already putting up those goddamn walls. "I don't know what to say."

"Let him do the talking."

"Wilder," my heart squeezes in my chest. "I love you."

"I know, Blondie," he replies.

"Can I come over after he leaves?" I ask.

"I, uh, don't think that's a good idea," he responds.

I wrap my free arm around my waist, knowing he's slowly going to start pulling away. "Tomorrow then?"

Wilder clicks his tongue. "We should keep our distance for now."

"So, that's it then?" I laugh in disbelief. "Cash comes back and it's just over?"

"I have to go," he says.

"Fine," I snap.

"Don't be like that, Blondie," he sighs.

"Goodbye, Wilder." I angrily click the red *End* button on the screen and turn to face myself in the mirror.

Tempestuous tears are forming, but I will them away. I'm angry—*so angry*—at Cash right now. He left. He upended my world. Now he's back doing it all over again.

I change out of my clothes quickly and slip into a pair of leggings and an oversized tee. I'm not dressing up for Cash. I'm not even sure why I let him inside.

"What do you want?" I ask him when I walk back into my room and see that he's sitting on my bed.

"I guess I deserve that," Cash hangs his head.

"So," I clear my throat. "What do you want?"

"I messed up, Ingrid." He sounds remorseful, but I'm not buying his crafty Allred act. "I was... there's a lot of stuff that's been going on. I haven't been honest with you."

I frown. "Like your mom stealing money from my dad's company, framing him, and then getting him fired?"

Cash's mouth drops open. "How did you find out?"

"Your mom's loose lips," I roll my eyes.

"She wore me down, Ingrid," he licks his lips nervously. "She threatened me with all kinds of things. I couldn't think straight anymore. So, when there was an opportunity to get away from it all, I took it. I know I shouldn't have but living with all that... all that chaos... it was draining."

"You should have told me the truth," I shake my head. "You owed me that much."

"I know," Cash stands and crosses the room. He tries to touch me, but I take a step back. "I messed up. And I don't expect you to forgive me. I just... I needed to see you."

"Why?" I counter.

"Because I love you," he inhales sharply. "And being without you is too hard."

"You're going to Johns Hopkins," I remind him. "You were going to be without me, anyway."

"No," he raises his eyebrows. "I'm not going."

"Wh-what?" My mouth drops open in surprise.

"My parents were using tuition to threaten me, so I dropped out. I'm not going to school in Maryland. I'm staying here."

I try processing what Cash is saying, but I don't understand. "Johns Hopkins has been your dream for years."

"No," he smiles. "It was my mom and dad's dream."

"You broke up with me," I huff. "You left me, and you left Wilder, too. You didn't even say goodbye to him."

"I know," Cash takes an unsteady step forward, his blue eyes bright like turquoise lake water. "I couldn't face Wilder, though. He would have seen right through me. He always does."

"He's your best friend," I defend Wilder. "He deserved a goodbye."

"I will make it up to him," Cash promises. "I need a place to stay, so I was kind of hoping I could crash with him."

"Why do you need a place to crash?" I furrow my brow as his fingers run along my arm.

"My parents kicked me out," Cash shrugs. "When I told them I wasn't going to Johns Hopkins, they told me to leave. You and Wilder have always been my real family. The only real family I've ever known. So, I thought I'd come here first to tell you how sorry I am for leaving you the way I did. Then, I'm going to apologize to Wilder."

My head hurts as I stare up at Cash. The boy who stole my first kiss. The boy I used to dream about a future with. The boy who left me when things got too hard.

"I'm not sure what you're expecting," I chew on the inside of my cheek, "but I'm not at a place where I see us getting back together."

Cash's face falls. "Why not?"

I briefly close my eyes. "Because I've had more fun this past summer than I did the four summers I spent with you."

"I—"

"I'm not trying to hurt you," I continue. "I just... I don't want to pretend to be someone I'm not anymore. And being with you, that's all I did."

"I know," he nods. "I know it's my fault. I shouldn't have... I should have done more to make you feel comfortable. I should have tried harder to show you how much I love you."

"Don't beat yourself up over the past," I hitch a shoulder. "I don't hate you, Cash. I just don't want to be someone I'm not."

"I won't let you," he whispers as he moves closer. "I'm not going to disappoint you anymore."

I don't want him to touch me. I don't want him to need me. I don't want him to be here, trying to prove that he's different. I don't want him to give up his future.

I want Wilder.

But I don't think that's going to happen now. Not after everything Cash has revealed.

"You should go see Wilder," I suggest.

Cash gnaws on his lower lip. "Will you walk down with me? I, um, I'm afraid he might punch me in the face for being a terrible friend. If you're there, he might think twice about violence."

"Yeah," I say half-heartedly.

We walk slowly, Cash's arm bumping into mine every few steps. I don't want to show up on Wilder's doorstep next to his best friend. But I need to see Wilder. Just a glimpse. Just a moment.

Cash knocks on the front door and takes a step back. I cross my arms over my chest and wait, my heart thumping against bone and flesh.

The door creaks open and Wilder sees me first. His face is solid stone, his emotions a wall of impenetrable rock.

"Hey," Cash steps into his view. "Before you punch me, I want to apologize."

Wilder's eyes slide from me to his best friend. "You don't owe me an apology."

"I left without saying goodbye, and I'm sorry. I was a shitty friend, and I'm sorry."

"Did you just say *shitty*?" Wilder raises his eyebrows.

"Seemed like the best word to describe myself," Cash admits.

"I'm sure you had your reasons," Wilder lets him off the hook. *Too easy*, in my opinion.

"My parents kicked me out," Cash explains. "I'm not going to Johns Hopkins. Paying my tuition was their way of holding everything over my head. I don't have anywhere else to go. I thought—I was *hoping*—I could crash here until I get a job and save up for a deposit on an apartment."

"They kicked you out?" Wilder shakes his head in disbelief.

"Yeah," Cash answers. "They've been doing some shady things, and I can't take it anymore. That's why I came back early. I can't keep running from them. I told Ingrid that you guys are my real family. The two of you."

My heart sinks as Wilder refuses to look at me.

"Yeah, you can stay here," Wilder stands back to let him in.

Cash takes a few steps forward, then turns to me. "You coming?"

"I-I, uh..." I stutter.

"Blondie can find her way home," Wilder coldly interjects.

My chest burns with blinding pain.

"No," Cash steps between us. "If she's not welcome here, then I'm not staying."

"It's fine," I force out. "I have stuff to do anyway."

Cash holds a hand out and I awkwardly touch his fingers. "I meant what I said. I'm not going to disappoint you again."

Wilder's mask slips for a split second as his eyes flash with pain. But then, he rearranges his features. *Indifference*. That's all I'm ever going to get out of him, isn't it?

Cash drops my hand and brushes past Wilder. But Wilder stands rooted in place, his eyes locked on mine.

My eyes prick with tears as I stare at him. An hour ago, I was lying in his arms as he kissed me beneath the shade trees at the creek. *Strangers*. That's what he's acting like we are now.

"I'm..." I trail off, not knowing what to say.

"Go home, Blondie."

Tears spill out of my eyes as I nod. "I guess I'll see you around."

Wilder takes a step forward and quickly shuts the door behind him. He reaches for my forearm and runs his fingers over the lightning bolt tattoo on my wrist. "Thank you."

"For?" I glance up at him through a haze of tears.

"This," he says as his thumb presses lightly over the tattoo.

I let out a heavy breath before pulling my hand out of his grasp. I leave him standing on his front porch and make my way home.

Cash is back now, which means Wilder, and I are over.

One door is closing while the other is reopening.

The problem is that I want what's behind that closing door, knowing it'll never be mine again.

Chapter 28
The Obnoxious Snorer

Wilder

Cash is sleeping on my floor, his obnoxious snoring keeping me awake. I grab my phone and stare at the time. 3:31 am. At least tomorrow—er, *today*—is Sunday. I can sleep in.

I take a breath and wince. Every time I breathe in, my heart stings and spasms.

Blondie can find her way home.
Go home, Blondie.

I didn't think breaking her heart would mean breaking my own. But I think that's what I've done.

I toss and turn, shoving another pillow under my head. I'm restless. I've never been this restless before.

All I can think about is Ingrid. I'm not sure when she stopped being Blondie for me. Maybe when I walked in on her recording herself naked. Something happened that day and it changed everything. She's not some nickname anymore. She's Ingrid.

She's Cash's Ingrid.

I wince from the pain again, wishing I could ignore it. Push it away. Pretend long enough to trick my heart into actually believing I feel nothing for her.

Instead, I'm in physical pain. The kind of pain I felt when my dad left. Almost as if a piece of myself has been torn off, and I have to learn how to live without it.

This is all my fault. I knew this would happen. I knew Cash would come back for her. Despite how shitty he's treated her over the years, I know he's never loved anyone like he loves her. That's not an excuse for breaking up with her and ditching her for the summer. It's just a fact.

Cash Allred might be a nice guy, but he's still an Allred. And the Allreds always get what they want in the end.

I should stay out of his way and let him win. I should do that. The thing is, if I can't have Ingrid, then I don't think he should either.

Another loud snore echoes through my room, rattling the windows. I grab one of the pillows I'm propped up on and propel it at Cash's big head.

"What was that for?" he groans loudly.

"You're snoring and I can't fucking sleep," I grumble.

"Sorry, Wild. I haven't been able to sleep in weeks. This is the first night I've fallen asleep comfortably."

Great, now I feel bad. His life is so fucked up he sleeps better on the carpet in my room than in his big mansion across town.

I blow out a tired breath. "Just keep it down, okay?"

"Okay."

I roll over and close my eyes, trying hard not to think about Ingrid. Not about her brown eyes or her soft hair. Not the way she slid out of her bikini at the creek and crawled on top of me, her pert nipples running along my chest. Not about how warm and wet she was. Not about the hours we laid on the rock, limbs tangled as we kissed.

If I had known it was going to be the last time I held her like that, I would have held on a little tighter.

***

My eyes open slowly, hoping everything that happened yesterday was a bad dream. But Cash is standing in the doorway, staring at me.

"Hey, Sleeping Beauty," he gives me a shit-eating grin. "You've been asleep for hours."

"You snore worse than my grandpa," I stretch my arms over my head.

"You gonna tell me why you have her nickname tattooed on your arm?" Cash gets straight to the point.

I freeze. *Shit*. I forgot about the tattoo. We never came up with a story. Or an excuse. I can't tell Cash the truth.

"I lost a bet," I clear my throat and sit up.

"What bet?" Cash crosses his arms over his chest.

"Pool," I offer quickly. "Turns out Blondie isn't terrible at it." She is, for the record. She sucks.

"You guys spend all summer together?"

Yep.

"We hung out a few times," I tell him. "Played pool once and we swam at the creek."

"I didn't think you two liked each other," he nonchalantly yawns.

"You abandoned us, Cash," I remind him. "She needed to talk to someone."

He runs a hand through his blond hair. "I screwed up, Wild. I never should have left her."

"Why did you?" Not sure I want to hear his answer, but I know I need to.

"My mom did something really bad," Cash admits. *Oh, you mean frame Jason Winthrop?* "Like, something illegal. If I didn't leave, she was going to cause a lot of problems for Ingrid."

"So, what? You thought by leaving you were protecting her?"

"I thought so," he frowns. "I see now that I wasn't. I've lived under my mom's control for so long, I didn't even realize she was manipulating me. Going to Europe was good for me. I could finally think without her breathing down my neck."

"If she didn't like you with Blondie," I lick my lips, "why didn't you just break up with her sooner?"

Cash scoffs. "You know why. I love Ingrid. I want to marry her. I... I can't see my life without her in it. Ingrid's the best thing that's ever happened to me. But I'm pretty sure she told me I'm the worst thing that's ever happened to her. She said she's had more fun this summer than she did the summers that we were together."

Funny, she told me the same thing.

I scratch the side of my face. "What are you going to do?"

"Win her back?" Cash blows out an unsteady breath. "If I can. Try to prove to her that I never meant to hurt her. That I was so exhausted from the endless nagging and negativity that I had to leave. Not her. Just everyone."

"You think she'll forgive you?"

He shrugs. "Ingrid isn't like my mom. She's not harsh or manipulative. She doesn't make threats or guilt trip me. She's never demanded anything from me. So, probably not. Why would she? After everything my mom's done, I'd run in the opposite direction."

I click my tongue. "You want to do something today?"

"I was kind of hoping we could mini golf with Ingrid," Cash proposes. "If you invite her, maybe she'll come."

"You want me to invite her?" I guffaw.

"Yeah," Cash raises a hopeful eyebrow.

"Doubt she'll come, but I can try."

"I'm going to jump in the shower," Cash throws a thumb over his shoulder. "You'll give her a call?"

I don't want to. I need to keep my distance. But watching Ingrid reject Cash during a round of mini golf isn't the worst way to spend a Sunday afternoon.

"What?" she answers on the first ring.

"Cash wants to know if you want to mini golf," I exhale.

Silence.

"Ingrid," I breathe out.

"Don't call me that," she chastises me.

"Blondie," I try again.

"I'll play mini golf with you two idiots," she smirks, "but I want something in return."

"What?" I ask.

"Send me a nude photo, Wilder."

"What?" I furrow my brow.

"We need to finish our bucket list," she states. "I want a nude photo of you."

"I can send one." My dick raises to attention.

"I'm sure you can," she snorts. "How many girls have you sent dick pics to?"

"None," I honestly answer.

"Bullshit."

"I've never sent one," I say again, not caring if she believes me. "But I'll send you one."

"And Wilder," Ingrid's voice lowers an octave, "make sure your dick is hard in the picture."

I smile. "I can do that."

I hang up with her and lock my bedroom door. I strip out of my boxers and stand in front of the full-length mirror stuck to my door with gorilla glue, my dick hard as a fucking rock. All I can think about is how wet her pussy was yesterday. Tight, wet, and warm.

After Olivia-Sophia, I had a one-and-done rule. Sleep with them once, and then move on. Not that there's been as many girls as Ingrid seems to think. I don't date. Don't get involved. Don't have unprotected sex.

I snap the picture and send it to Ingrid. She texts back immediately that she'll be down when she's done getting ready.

Then, she sends a follow-up text.
You with Cash?
Nope. I reply.
Tell me when you are.
OK?

By the time I'm dressed, and my bedroom door is unlocked, Cash strolls into my room with a white towel tied securely around his waist.

"Can I borrow a pair of shorts and a tee?"

I point to my dresser. "Have at it."

Then, I slyly send Ingrid a message. *I'm with Cash.*

A few seconds later, an image pops up. Ingrid is completely naked, kneeling in front of a mirror. Her bright, pink pussy is on full display.

I fumble with my phone, trying to quickly click out of the message.

"You okay over there?" Cash asks.

I rub my forehead with my hand. "Yep."

"Did Ingrid say she'd mini golf with us?"

My throat feels dry as the nude she sent me sears itself into my brain. "Yep. She'll be down when she's ready."

"Yes!" Cash fist-pumps the air.

An hour later, we're piling into Cash's truck. That's the only thing his parents let him keep when they kicked him out. Lucky him. The only thing my dad gave me as a parting gift was trust issues.

"You look stunning," Cash wiggles restlessly in the driver's seat as Ingrid buckles her seat belt.

I put my sunglasses on in the backseat, annoyed. I haven't worn them much this summer. I used to wear them so I could stare at Ingrid without anyone noticing. Guess we're back to that. Quietly pining away for her from a distance.

"Thanks," Ingrid replies as she adjusts the tiny strap on her top.

"Is the air blowing cold enough for you?" Cash asks her.

"I'm fine," Ingrid assures him.

"You look beautiful," Cash tries again.

"I got it," Ingrid snaps.

"Sorry," he apologizes.

I watch as Ingrid's shoulders stiffen the moment Cash's fingers begin inching closer to her side of the cab.

"No," she forcefully mutters as her eyes dart from his hand to his face. "Don't touch me."

I can't hide the smile that spreads across my face.

My cell phone vibrates in my lap. I grab it and open the message from Ingrid.

Did you like my photo?

I loved it, I send back.

I have more.

I swallow hard as I stare at the words on the screen. What am I doing? I can't be hot and cold with her. Cash wants her. Cash has history with her. Cash will win in the end. He always does.

Send them to Cash, I write.

I took them for you.

He wants to get back with you.

An audible huff leaves her mouth before I get the next message.

He doesn't know what he wants.

What do you want, Blondie?

You. Only you.

I don't reply to her message even though I want to. I want to tell her I feel the same way, but I know something she doesn't.

My dad left. I watched him walk out the front door one day and never look back. Like it was as natural as breathing. I know how easy it is to leave. To get into the car and drive away without glancing in the rearview mirror.

I'm afraid that if things get too hard, I'll bail the same way my dad did.

And Ingrid? That's the last thing she needs. Someone else leaving her when she trusted them.

Chapter 29
The Video Reveal

I can feel Wilder's eyes staring at me through his stupid dark sunglasses. His gaze is burning into my shoulder as Cash pays for us to play mini golf, but I try ignoring him.

Which begs the question: if Cash got kicked out of his parents' house, why does he still have his truck and credit card? That's suspicious.

"Whew," Cash playfully wipes his forehead with his forearm. "They haven't canceled my credit card yet."

Oh. I guess that's why.

"Enjoy it now," Wilder yawns, "because it won't last forever."

"Nothing does, does it?" I glare at Wilder. I can't see his eyes, but I know he's staring back at me.

"What's that supposed to mean?" Cash interrupts our stare-down

"All good things must come to an end," I cryptically answer as I narrow my eyes at Wilder.

"Yeah," Cash frowns. "I suppose it does."

"You guys ready to golf?" Wilder interrupts the tense moment.

"Yep," I click my tongue.

No one talks after that, and I follow behind Wilder and Cash as they lead the way to the first hole. When we reach it, Cash tells me I'm up first.

Oh, joy.

I grab my pink mini-golf club and place the orange ball Cash hands me on the tee.

"You're going to want to—"

"I know how to golf," I hold up at hand, stopping Cash.

"You do?" He tilts his blond head to the side.

Yeah, dumbass, I do.

"What I find so interesting," I turn my upper body to face him, "is that you spent years coming up with excuses to play golf with your dad at the country club *without me*. A game you love and play often. But you never took me to play it *with you*. Instead, I get the cheaper, smaller, washed-up version of the country club in the form of mini golf. If you want to give me pointers, save it. You should have done that before you left me."

"Okay," Cash shoves his hands into the pockets of what appears to be Wilder's shorts. "I deserve that."

"You do," I flash my eyebrows at him.

"So, when did you learn how to golf?" Cash asks.

"Wouldn't you like to know," I raise my eyebrows, annoyed.

"I would," Cash tries. "That's why I asked."

"Well, guess what?" I snarl. "You don't get to know because you dumped me for Europe."

"Ouch," Cash takes a wounded step back.

"Careful," my nostrils flare, "wouldn't want you to fall on your ass. Oh, wait, you already did. Otherwise, you wouldn't be here with Wilder and me right now."

"Blondie," Wilder interjects.

I let out an exaggerated huff. "What?"

"Would it kill you to be nice?" he lowers his voice.

"Yeah, I think it would."

"Someone's in a mood today," Wilder grumbles.

"Anyone else have something they need to say before I hit the ball?" I smack my lips together. Wilder and Cash shake their heads in unison. "No? Good."

I take a breath, my toes wiggling in my shoes. I need this ball to go in on the first try. I need it to curve just a little to the right, over that hump. I need to prove to Cash that I'm not the girl he left confused and hurt on the front porch. I'm the new, improved Ingrid who doesn't need him or his bullshit.

I carefully swing the club back before letting it slide forward. The ball soars over the straightaway, curving just slightly to the right, barely climbing the hump, and coming to rest in the first hole.

I smile triumphantly before rearranging my features into a mask of indifference. "Who's up next?"

Cash steps forward. He finagles the ball a thousand different ways as I stand beside Wilder, his skin so close I can feel the heat coming off it.

"Go easy on him," Wilder whispers.

I sigh, bored. "No."

"He's had a rough couple of weeks."

I laugh quietly in disbelief. "And I'm supposed to feel bad about that because?"

"Because he slept on my floor and snored all night long," Wilder grumbles.

"I'll be nice but I'm going to need something in return," I wager.

"What?"

"I have to go the bathroom," I say loudly.

Cash glances over his shoulder. "What?"

"I don't know where the bathroom is," I lie. "I need to go. NOW!"

"Wild," Cash's eyes widen as he glances at Wilder, "can you take her?"

Wilder exhales dramatically. "Sure."

We walk silently over to the only concrete building on the premises, the crowd surprisingly sparse for a Sunday afternoon.

"What do you want?" Wilder gets straight to the point.

I open the bathroom door. "I already told you. I want you."'

"Ingrid," he rolls his eyes.

"What happened to Blondie?"

He drops his head a little, moving his face closer to mine. "I can't give you what you want, okay?"

"I think you can," I bargain. "Especially if you want me to stop being mean to Cash."

"What *specifically* do you want?" he tries again.

I step inside the bathroom. "I want you to kiss me."

"That's not a good idea," Wilder removes his sunglasses, his hazel eyes cold and hard.

"I love you," I ball my fists at my sides. "I love you so much that the thought of never kissing you again makes my heart *hurt*."

"It's o-over, B-blondie," he stumbles over his words. "It was just a summer fling."

I hold my wrist out showing him my tattoo. "This isn't some fling to me. This is permanently marked on my arm. *Forever*. Just like yours. It's not a summer fling and you know it."

"He's in love with you," Wilder harshly replies. "He's given up everything *for you*. I can't tell him that I..."

"You can't even admit it to yourself, can you?" I shake my head. "You love me. You want to be with me, too."

"It doesn't matter what I want."

"It does," I place a hand on his chest. "It matters to me."

"He's not going to Johns Hopkins. If he was going, then maybe we wouldn't have to stop. He wouldn't be around long enough to figure it out. But I can't keep this from him. I can't lie to Cash any more than I already have."

"I'm not giving up," I warn him. "I'm not going to make it easy for you to walk away from me."

He gives in for a moment, his fingers tangling with mine. "I can't give you what you need."

"I don't need anything special. I just want you."

"Ingrid," he swallows hard. "We live in a small town. We're going to college in a small town. We're not going to make it out alive if we screw over an Allred."

I move closer, inhaling the smell of him. Laundry detergent with a woodsy hint. "Kiss me, Wilder."

"It's just going to make things worse," he says quietly, his resolve slipping.

I slide my hand from his chest up to his neck. "Kiss me."

"And you'll stop being mean to Cash?"

"For one day," I make clear.

Wilder sucks in a harsh breath as he wraps his arms around my waist and pushes me into the bathroom, the door closing behind us with a resounding *click*.

I cup his face in my hands, stubble poking my palms as I stare into his eyes. He doesn't kiss me right away as his arms tighten their hold on me and we take each other in. Twenty-four hours ago, we were swimming in the creek, unaware that all of this was waiting for us hours later. Now, we're reduced to a single stolen moment in a public restroom.

"It's not fair," I breathe out. "It's not fair that he gets to come back and ruin everything."

"The first Christmas after my dad left," Wilder sucks in a harsh breath, "we were tight on money. My mom told me we weren't celebrating Christmas that year. She said as soon as she received the first child support payment my dad was supposedly sending, she'd buy me whatever I wanted. Well, Christmas came and went, then months passed, and my dad didn't make a single payment. He worked under the table and put everything in Margot's name. Even his bank account. He was, virtually, untouchable."

"I'm sorry."

"My mom struggled, but Cash knew I really wanted a new bike. Mine was too small, and the chain fell off every time I rode it. Cash mowed lawns that summer and saved up enough to buy me a bike for Christmas."

"That was nice of him," I say as I resist the urge to roll my eyes.

"Cash is selfish and self-absorbed sometimes," Wilder shrugs against me, "but he was raised in a mansion. He's a product of his upbringing. Except he's not just selfish and self-absorbed, he's also thoughtful and loyal. He screws up and then he makes things better. He's the guy who broke up with you to selfishly get away from his parents but then he came back home and gave up everything because he loves you. Because it's the right thing to do."

"But he left me."

"He came back," he argues.

"I'm not getting back together with him," I stand firm.

"I'm not asking you to," Wilder's fingers run through my hair. "I'm just asking you to be nice to him."

"You confuse me."

"I confuse me, too," he admits.

We stare at each other for a long moment before he moves his face forward and I hurry to kiss him. His mouth is warm and wet and welcoming as I run my tongue along his. He tastes like mint and summer and everything I've ever wanted.

I hold on tight, tighter than I've ever held onto anything in my life. Wilder's lips move slowly, savoring every moment.

When he finally pulls away, I feel my heart plummet to the cold concrete floor below. He carefully removes his arms from me and takes a step back. "You'll be nice to him now?"

"If that's what you want," I reply.

"Ingrid," he says my name again like it's his favorite word.

"I'll be nice," I promise.

Wilder walks in front of me as we make the short trek back to Cash. He's standing off to the side as a group finishes up their first round.

"Your turn," Cash gives Wilder a small smile.

I stand back a little, my heart and head woozy. I'm not giving up. I'm not letting Wilder walk away so easily. Not when I feel like this.

"Wait," Cash lightly smacks Wilder's arm. "We need a photo."

"Of what?" Wilder groans.

"Of the three of us."

"I'm good," Wilder runs a hand through his hair, his sunglasses hiding the fact that he's staring at me.

"No, Cash is right," I speak up. "We should take a photo. The three of us finishing out the last week of summer together."

I slide my phone out of my back pocket as Wilder's mouth drops open. Not sure what he expected. This is me *trying* to be nice.

I hand my phone to Wilder as he stands on one side of me, Cash on the other. Wilder snaps an unenthusiastic selfie as I force a smile.

"Alright," Wilder hands me back the phone. "It's my turn."

"Can I see the photo?" Cash asks.

I open up the Gallery on my phone and hand it over to Cash. "Yep."

I step around my former boyfriend, watching Wilder as he stands over his ball. Wilder knocks the green ball with the club, sending it halfway down the small stretch of turf. It stops three feet from the hole.

"*Pathetic*," I yawn.

"I'm just getting started," Wilder scoffs.

"You still need some time to warm up?" I tease.

"I'm going to win," he proudly boasts.

"What are we going to wager this time?" I cock an eyebrow and cross my arms over my chest.

Wilder rolls his head on his shoulders. "Cash's front seat."

"If you win, you want the front seat?"

"I do."

"And what do I get if I win?"

"What do you want?" Wilder repositions himself over the ball.

"You already know that answer," I return.

"Try again," he quips.

"If I win," I laugh, "you have to get waxed. By Pierre."

Wilder straightens. "Are you serious?"

"Dead serious," I challenge.

"Fine," he accepts.

Just as I'm about to respond, Cash's elbow bumps mine. My eyes slide over to my phone, my naked body on full display. Except it's not the set of nudes I took for Wilder. It's the video. The one we made weeks ago on my bed.

Before I can grab it from Cash, Wilder's naked body steps into the frame, climbing onto the bed behind me. Cash drops my phone as his eyes dart from his best friend to me.

"Wh-what the hell happened this summer?"

Chapter 30
The Friend Feud

My life is flashing before my eyes. Every moment this summer reduced to a blinking line of images popping up in front of me, then disappearing.

My phone is free-falling through the air and suddenly crashes to the ground below.

Cash's face is white as a ghost. Wilder's bright green ball is rolling across the dull green turf. A warm breeze is ruffling my hair.

"Wh-what happened this summer?"

The words hang in the air like a rancid smell. Hot, overwhelming, and putrid.

I quickly swoop my phone up off the ground but the sounds of moaning and hushed words slip out of the speaker, alerting Wilder to the shit show that's about to unfold.

His hazel eyes fill with trepidation as panic races through my body.

"What happened this summer?" Cash demands an answer.

Wilder stands frozen in place.

"Is someone going to tell me what that was?" Cash's chest rises and falls as he points to the phone in my hand.

I'm not sure what to do. I want to wait for Wilder to respond, but I know he can't. He can't even move his limbs let alone his lips. So, it's up to me.

"Cash," I say quietly as I hold the incriminating evidence against my chest, "it sort of just... happened."

Cash's cheeks turn red. "I wasn't asking you."

I take a step in front of Wilder, protecting him from Cash's rage. "It was me. All me. Wilder was—"

"Get out of my way, Ingrid," Cash's nostrils flare.

I quickly step back, putting myself right in front of Wilder so close I can hear his heart pounding against his ribcage. "You left me. You walked away when things got too hard."

"You know why I couldn't stay." Cash's knuckles turn white as he grips the golf club in his hand.

"Yeah, but I didn't know why you left," I try to reason with him. "You didn't tell me what was going on. You made it seem like you were done with me and wanted a summer of freedom."

I reach behind me and find Wilder's hand. It's clammy and hot. I hold onto it, reassuring him that I'm not going anywhere.

"Move out of the way, Ingrid," Cash raises his eyebrows. I know he wants to hit Wilder, but I'm not going to let him.

"No," I stand firm.

"Get out of the way," he tries again.

"You're not punching him," I lick my lips nervously. "He didn't do anything wrong. It was me. All me. I pursued him. I-I talked him into doing—"

"*He's Wilder*," Cash angrily interjects. "You can't force him to do something he doesn't want to do. I saw that video. Or some of it. *I saw*. You didn't hold him down and force him to fuck you."

I glance around as a few passersby notice our tense exchange. "No, but I didn't give up. I didn't stop until I got what I wanted. And I wanted him."

It's not exactly what happened, but Cash doesn't need to know that. If I can somehow salvage Wilder and Cash's friendship, I'm going to. Whatever Cash and I had, it's over *for good* now. Cash can barely even look at me. But Wilder and Cash have a history that's long and deep-rooted. I'm not worth giving that up over. Am I?

"Get out of the way, Ingrid," Cash warns.

I shake my head. "You can get in your truck and go home. I'm not moving."

"I don't have a home," Cash says, exasperated. "I have nowhere to go. Not now. So, move out of the way and let me give him what he deserves."

"No," I lift my chin, fighting against years of giving in when Cash demanded I do so. "I'm not moving. Stop telling me to."

"You weren't like this before him," Cash exhales as he tosses an annoyed hand at me. "You didn't treat me like this before you let him—"

"I wasn't like this before *you left me*," I clarify.

Cash nods. "You can hate me all you want for leaving, but he knows how much I love you. He knows I'd never leave unless I had to. Ask him!"

I can tell Cash is grasping at straws. At anything that might get me to move. But I don't. I stay rooted in place, protecting Wilder. After all the people who have stepped to the side and knocked Wilder down when he didn't deserve it, I'm not moving.

"Blondie," Wilder mutters behind me as his fingers tighten around mine.

"I'm not moving," I say to Wilder as I glare at Cash.

"You know what?" Cash throws his arms up. "You two can have each other. I'm done. I gave up everything for you, Ingrid. And Wild? All those years I helped you when no one else would. What a waste. You've both been the biggest waste of my time."

Cash angrily walks away as I let out the breath I was holding.

"I... I..." Wilder stumbles over his words.

I turn to face him, our fingers still interlocked. "I'm sorry. I shouldn't have handed him my phone. I forgot the video was on there."

The color slowly returns to Wilder's face. "He's never going to forgive me."

"He will," I try. "In time, he will forgive you."

"You don't know Cash then," Wilder pulls his hand out of mine. "He's not forgiving. Not like you."

"I love you," I say as I feel tears filling my eyes. "And so does Cash. When you love someone, you forgive them."

Wilder hangs his dark head. "I don't think you understand what we've done, Ingrid."

"I love you," I repeat. "I haven't done anything wrong. *We* haven't done anything wrong."

His strong hands cup my face. "You're right. You haven't done anything wrong. But I have. I betrayed my best friend."

"He left you," I mumble.

"Everyone leaves me," he sighs with resignation. "But Cash, he came back."

"Did he?" I furrow my brow.

"He did." He chews on his lower lip.

Cash came back, but it was only after he realized what he lost.

I know what I might lose, and I'm not willing to lose him. I'm not willing to lose Wilder.

"I'll call my mom and have her pick us up," I suggest.

Wilder shakes his head. "I think I should find my own way home."

"You live three doors down," I remind him. "It's not like Jill will be going out of her way."

Mom arrives twenty minutes later to pick us up with a large German Shepherd in her front seat. Wilder and I pile in the back as classical music echoes through the car.

"Gerardo likes instrumental tunes," Mom informs us.

"Who's Gerardo?" I ask.

Mom motions to the dog. "The big fella sitting beside me, Ingrid. Duh."

Oh. I don't respond as I glance over at Wilder. He has his forehead pressed to the glass window, his eyes closed.

Hesitantly, I reach out to touch him. He doesn't recoil or react when my fingers run along his arm. But it still feels like rejection.

"Don't let Cash ruin this," I whisper.

He exhales heavily. "It's already ruined. When are you going to accept that?"

"You're saying we have no future?"

"I'm saying," Wilder's eyes open, "stop trying to make this something it's not. I can't be with you. I've told you that from the beginning."

"You also told me you don't," I pause to see if Mom's paying attention. In true Jill Winthrop fashion, she's too worried about Gerardo enjoying himself in her front seat to notice. "You wouldn't fuck Cash's ex, but you did."

"I didn't fuck you," he inhales. "That wasn't what we did."

I want to tell him I love him for the millionth time even though I know he won't say it back. I know I shouldn't. It hurts every time he refuses to say it back. So, instead, I stroke his Blondie tattoo with my thumb, memorizing the sharp, jagged edges of the text and the soft feel of his skin.

"If you want me to leave you alone," I let out a shaky breath, "then I will." *But I don't want to*.

He doesn't respond right away as he sits up straighter and peers over at me. He reaches for my hand, and I feel my chest shake and shudder and stumble. Whatever he says next is either going to make my heart soar or shatter.

"I don't see a way this could work," Wilder reveals. "Either way, you lose. Cash will destroy your name and reputation, along with mine, if we keep doing what we're doing. If we stop, maybe we can convince him not to."

I want to argue and tell him that I spent the last four years living in fear of what everyone would think. Did they think I was pretty enough to be Cash Allred's girlfriend? Did they think I was rich enough? Worthy enough? Smart enough?

I'm tired of living in the Allred's shadow, but Wilder isn't there yet. He's still bound to Cash in ways I'm not. In ways I never have been. I've outgrown whatever it was we had. I've outgrown who I used to be.

"If that's how you feel," I give in, waving a white flag in surrender, "then I understand."

We hold hands as Mom pulls into the driveway and unloads Gerardo to finish their jaunt around the neighborhood. She was mid-walk when she ran home to grab the car and pick us up.

We stay seated in the backseat as the sun disappears behind the trees, knowing the moment one of us opens the car door, what we are—*what we were*—becomes a thing of the past.

Wilder lets my hand go first as a tear falls down my cheek. I know there will be more. Lots more. I'm not going to cry once for Wilder and move on the way I did for Cash.

No, this is going to be an earth-shattering heartbreak. The kind that I'll never get over.

I don't think I'll ever get over Wilder.

Another tear falls. Then another. They keep falling onto my lap and soaking into my shorts.

"I'm sorry," Wilder mutters before he opens the door and gets out.

I know I should get out, too. Maybe ask for a hug or watch him walk home. But I can't move. Can't breathe. Can't feel.

I'm immobilized by pain.

I lay down in the backseat and close my eyes as teardrops cascade down my cheeks, over my ears, and onto the cloth seat. I reach for my phone, my limbs heavy with sorrow, and turn on the thunderstorm app on my phone. The weather understands me better than most people do.

"Ingrid," I hear Isla as the car door opens. "What's going on?"

"Hurt," I tell her.

"What's hurt?" Her eyes frantically search for the wound.

"Here," I point to my chest.

My selfish sister kneels on the concrete driveway and runs her fingers through my hair. "Ing, you have to come inside. If you suffocate in the hot car and die out here, I'll never get over you leaving me alone with Mom and Dad *for a lifetime.*"

"I-Is that s-so?" I hiccup as a fresh wave of tears soaks my face.

"I will find every medium and psychic I can to haunt you into the afterlife," she promises. "We are Winthrop's. We're survivors. Now, get up before I call 911 and have you committed."

I slowly push myself up and feel my head sway from side to side.

"Isla?" I wipe the tears off my face.

"Yeah?"

"When you get your heart broken next time, do you want me to tell you all the things you just said to me?"

My older sister smiles. "You better."

She drapes a dramatic arm over my shoulder and steers me in the direction of the house. I'm not sure what tomorrow will look like, but Isla's right. I'm a Winthrop. And like my sister, no matter how many times I'm knocked down, I'm still going to stand back up and fight.

I just have to figure out how to fight for Wilder without him knowing.

Chapter 31
The Awkward Conversation

I drum my fingertips on the desk, the afternoon light streaming in through the glass window and shimmering across the tiled floor of Loretta's Laser Hair and Wax Removal. It's been quiet today. Guess everyone is slowing down on their summer waxing plans and preparing for the impending cold around the corner. *Autumn*. The subtle reminder that everything changes—even the leaves.

I've changed, too.

Before the summer started, I thought I knew what I wanted. A life with Cash Allred. Country club dinners and fancy chandeliers hanging over an exquisitely decorated dining room table. Vacations in Aspen, Cancun, and Jackson Hole. Children with Cash's blue eyes. Christmas pictures in the snow. A life pretending everything was perfect. A shallow life. Not one that would have made me happy.

But then I spent the summer with Wilder, and I fell in love with how he made me feel. I fell in love with all the fun we had. With just being me. No pretending. No wondering if I was saying the wrong thing or thinking the wrong thing. For once, I just got to be me.

There's no comparison. One summer with Wilder is better than a lifetime of summers with Cash.

"Why are you frowning?" Pierre *tsks* me as he strolls into the room looking bored.

"I look pitiful, don't I?" I groan.

"What happened?"

"Wilder broke up with me, I guess." I'm not sure how else to explain it. He didn't really dump me because we never put a label on what we were.

Whatever label-less thing we were doing is over now.

"You've gotten dumped twice this summer," Pierre notes. "Kind of seems like the common denominator here is *you*."

"I'm aware," I roll my eyes. I'm also aware that both of these so-called break ups didn't have anything to do with me. I mean, of course, they did. But they had more to do with Cash's blackmailing parents and Wilder's loyalty to Cash.

"You want some advice?" Pierre offers with a flick of his wrist.

"I'd rather not—"

"The summer before last," he interrupts. "I was dating Yani Habid. He was gorgeous. Dark, luscious hair, tanned muscles, and an enormous—"

"Please don't finish that sentence," I hold up a hand.

"Anyway," Pierre continues, "his parents found out about us and forced him to end things."

"I'm sorry, Pierre. That's horrible."

"I wasn't too heartbroken over it," he clarifies. "I liked him, but Yani was afraid to be who he really was. He's engaged now to a New York socialite, Luna Lawrence. He has one life and he's going to waste it trying to make his parents happy. It's a shame."

"Is this the advice?"

"No," Pierre stares at his nails. "First, you chose the wrong person at the right time. Then, you chose the right person at the wrong time. You're doing everything backward."

"Like Yani did?" I try to connect the dots.

"Yani keeps choosing the wrong people at the wrong time."

I run a hand over my face, annoyed. "I'm not getting your point."

"The point is that we're all trying to figure out who's best for us while living under a microscope. You're allowed to mess up, Ingrid. You're allowed to get your heart broken and figure out who you are. Yani is going to learn that lesson too late in life. But you? You have a chance to do it now. So, ignore the microscope."

"I don't want to be Yani."

"Me neither," Pierre winks.

"What if I never figure it out?"

"What if you do?"

"I thought I had."

"Did you?"

I exhale heavily. "You're giving me a headache."

"This town is a worn-out microscope, but you are not Yani Habib. You're Ingrid Winthrop, and you're going to be talked about, put down, and pressured into things because that's what small towns do. They force you to conform. You don't have to, though. You can choose to figure out what's best for you without worrying about what everyone thinks."

"I don't worry about what everyone thinks," I raise my eyebrows. "But Wilder does."

"He's been through a lot," Pierre reminds me. "Lots of gossip over the years. Maybe he's tired of it."

"Maybe he is."

Maybe he's tired of being the screw-up. The odd man out. The guy trying to find himself in a town that lets the rumor mill run rampant.

"Thanks, Pierre," I say as I stand and grab my purse.

"Where are you going?" he whips his head back. "You're not off the clock for another half hour."

"I have to go talk to the microscope."

"Ah," Pierre grins. "You get it now."

I rush out the door, hoping I'm not too late to make things right.

Because Pierre is right.

This town might try to tear me apart, but they won't be able to if I don't let them.

The faded red paint on the wood door brings back a plethora of memories. I raise a steady hand and firmly knock on the wood. It swings open with a vengeance as Fanny Allred and her plastic nose come into view.

"Ingrid," she smirks. "Back so soon?"

"I'm here to see Cash," I tell her.

"He doesn't live here anymore," Fanny stares down at me over the bridge of her upturned nostrils.

I glance at the driveway. "Then why is his truck here?"

Fanny blinks slowly. "What do you want?"

"I want to speak with Cash," I tell her. "And after all you've put my family through, the least you can do is step aside so I can."

"I don't want you anywhere near him," she narrows her beady eyes at me.

"I'm not getting back together with him," I explain. "I just need to talk to him. It's important."

"Mom?" I hear Cash's heavy footsteps.

I maneuver around Fanny and greet Cash with an awkward wave. "Can we talk?"

Cash crosses his arms over his chest. "I told you we were done."

"I know," I tug at my fingers. "I still need to talk to you, though."

"Cash, dear," Fanny glides across the floor. "You have that golf lesson in twenty minutes. You can't be late for that. Not if you're planning on re-applying for Johns Hopkins."

"Two minutes," he says as he holds up two fingers. "Then I have to go."

I head toward the driveway with Cash following behind me. When we're out of earshot, I frown. "I thought you didn't want to go to Johns Hopkins anymore."

He raises his blond eyebrows. "I don't."

"Then why did she—"

"It's not your problem anymore, Ingrid. What do you need to say to me?" Cash cuts me off.

"It's about Wilder," I lick my lips nervously.

"What about him?"

"He's your best friend, Cash. You can't ruin a lifelong friendship over a summer fling."

The words physically hurt as they leave my mouth. Wilder is so much more than a summer fling, but if I'm going to fight for him, then I have to try to fix what he thinks is beyond repair.

"Doesn't matter," Cash scoffs. "He had sex with you."

"Why didn't we have sex very often during the last few months of our relationship?" I tap my foot restlessly.

"What?"

"We used to have sex all the time," I recount. "Any time you could get me naked, you would. But the last two and a half months before you went to Europe, you barely gave me the time of day."

"I told you already," he fidgets with the hem of his polo, "my mom was blackmailing me."

"Yeah, but most people rebel when their parents don't like their partner. Why didn't you?"

Cash shrugs. "I'm tired."

"Of?"

"Always doing the wrong thing in their eyes," he answers. "I was tired. Tired of the nagging and the endless threats. Tired of trying to be a good boyfriend knowing I was pissing my mom off every time we hung out. Why do you think I brought Wilder with us everywhere? If I was hanging out with Wilder, she couldn't bitch at me."

I'm not letting him off the hook, but this explains so much now.

"You could have talked to us," I offer.

"And say what? My mom hates you, Ingrid, and she only lets me hang out with Wilder because he's her charity case. Do you know how many times she used Wilder to make herself look good?"

"We were your friends," I counter. "You could have trusted us."

"I could have," Cash gives in. "But I didn't want anyone to hate me."

"We wouldn't have," I reassure him.

"Why him?" Cash furrows his brow.

I rub my arm, trying to comfort myself. I didn't show up here to have a heart-to-heart about why our relationship ended and why I fell into bed with Wilder. I came here to fix what I helped break.

"It just happened," I honestly answer. "We were both sad you left us for the summer. You didn't even say goodbye to Wilder. You were a shitty friend, Cash. We decided to make a bucket list and do all the items on it before the summer ended. I suppose... I suppose we realized we had more in common than just you."

"I'm pissed, Ingrid."

"I know," I inhale sharply. "But it doesn't have to end your friendship."

"It does," Cash scoffs. "It does."

"When you needed a place to crash, Wilder didn't hesitate to share his room with you."

"Oh, wow, one time," Cash blows out a breath of hot air.

"Junior year, you accidentally got drunk at that birthday party we went to at Craig Drummond's house. Wilder covered for you and sobered you up in time for church the next morning. Sophomore year, when you were failing math, Wilder spent every night for two months tutoring you. You passed Algebra with a B+. You guys have been there for each other through every high and low. I'm not worth throwing that away on."

"No, you are not," Cash agrees. "But it's the loyalty part I can't get over."

"He chose you," I whisper. "When I begged him to choose me, he chose you. He ended things. We're over. He doesn't want anything to do with me." I place a hand on my heart, willing the tears forming in my eyes not to fall down my face. "He chose you knowing you were done with him."

"Is that supposed to make me feel better?"

"I'm not sure," I shrug. "But his loyalty isn't the problem. It's the fact that you had something, and you think he took it without asking."

"You will never understand," he mutters as he shakes his head.

"Then explain it to me," I challenge.

"I thought I was making a big, sacrificial decision. I knew it was going to be hard, but I figured you'd spend the summer missing me and waiting for me. When you didn't, it was... it hurt. You moved on so fast, Ingrid. You moved on with Wilder in record time."

"I know," I run a hand over my face. "I'm sorry."

"I wasn't blind, you know?" Cash forces a smile. "I heard all the fights, and I witnessed all those intense staring contests you two had. But I never thought you'd move on so fast."

"You left me," I reiterate. "Before that, you ignored me, barely acknowledging my existence. And every time we went somewhere, Wilder went with us. We... we weren't in a relationship those last few months. It didn't feel like it. So, I did move on. Not because I didn't love you but because I had already grieved all the good parts of our relationship."

"I never meant to hurt you," he clicks his tongue as he sways back and forth.

"But you did."

"I'm sorry," he apologizes. "I thought I was doing the right thing."

"We live under a microscope," I say. "One that's hard to get out from under. You know that better than anyone."

"I'm not going to Johns Hopkins," he reveals.

"Then why does your mom think you are?"

"Because I have proof she embezzled money from your dad's company," he grins. "And I'm going to make sure she pays for everything she's done to you over the past four years."

"You h-have proof?"

"We're having a dinner party tomorrow night. Would you like to come as my date?" My face flashes with worry before Cash adds, "*Platonically*. Just as friends."

"And prove that your mom framed my dad?"

"Yep," Cash sinks his top teeth into his bottom lip.

"Then, I'll be there."

"Cash, dear!" Fanny sings from the front porch. "Time for that golf lesson."

Cash takes a step back. "I'll pick you up at six tomorrow night."

"I'll be ready," I promise as I watch him jog over to his truck.

When he opens the door, he glances back at me and gives me one of his famously breathtaking Cash Allred smiles. As I watch him go, I realize that this is the first honest conversation we've had in four years.

Chapter 32
The Dinner Disaster

I'm standing on the front lawn, my black, body-hugging dress clinging to my thighs the same way my heart is still clinging to the hope that Wilder will realize he's making a mistake. I keep glancing down the street, hoping he'll appear like he used to. I don't want to bother him, but I miss him. And this gaping hole he left in my heart is refusing to heal. I think it's getting bigger and bigger as the hours wear on.

Missing Wilder Cox is like trying to breathe while underwater. My lungs are screaming for air, but I keep sinking closer to the sandy lake floor, praying that someone throws me a life jacket.

Cash's truck appears down the road, and I take a sobering breath. I can't think about Wilder right now. Right now, I have to focus on proving Fanny Allred is nothing more than a gossiping menace to our small-town society. Then, maybe I can salvage the Winthrop reputation and convince Cash to give Wilder a second chance. The lifelong besties need to be reunited and maybe Cash can crash at Wilder's again.

It's just that doing all of this—saving reputations and friendships—doesn't get me

Wilder back. If anything, it'll just push him farther away. I still want to do it, though. Wilder depends on Cash's friendship. It's the one constant in his ever-changing world. I want him to have that back. But I was a constant, too. I was always there. I was always around. Doesn't matter. He's made it clear he's not interested in letting me be there for him.

Maybe someday.

Cash rolls the truck window down and waves as I take several steps forward. Once I get in that truck, I know everything that happens after tonight will be a domino effect. If Fanny goes tumbling down, then a lot of us will follow. But I'm willing to scrape my knees and elbows to make sure she can't hurt anyone else the way she's hurt me and the people I love.

"You look nice," Cash offers as I buckle my seat belt.

"So do you," I give him a small smile. He looks great in a navy button-down and khaki pants. "Do you ever think about wearing something other than khaki?" I never would have asked him that question a few months ago, but things are different now.

Cash chuckles. "I would like to, but the country club has a strict dress code."

"I know," I sigh as I think back to dinner with Wilder. The dinner where we uncovered Archibald Allred and Clementine Church's affair. "Can I ask you a question about your dad?"

He nods his blond head. "Sure."

"Do you know about his affair with Clementine?"

Cash's fingers grip the steering wheel so tight his knuckles turn white. "Yes."

"Do you know how long it's been going on for?"

"Four years," he exhales.

"Oh."

"I found out around the time we started dating."

"You should have told me," I purse my lips.

"I should have told you a lot of things, Ingrid," he sighs, "but my parents like secrets."

"I've noticed."

"My dad pays for Clementine's house around the corner," Cash reveals, "and he spends most nights there after dinner with my mom."

"That sounds awful, Cash," I reach out a hand and gently pat his forearm.

Cash's blue eyes land on my fingertips. "It's not so bad."

"Believe it or not," I look over at him, "I do understand why you ran away to Europe for the summer. If I had been in your shoes, I probably would have done the same thing."

"You're not mad at me?"

Mad? No. I mean, would I have fallen *madly* in love with Wilder if Cash hadn't left? Probably not. I'd be stuck where I was two months ago; trying to figure out a way to maintain a long-distance relationship with Cash. I am annoyed, though. Annoyed that he left without telling us the truth and returned expecting things would be just as he left them.

"I think the way you left was really shitty. I also think the way you came back was just as shitty. And how you're treating Wilder, that's also—"

"Shitty," Cash finishes. "I've got it."

"You can be mad about what happened," I tell him, "but I'm not apologizing. I'm not sorry I spent the summer with Wilder."

I gaze out the window. It hurts to say his name. Hurts to remember not that long ago, we were blissfully swimming in the creek as the day was coming to an end.

I want to go back. Why can't I go back?

"I still love you," Cash mumbles barely loud enough for me to hear.

Frustrated, I cross my arms over my chest. "What do you want me to say to that?"

"Nothing," Cash replies. "I just wanted you to know."

"Okay."

After our exchange, there's a lull in conversation. I don't speak, and neither does Cash. In a way, it feels like old times. Back before he left for Europe. There were so many quiet car rides. *Years* of quiet car rides. Rides where I'd wonder if this was normal—the deafening silence.

With Wilder, there was never any awkward silence. There was just him and me. Two people with the same wound who never ran out of things to say to one another.

God, I miss him.

The Allred mansion is decorated in deceptive bright lights as we pull into the driveway. It's surreal to think I used to walk into that house believing Archibald and Fanny had a great marriage. That they were superior to the rest of us because they'd managed to build a life of luxury. But they didn't. Instead, they built a home full of loneliness and decided to hide it from the world.

"You ready?" Cash holds out a hand.

I close my eyes and give myself a moment to tap into Old Ingrid. The one who always put a smile on her face, convinced being Cash Allred's girlfriend was a privilege she didn't deserve.

"Ready," I smile wide.

Holding Cash's hand isn't as uncomfortable as I thought it might be. My heart doesn't flutter as his thumb rubs the back of my hand. It doesn't excite me. Honestly, I don't want to be holding Cash's hand, but I can't think about that right now. I have to focus on tonight. Getting the job done, then moving on with the rest of my life.

There's a group in the sitting room as a local artist plays the harp and bubbly champagne is passed around. Familiar faces whisper to each other after noticing our late arrival. Cash grabs a glass flute and takes a long sip.

He offers it to me, but I shake my head. "I'm good."

Cash squeezes my hand as Archibald and Fanny enter the room. Fanny giggles and points to Archibald's crooked bowtie. She adjusts it as his hand slowly finds her backside and he pats it playfully. *An act.* One they've perfected over the years. Just like I had. Before Wilder showed me what life outside of the deceptively bright Allred mansion looks like.

"We're so glad you could join us," Fanny beams as she's handed a glass of champagne. She scans the room, her eyes taking in the twenty or so of us spread out in her floral-decorated sitting area. When her gaze lands on me, anger flashes across her face before she subtly elbows Archibald, who immediately notices Cash's hand tangled in mine.

"Dinner will be served soon," Archibald announces as he narrows his eyes at me. "Why don't we all make our way into the dining room."

I swallow hard, willing myself not to lose my nerve.

"Ingrid," I hear Cash to my right. I look over at him. "Look at me. Don't look at them."

A small part of my heart throbs at his words. I needed to hear those words so many times when we were together. Why is he saying them now? Now, when they mean nothing.

"Cash, dear," Fanny calls out to her son.

He ignores her as his free hand raises to my face and he slowly slides a curl behind my left ear. "Just keep looking at me, okay?"

I do, my breathing evening out as Cash's blue eyes glow with an emotion I'm not sure I'll ever return again.

"Cash," Fanny interrupts our weird moment.

His eyes slide to his mother. "What?"

"You didn't tell me you invited Ingrid."

"I told you I had a plus one."

"I assumed," she gives me a forced smile, "you meant someone else."

His arms slip around my waist. "We're working things out."

"*Wonderful*," she says before walking toward the dining room. "You two coming?"

Cash licks his lips. "Uh, we'll be there in a minute."

It's *go* time. That was a sign to let me know Cash is ready to steal proof that Fanny Allred is an embezzling blackmailer.

He tugs me in the direction of the stairs as Fanny stomps an agitated heel against the marble flooring.

Cash leads the way, one step ahead of me. It feels strange to be rushing up the stairs the same way we used to when we were younger. Except stripping our clothes off and falling into his bed with our limbs tangled isn't what we're about to do. It's just a cover. One Cash brilliantly came up with.

"Guard the door," Cash warns as we sneak into his father's office. The one Fanny uses because Archibald prefers his spacious setup over at Clementine's.

I peek out the sliver in the doorframe as Cash sits down at the computer. I hear him typing away as my heart pounds restlessly against my ribcage, the darkness eerie and excruciating.

"I found it!" Cash whisper-yells across the room to me.

A wave of relief washes over me as I glance over my shoulder. The glow from the computer screen lights up Cash's determined face.

"Just gotta save it all to a flash drive and we can get out of here," he continues.

But I hear footsteps and my heart freezes in my chest. I can't make out who is walking down the dark hallway, so I hurry over to Cash. *Someone's coming* I mouth at him as his eyes widen.

In a split second, he turns off the monitor and pushes me up against the desk, his fingers tangling with my hair.

"Sell it, Ingrid," he says in my ear before his lips crash against mine and I instinctively snake my arms around his neck.

Cash's heart pounds against my chest as we kiss, and his hand inches up my thigh. Not far enough to be considered inappropriate but sordid enough to sell our fake cover.

I ignore my heart as it screams at me, telling me to stop this madness. I can't stop. I can't stop kissing Cash if it means freedom. Freedom for all of us.

If Archibald or Fanny finds us up here stealing information, the truth will never see the light of day.

So, I keep kissing Cash until the door creaks open and someone flicks on the light. As my eyes adjust to the brightness, the one person I never expected to see at the Allred Mansion stares back at me.

Wilder.

Chapter 33
The Compromised Cover

I can't tell if he's hiding how he feels or if he's *not* all that surprised to see Cash and I entangled on the office desk. Wilder has always been hard to read. Even harder now that he's standing in front of us, his face stoic and bored.

"Hey," Cash lets go of me. "What are you doing here?"

I wipe Cash's slobber off my mouth as my face turns red. I'm embarrassed and frustrated. Why is Wilder here? Why did he have to be the one to walk in on us? Out of all the people in the world, why did the one boy I'm in love with have to catch me in a compromising position with my ex-boyfriend and his former best friend?

"I needed to talk to you," Wilder answers, his voice steady. "You haven't answered my phone calls. I guess you've been... *busy*."

Cash's eyes dart to me for a split second. "This isn't what you think, Wild. We're, uh, can you... it's not what it looks like."

Grateful Cash is trying to tell the truth, I reach over and turn the monitor back on. The files are still saving to the flash drive.

"Come here," Cash says as he motions to the computer screen.

"I thought you were Fanny," I whisper to Wilder. "I wouldn't have—"

"Don't worry about it, Blondie."

Blondie. We're back to that. Good to know.

"I just need to finish saving these files," Cash tells Wilder, "then we can head over to the police department."

Wilder scrunches his face. "Why?"

"I'll explain in the car," Cash answers before looking at me. "Ingrid, can you keep watch?"

I nod and scurry around Wilder, happy to put distance between me and the boys. The hall remains empty as Cash keeps the conversation going.

"How did you know we were in here?" he asks Wilder.

"Your mom said you were up here," Wilder answers. "When you weren't in your room, I started looking around."

"Oh," I hear Cash inhale sharply.

"Why?"

"Just wondering if my mom planned this whole thing."

"What thing?"

"The *you-seeing-me-with-Ingrid* thing," Cash replies.

"She didn't mention Blondie when she answered the door," Wilder explains.

No one speaks after that, but I can feel the tension oozing from every corner of the room. Tension so thick that I feel like I'm suffocating.

"It's done," Cash finally speaks after an excruciatingly long five minutes. "Let's go."

The hallway is still clear when we leave the office behind, turning off the light and shutting the door quietly behind us. Cash and Wilder walk ahead of me, and I feel like the third wheel.

Sometimes, I wonder if that's all I ever was. The third wheel in Cash and Wilder's friendship.

As we're descending the stairs, Fanny's livid face halts us in our tracks. "Where have you been?"

Cash peers over his shoulder at me. "Ingrid isn't feeling well. We're going to take her home."

"Wilder can take her," Fanny flashes her eyebrows up at her son. Even though she's a whole foot shorter, she seems to stand taller than Cash. "If you want to stay in this house, we will be a united front. And you will march in there and enjoy dinner with all our guests."

The back of Cash's neck visibly tenses. He fishes his truck keys out of his pocket before handing them over to Wilder. "Drop her off then come back? We still need to have that talk."

Wilder nods before grabbing my elbow and leading me to the front door. I can feel Fanny's searing gaze on my back as we step over the threshold.

The warm August night is a nice change from the Allred mansion chill.

I open the passenger door to Cash's truck when we reach it and climb inside. I watch out of the corner of my eye as Wilder runs a hand over his face before he gets in.

"It's not what you think," I rush to get out. "It was just a cover. Cash and I are not getting back together."

"Doesn't matter if you are," Wilder shrugs before turning on the ignition. "Not my business."

"We're not," I reassure him, my hand reaching across the center console to touch him.

He recoils in protest, and I feel more of my already broken heart ripping apart as I pull my arm back to my lap. Eventually, all those tiny rips will morph into one cataclysmic tear, and I don't know if I'll ever be the same again.

"You don't have to believe me," I manage to get out, "but it's the truth."

"You two looked pretty cozy," Wilder snarkily replies. "His hand was so far up your dress, I couldn't tell where your thigh began and his arm ended."

My throat burns. "I promise you it was not what it looked like."

"Actions," Wilder smirks, "speak louder than words, Blondie."

"I love you," I remind him. "I don't want anyone but you."

"You have a funny way of showing it," Wilder scoffs.

"We stole proof that Fanny framed my dad," I try explaining. "We needed a cover in case Fanny or Archibald caught us. One that was believable."

"Like I said, it's none of my business," Wilder dismisses me as he backs out of the Allred's driveway.

"You're pissed right now," I take a sobering breath. "One day, though, you're not going to be. And when you're done being angry, you're going to see that everything I've been doing over the past few days is for you."

"No," Wilder chuckles cruelly. "It's for you. For your family. Not for me."

"You miss Cash," I say quietly. "I know you do. I figured if I helped him, maybe I could help him see that you aren't the bad guy here. I am."

"Why are you the bad guy?" he humors me.

"Because I seduced you, of course," I smile sadly, remembering how good it felt to lay in his arms.

"No one sees it that way except for you," he shakes his head.

"If Cash hadn't come back, would you have kept seeing me? Kept sleeping with me? Kept going places with me? Kept having dinner with me?"

Wilder scratches the back of his neck. "Probably, but it doesn't matter now. Cash is back, and he's staying. For good."

"I miss you," I twist in my seat to look at him. "I miss you so much I can barely breathe. Do you miss me the same way?"

Wilder stares straight ahead. "You have to stop saying shit like that to me."

"I can't help it," I place a hand on my wailing heart.

"It makes things harder, Blondie."

"Harder for you?"

"*For you.*"

"I don't understand why you're being this way," I drop my head into my hands. I have to stop doing this. Have to stop begging him to be with me. What's that saying everyone keeps blasting on TikTok? If he wanted to, he would.

He doesn't want to be with you, Ingrid. Let him go. Move on.

"There's never been a future for us that would make you happy," he deals what feels like the final blow. The final fissure that splits my heart in two. "I can't love you the way you want me to. I don't even know if I want to get married or have kids."

My body shakes as the break reverberates through my body. "I don't know what I want, Wilder. I'm only 18. I don't have my future planned out. I just..."

"You just what?"

"I guess," I hitch a shoulder, "I thought we could figure things out together."

He doesn't respond as I lick my lips, my heart aching like a broken bone.

I know I'm beating a dead horse. I know he's just going to keep putting up walls. I know fighting for him is a losing battle. I know all of this, but I still want him.

I want all of Wilder. The good parts of him. His loyalty and his strength. And the bad parts. Like the cold, aloof version I'm getting right now.

There's nothing more I can say. Nothing more I can do. I keep baring my heart and soul and he keeps rejecting me.

Cash rejected me and I cried for a minute, then moved on.

I can't move on this time. Why can't I move on?

"Can I tell you something?" Wilder interrupts the heartbreaking silence.

"Yeah, of course."

"I have a rough past," he frowns as an oncoming car's headlights dash across his face. "I come with baggage. Baggage I haven't looked through. Baggage that's made it hard to let people in. The example my father set is a terrible one. When things get too hard, choose the second family you made and leave the first one. That's what he taught me. I have a rough past, Ingrid. I can't drag you into that."

"Your dad isn't the only one who's set an example for you," I raise an eyebrow. "Look at your grandpa. He welcomed you into his home with open arms. He's taken care of your mom, you, and your grandma for years. He's spent his weekends doing yard work with you and taking your mom to work. Or you to work. He's always been there for you. Your dad isn't the only example, Wilder. He's just one. A shitty one at that. You have another example. You're not broken beyond repair. We all have baggage. I'm not afraid of yours."

He parks alongside the curb in front of my house and peers over at me. "It's complicated."

"Everything is complicated," I swallow hard. "I won't keep asking you to choose me. I know you won't. I just want you to know even though you chose Cash instead of me, I still love you. I still want you. I still want all the baggage and all the examples that have been set for you."

"Ingrid," he exhales.

"I won't keep begging you to want me, Wilder," I grab his hand and hold onto it, melting against the way his calloused palm feels like home against my skin.

"I..." he trails off.

"I admire your loyalty to your friendship with Cash," I play with his fingers, wishing I could hold on forever. "But sometimes, we outgrow our friends. Or maybe they outgrow us."

"You don't have any friends," he teases me with a smirk.

"I had you," I sigh. "Now, I have no one."

"I'm sorry," Wilder mutters. "I didn't realize..."

"It's okay," I assure him. "I'm not like all the other people in your life. There aren't any conditions attached to my feelings for you. I'm not expecting anything in return. You don't have to prove to me that you're worthy of me. You don't have to give up all the things that make you happy for me. I'm not your dad, and I'm not Cash."

Wilder inhales sharply. "You say that now. But when I disappoint you enough times, there will be conditions. You'll stop loving me like everyone else."

"There's only one way to find out," I chew on the inside of my cheek.

We stare at each other, my heart yearning to be closer to him.

"You should go," Wilder urges. "I need to get back to Cash."

I nod. "If you ever need me, I'm only three doors down. I'm not going anywhere."

He holds my hand tighter before letting my fingers fall through his. I get out of the truck and wonder if there will ever be a day that Wilder Cox lets himself have the things he longs for.

Chapter 34
The Toxic Mentality

Wilder

I watch her walk up the dark stone pathway to her house, my stomach in knots. I don't know what to do. Walking in on Cash and Ingrid sucking face was brutal. I'm not sure what I expected, but it hit me like a ton of bricks. Heavy, heart-crushing bricks. I want her. I've always wanted her. And she was mine for a little while. Pushing her away feels like punishment.

I miss you. I miss you so much I can barely breathe. Do you miss me the same way?

I guess I thought we could figure things out together.

We all have baggage. I'm not afraid of yours.

I still want you.

I'm not like all the other people in your life. There aren't any conditions attached to my feelings for you. I'm not expecting anything in return. You don't have to prove to me that you're worthy of me. You don't have to give up all the things that make you happy for me.

No one's ever said those things to me before. No one's ever told me they've loved me as many times as Ingrid has. Not even my mom. Truth is, no one's ever loved me the way Ingrid loves me.

I know I should leave her alone. Especially after the image of Cash sliding his hand up her thigh has burned itself into my retinas. But I don't want to.

I can keep pushing her away, and eventually, she's going to stop coming back. I'm not sure that's what I want. I know what I don't want, though. I don't want to watch her walk away from me anymore wondering if she might come back.

It's toxic, this mentality.

My fingers grip the truck door handle and I make a run for it. She's stepping on the front porch when I reach her, and I grab her shoulder, spinning her around in surprise.

Her forehead furrows as I take a deep breath. "I love you, too."

Ingrid's brown eyes grow impossibly large as she stares up at me. "What?"

"I love you," I say, watching as her face softens. "Really?"

"Really," I frown. "I should have said it sooner. I'm sorry I didn't. I... I thought I'd lose my best friend if I let myself love you."

"You haven't lost him yet," she smiles as she wraps her arms around my neck.

"Cash isn't my best friend," I reply as I run my fingers through her hair. "You are."

She melts against me like snow on a warm winter day. "You don't mean that."

I do, actually. Instead of arguing with her, I bend down and kiss her. She moans against my mouth as my hands find her backside and I pull her closer. She smells like honey and cinnamon.

My lips move against hers as my lungs fill with air for the first time in days. I didn't realize how much I needed her before now. She's oxygen. The only thing keeping me alive.

"I missed you," she says when she breaks the kiss and presses her forehead to mine.

"I missed you more," I tell her.

"Come upstairs," she raises a hopeful eyebrow. "I know you have to get back to Cash, but—"

"Cash can wait," I interrupt as she grabs my hand and tugs me onto the porch.

I don't hesitate as she pushes the front door open and waves to her parents. Jason and Jill are parked on the couch, fast food takeout containers and a six-pack of beer spread across the coffee table in front of them.

"Hi Wilder," Jill gives me a small wave. "Glad you used the front door this time."

Ingrid groans dramatically. "Mom, be cool."

"I am cool," Jill takes a sip of the beer bottle in her hand. "I am the coolest."

"Jill," Jason chastises her. "Let the kids have their fun."

Fun. I used to think Ingrid and I were just having fun. I didn't realize while we were, I was falling in love with her.

Ingrid slams her bedroom door shut behind us and wraps her hands around the front of my shirt.

"You're sure you love me?" she smiles.

I nod my head. "I'm sure."

"Then strip," she instructs as she shimmies the black dress material up her hips. "Start with your shirt."

"Shouldn't we lock the door?" Wilder throws a thumb over his shoulder. "Just in case."

"Jason and Jill know not to bother us," she hums. "Shirt. Off. Now."

I laugh as I pull it over my head and throw it behind me. Ingrid slides the body-hugging black dress over her head as a wave of jealousy washes over me.

"What?" Ingrid notices the apprehension on my face.

"Sorry," I shake it off. "I'm just trying to get the image of Cash and you out of my head."

Ingrid's face falls. "I-I wasn't thinking when Cash suggested we use our past as a cover. I never would have agreed to it if I knew we'd end up kissing on that desk."

"I know," I snake my arms around her bare waist. "I just... it bothered me."

She tilts her blond head to the side. "Why?"

"Because I don't want you to kiss anyone else," I admit. "I only want you to kiss me."

"Good," she exhales heavily, "because I don't want to kiss anyone else either."

Ingrid unbuttons my jeans and sinks to her knees, slipping my pants down my legs. She smiles up at me as she wraps a hand around my hard dick and licks the tip, massaging my balls before she greedily takes me into her mouth. I watch as she sucks and licks and moans against my cock, leaving me aching for release.

"I want to come inside you," I tell her as my fingers find her chin. "Stand up."

My dick pops out of her mouth, and she uses a finger to wipe the saliva off the corner of her lips.

"Get on the bed, Ingrid."

She obeys and spreads her legs apart, her pink, swollen slit soaked. "I've missed you, Wilder."

"I've missed you, too," I sigh as I climb onto her bed and cup one of her breasts in my hand. "I'm sorry."

"It's okay."

It's not, but I'm going to make it up to her. I'll do whatever I have to.

"You are the best fucking thing that's ever happened to me," I proclaim.

She raises her head off the grey comforter and kisses me. "I love you, Wilder."

"I love you, too, Ingrid," I return as I push into her, my heart no longer aching.

"Where have you been?" Cash whisper-yells at me as I step out of his truck feeling incredibly guilty.

"Dropping Blondie off," I remind him. "Like you asked."

We might have had sex three times on her bed with her parents downstairs, too, but it didn't take that long. I was... *excited,* if you know what I mean.

"Did you get lost on your way back?" Cash grumbles as I hand over the keys.

"We need to talk." I shove my hands in my pockets.

"I know," Cash glances nervously over his shoulder. "Can we do it while I drive to the police station?"

"Yeah."

Cash fiddles with the rearview mirror as I buckle my seatbelt. "What did you want to talk about?"

I swallow the fear rising in my chest. "Blondie."

"What about her?" Cash rubs his eyes before backing out of the driveway.

I'm in love with her. I'm going to keep seeing her even though you're back. I understand if you want to punch me in the face.

"You know," Cash continues before I work up the nerve to tell him the truth, "she's not the same girl I left when I went to Europe."

"I guess that's my fault," I say as I scratch the back of my neck.

"I didn't mean it in a bad way," Cash corrects. "I meant that she's different. She's the Ingrid I remember before we started dating. The one who didn't change to make my parents happy. She's... herself again."

Oh.

"I don't know what happened while I was gone," Cash taps his fingers on the steering wheel as he drives, "but she's better without me, isn't she?"

"I think she'd be better without both of us," I honestly answer.

"I don't think so," Cash smirks. "She needs you, Wild. I think she's always needed you."

I've needed her far more than she's needed me.

"I never meant to fall in love with her," I exhale.

"You love her?" Cash repeats.

I rub my temples with my fingers. "Yeah, Cash, I do."

"Does she love you?"

"I think so," I close my eyes and breathe through my nose. Any minute now, he's going to punch me. I peek one eye open and see him deep in thought.

"I've been thinking," Cash leans back in his seat. "I was going to leave. I was going to pack all my stuff and move to Baltimore. Ingrid and I wouldn't have lasted. Not with the distance and our demanding schedules."

"Cash," I furrow my brow, "you don't have to—"

"I'm not saying I've accepted it," he warns. "I'm just saying maybe it would have happened anyway. You and Ingrid might have found each other anyway."

"You don't have to accept it," I tread lightly, "but I'm not going to stop seeing her."

"For what it's worth," Cash's shoulders slump, "I would have loved her better in Baltimore than I loved her here."

"Because your parents wouldn't have been around?"

"Yeah," Cash sighs. "But she would have been miserable either way. When I was in Europe, I sent her a ton of messages. She never replied. She ignored me, and she was fine without me. I was fine, too, Wild. I love Ingrid, but maybe we stayed together because we didn't know there might be something better for us out there."

"You both loved each other," I try.

"You'll take care of her?" he inhales sharply.

"I'll do my best," I promise.

"She doesn't really do well on her own and she doesn't like going places alone. You have to make sure you tell her she's beautiful because Isla has spent years telling her she's not. Her parents mean well, but they don't always know how to make things better for her. A tub of ice cream and a funny movie usually help. And, Wild," Cash pauses for a second, "when she's sad, she likes to cry while listening to the thunderstorm app on her phone. She forgets to turn it on. Make sure you turn it on for her. She'll tell you that the weather understands her better than most people. I'm not sure it's true, but it's what she believes."

I feel something strange tickling my chest. A mix of gratefulness and grief. Grief in choosing Ingrid, I'm losing Cash. Gratitude that he seems to understand, even if it's painful for him.

"I'll remember all that," I take a sobering breath.

"I've messed up," Cash smiles to himself, "but I'm making things right. Mostly for Ingrid. When she talks about me, can you do me a favor?"

"Yeah," I manage to get out.

"Can you let her have the good memories? Don't taint them with the way I left or how terrible I let my mother treat her."

"You're not going anywhere," I swallow hard. "We're still friends. All three of us."

"You guys don't want me to be your friend."

"We do."

"I'll need time, Wild."

"We'll be waiting."

Cash parks in front of the police station. He grips the flash drive in his hand and tosses me his keys. "I'll be here for a while. You mind waiting?"

He sounds nervous asking me for one last favor, but I'm not going anywhere. Not now. Not ever.

"I'll be here."

He gets out of the truck and walks into the police station, glancing over his shoulder at me before disappearing into the building.

Chapter 35
The Last Hurrah

The sun is shining bright as I look over my class schedule. A late August breeze wafts through the front yard, wrapping itself around me. This is my last free weekend before I'm officially a college student. Until Wilder, Cash, and I are all students at the *same* college. At least for this semester.

I'm not sure what happened, but Wilder and Cash seem to have worked out their differences. I wouldn't say they're friends like they used to be, but Cash doesn't act like he hates Wilder anymore. And Wilder doesn't think Cash is going to destroy him.

There's distance. The kind that makes the silence uncomfortable and the underhanded remarks painful.

But like Wilder, Cash has trauma of his own. Trauma that needs to heal. Trauma that can't be fixed with an apology.

"What are you thinking?" Wilder asks as he kisses my bare shoulder.

I turn my head and smile up at him. "I was thinking about healing."

Wilder runs his fingers through my hair. "What about it?"

"I was thinking about Cash," I admit, "and how he's going to have to heal from the mess his parents created."

"Archibald wasn't involved in the framing scheme," Wilder reminds me.

"No," I shake my head, "but with Fanny posting bail, Cash has a long road ahead of him. He turned his mom in. Fanny Allred isn't going to forget that any time soon. And Archibald abandoned his son. Cash told me he moved in with Clementine and hasn't spoken to him much since."

"At least Archibald and Clementine can finally be together," Wilder rolls his hazel eyes.

"What about you?" I turn it around on him. "When are you going to let yourself heal?"

"I'm not sure there's a way to heal what's broken in me," Wilder shrugs.

"You should talk to Elowyn," I encourage him. "I know she's been texting you."

"Right," Wilder scoffs. "I should reply to the half-sister who stole my dad."

"I think you've always been better off without your dad," I tell him. "But having a sister, I mean, it's not so bad."

Even Queen Isla has her moments.

"What do you want to do today?" Wilder asks me.

"I was thinking," I grin, "we could have one last hurrah at the creek before school starts."

"You and me?"

"And maybe Cash?" I scrunch my face.

"He said he needs time, Ingrid," Wilder says gently.

"It would feel weird not to invite him," I raise a hopeful eyebrow. "I can be the one to send the text."

"Cash and I are literally sharing a room right now," Wilder reminds me. "And we have three classes together. We have no space. The creek would be too much."

"Oops," I laugh as I hit send on the text I already drafted to Cash. "I sent it."

"*Ingrid*," Wilder groans.

"He'll probably say *no*," I wave him off.

Cash responds to my *Wanna go to the creek with Wilder and me?* text instantly.

"He said he'll head this way in five minutes," I smile, triumphantly.

Wilder shakes his dark head at me. "You think he's really ready to hang out with us?"

"He hangs out with you every day," I twist to kiss him. "And he keeps me up to date on the Fanny front. The sooner we rip off the Band-Aid, the better."

"He's in a fragile state," Wilder endearingly explains. "I don't want him to—"

"We will make sure he has a good time," I interrupt. "I promise."

"You got a tattoo, too?" Cash crosses his arms over his chest as I toss a bag of towels into the back of my car.

"I did," I answer as I close the trunk.

"You never would have gotten one when you were dating me," Cash challenges.

"That's because your mom would have *crucified* me," I quip.

"Yeah," Cash chuckles, "she probably would have."

"It was a bucket list item," I hold out my wrist to show him the lightning bolt.

"What does it signify?"

I smile as I pull my arm back to my body. "Bottled-up lightning."

"I don't get it," Cash furrows his brow.

"You're not supposed to," I raise my eyebrows. "It's for me. Not for anyone else."

"That's dumb," Cash mutters as Wilder takes the keys from me. We decided it would be best that Wilder drive, Cash sit in the front seat, and I take the back. Less awkwardness that way.

The drive to the creek is quiet until Cash decides to plug his cell phone in and play Smashing Trout.

When Wilder sings along to one of the songs, Cash's mouth drops open. "You know this one?"

Wilder hitches a shoulder. "Blondie forced me to go to a concert this summer. I learned a few songs before we went."

"What did you two *not* do this summer?" Cash gapes at Wilder's profile.

I hide a smile, realizing Wilder and I did more this summer than we bargained for. We got tattoos, went to a concert, dined at the country club, played a round of golf, made an adult film, sent nudes, jumped out of the tree at the creek, snuck into the movie theatre, skinny-dipped at the lake, and fell in love.

"We didn't get to hang out with you," Wilder smartly replies. "I think that's really how we both saw our summer going."

Cash nods slightly.

"Tell us about Europe," I interject. "What was your favorite touristy spot?"

"You guys don't want to hear about—"

"We do," Wilder reaffirms. "Tells us everything."

Cash launches into a play-by-play of his European backpacking trip. He details the conditions of the hostels he stayed in, and the few friends he made along the way, but he fails to tell us which destination was his favorite. It's then that I realize Cash never went to Europe looking for culture or adventure. He was looking for *connection*.

"We're glad you're back," I offer from the back seat.

"You'll never guess what Blondie did at the creek this summer," Wilder winks at me in the rearview mirror.

"She finally went for a swim?" Cash looks over his shoulder, teasing me.

"Nope," I grin. "I jumped out of the tree."

Cash gives me a small smile. "I didn't think you had it in you."

"I didn't either," I answer. "But Wilder knew I could do it."

"Sounds like you've turned over a new leaf," Cash gives me a sad smile.

I don't know what to say after that, so I stay quiet in the back seat.

Wilder parks, and we climb out of my car. The sun is still high in the sky, but the shady oak trees shelter us from the harsh rays of light.

I lay a towel on the rock and make myself comfortable as the boys run and jump into the cold creek water. There's a part of me that's grateful Cash isn't punishing Wilder and me. But there's another part of me that knows he hasn't fully processed it yet. He has so much going on. Fanny is livid with him for turning her in. Archibald is distancing himself from Fanny and Cash because he doesn't want to become embroiled in their drama. Then, there's Wilder and me. I used to think Wilder had it bad, but Cash has problems we never even knew about.

And he's carried most of them alone.

I lay on my stomach, watching as Cash and Wilder cannonball into the creek. It feels like old times but I know we'll never go back to where we were at the beginning of the summer. Life has shifted and altered so much that finding a new normal will take time and patience.

I don't expect Cash to always be willing to spend time with us, but I'm glad he knows we want to. We still want him around, even if it's uncomfortable.

"You look deep in thought," Cash frowns as he grabs a towel from my bag.

"Just thinking about old times."

"Did you always like Wilder?" Cash asks, surprising me. "Or was it more recent that you started having feelings for him?"

I smack my lips together, buying time. "I think a part of me always liked him, but I didn't realize how much until you were gone."

"Did you, uh, think about him when we were together?"

I shake my head. "I thought about strangling him but other than that, no, not really."

"I don't know how to do this."

"Do what?"

"Be friends with Wilder and hang out with you. I still have all these feelings for you. Feelings that aren't going away, even though I'm pissed at you."

"Maybe we just take it one day at a time," I suggest.

"Guess I don't have much of a choice, do I?"

"You want to jump out of the tree?" I stand, changing the subject. We're here to have fun; not dwell on everything that's happened.

Cash glances at the tree branch over the creek. "Looks unsafe."

"It's not," I assure him. "Come on."

I motion to Wilder, and he wades out of the water. "What's up?"

"We're going to jump out of the tree," I inform him. "I'll go first."

"Ingrid," Cash puts out a hand to stop me.

"I'm fine, Cash," I smile. "I'll be fine."

I climb the tree with Wilder right behind me. Cash stays back, watching apprehensively.

The moment I'm standing on the sturdy branch above the water, Cash starts climbing up.

"You going to be okay?" Wilder mutters only loud enough for me to hear.

"I'm safe with you, right?" I hold out a hand and he grabs it.

"Always," Wilder squeezes my fingers.

I jump off the branch, letting out a shrill scream before the cold water covers my head. When I resurface, I see Cash crouched on the branch next to Wilder.

"See?" I yell. "It's fine!"

Wilder jumps next and swims over to me. We both peer up at Cash, who is staring down at the water. He doesn't look like he wants to jump, but he does anyway. He sinks right into the water as I shoot Wilder a triumphant grin.

As soon as Cash's head pops up, Wilder and I whoop and holler.

Cash floats in front of us, a big smile on his face. "That was fun."

"*Told you*," I sing.

"Wanna do it again?" Wilder asks us.

I watch Cash and Wilder race to the shore, knowing I'm stuck with them for life.

Cash and I have never been friends, but I think we'll figure it out. We have to.

Then, there's Wilder.

Wilder Cox has been—and always will be—the third wheel in my relationship with Cash Allred.

Except he's not anymore.

Now, Wilder Cox is mine. And I plan on keeping him forever.

Epilogue

9 months later...

"Wilder," I moan, "I'm going to be late for my astronomy final."

He chuckles against my thigh before planting a sloppy kiss on my balmy skin. His mouth is... *magical*. Wet and wonderful and *wild*. Just like him.

He licks a sultry path through my soaked folds before kissing my lower stomach. Goosebumps raise on my skin as I let my head fall back and close my eyes. Wilder peppers a trail of kisses up my torso before wrapping his mouth around a pebbled nipple and sucking hard. I sigh as his lips move to my neck.

"Wilder," I mumble, his teeth grazing my earlobe.

"*Ingrid*," he coos.

"I'm going to be..." but the words die on my lips as he slides his arm between us, and he positions the tip of his cock at my entrance. Slowly and methodically, he inches himself into me, his tongue running along my scorching skin.

I want him. No, I *need* him. He's like water, and I'm *parched* in the middle of a dry, dusty desert.

His arms slide around my waist, and he tugs me closer to the edge of the bed. My feet hang off as he pummels into me, his breaths shallow and jagged in my ear.

"You still feel amazing," he mutters as he tightens his hold on me. "Even after all this time, you still feel amazing."

I smirk against his shoulder, breathing in his musky scent.

"I love you," he whispers against my skin. The words alone undo me, and I clench around his veiny shaft as my stomach muscles constrict and contract. He follows shortly after, his bare stomach rubbing against mine.

We collapse on my bed, both out of breath.

"That was amazing," he smiles.

"You always say that," I hide my face in his chest.

"That's because it's true," he replies as he kisses the top of my head.

"We've been doing this for a while," I remind him, "you don't have to charm me every time."

"I would never," he laughs as my fingertips draw circles on his toned chest.

"I'm sure you've said that to all the girls," I tease him.

"You jealous?"

I shift to look up at him. "Always."

"I've been thinking," he tries to hide a smile. "We should—"

"Shit," I jump up, cutting him off. "I have my astronomy final in fifteen minutes."

As fast as I can, I grab my clothes off my bedroom floor and put them on as Wilder sits up and watches me.

"Blondie," he calls out to me.

"What?" I ask as I button up my shorts.

"We need to talk," he cryptically states.

"Good talk or bad talk?" I raise an eyebrow as I grab a clip off my dresser and throw my hair into a messy bun.

"Come here."

I am going to be late, but I walk over to him and stand between his legs.

"I love you," he grins as he grabs my left hand and slips something on *that* finger.

I swallow hard before my eyes slide to my hand. There's a white gold band with a tiny diamond heart in the middle.

"What's this?" I hold my breath.

"It's not an engagement ring," he rushes to get out. "I just... I love you. And I know we haven't talked about our future, but I want you to know I see one for us. This," he holds my hand up, "is a reminder that I'm serious about you."

"I already knew that," I tilt my head to the side and run my fingers through his hair. "And I want to talk about this, but I am so late right now."

"Go," he motions with his eyebrows.

I give him a quick peck on the lips before grabbing my bag and racing down the stairs.

I have 12 minutes to get across town, park, and arrive in time to take my final. No pressure or anything.

Cash is sitting on Wilder's front porch as I walk up the concrete pathway after the hardest final of the year.

"Hey," I say to him.

He glances up from his phone. "Hey. How were all your finals?"

"Okay, I think," I say, grimacing. "I felt good about English, math, and history, but astronomy is up in the air."

"Wilder forced me to study all weekend long, so I'm pretty sure I passed everything," he scrunches his nose. "Why is your shirt on backward?"

I groan. "I'm going to kill Wilder."

"I don't want to know details," Cash shakes his head.

"Any updates on your mom's trial?"

"Prosecution wants me to be a witness," he sighs.

"I thought your mom wanted you to be a witness for her," I take a seat beside him.

"In her dreams," he scoffs.

"You should only testify if you want to," I suggest wondering if they can force him to.

"My dad said I should be supporting my mom," Cash shrugs. "I guess he feels if I'm supporting her, then he doesn't have to."

"How's your new baby sister?" I ask.

Cash hitches a shoulder. "She looks just like Clementine."

"You always said you wanted a sibling," I nudge him with my shoulder.

"Not like this," he forces a smile.

"You and Wilder have more in common than I originally thought," I sigh.

"Yeah, but I see my half-sister more than once a year. He doesn't."

"You know what I think?"

"No," Cash runs a hand over his face. "And I don't want to know."

"I think you're too hard on him."

"He stole you from me."

"No," I hold up a hand, "you dumped me. You left me."

"You ever get tired of saying that?"

"No," I grin. "Never."

"You guys have plans tonight?" Cash throws a thumb over his shoulder.

"Yeah," I clear my throat. "We're playing pool. With you."

"I hate when you guys make me tag along."
"Why?"

"Because I hate being the third wheel."

"Get used to it," Wilder laughs as he walks out the front door. "You're not going anywhere."

"You're stuck with us," I add.

"Oh, joy," Cash rolls his eyes.

Wilder kisses my cheek, then pulls the keys out of his back pocket. Keys to his used Ford truck. With a single cab. Which means we're all in the front seat.

"Let's go," Wilder twines his fingers with mine.

"I'll meet you guys there," Cash raises his eyebrows.

"You sure?" Wilder frowns.

"Yeah," Cash answers. "I need to do something before."

Wilder and I walk to the truck and he opens the passenger side door for me.

"Thank you," I say to him.

He runs his thumb over the ring on my left finger. "Do you like your promise ring?"

I glance down at it. "I think promise rings are supposed to go on the right hand."

He shakes his head. "You're mine, Blondie. It's on the correct hand."

I don't argue as I climb inside the truck and wait for him to get in.

"What do you want to do this summer?" Wilder asks as I lay my head on his shoulder, content to sit in the passenger's seat as we drive through town with the windows rolled down.

"Just hang out with you," I reply.
"Sounds like a plan."
The problem with making plans is they seldom work out the way we want them to.

About the Author

Jessi Hansen grew up in sunny San Diego County before falling head-over-heels in love with an Oklahoma boy.

After moving halfway across the country to be with him, she quickly adapted to small town life. Now, she spends her days chasing children, chickens, and the occasional tornado.

When she's not microwaving her cup of coffee for the umpteenth time, reading stories to her children or watching her husband operate heavy machinery (swoon), Jessi is crafting stories about sassy, sensitive heroines and their complex male counterparts. Family, friendship and feel-good endings are her specialty.

You can find more stories by Jessi at
authorjh.com

Find Jessi on social media!
Goodreads – Jessi Hansen
Instagram – authorjessihansen
Tik Tok – authorjessihansen

More Books By Jessi Hansen

The Firsts Series
Firsts Are Always Messy
Sloppy Seconds
Third Time's A Charm
Ava's Choice
Managing Mia
Love Taylor
Inspiring Izzy

The Kit Clark Series
Lede
Beat

Fused Fates Series
Fire
Fury

Standalones
Give Yourself Away
This Ain't My Town

Milton Keynes UK
Ingram Content Group UK Ltd.
UKHW012014280324
440101UK00004B/438